DYSENFRANCHISED

LOVERS

BY

BRIAN L. KING

Brian L. King

Brian L. King   Dysenfranchised Lovers

Published by King4life Publications

Copy Right: 2009 © King4life Publications
Brian L. King
ISBN: 978-0-983-68090-1
        093-6-8090-6

This book is a work of fiction. It is not meant to depict, portray, or represent any particular gender, person or group. Places, names, incidents, and characters are products of the writer's imagination are not to be construed as real. Any resemblances to actual events, people living, or dead, locality is entirely coincidental.

King4life Publications
www.king4lifepublications.com

ACKNOWLEDGEMENTS

Thanks to everyone who has supported me and never had any doubts in my ability to accomplish anything I've set out to do. To my family you have always stood behind me and told me I could do it. To my mother, my favorite supporter you were always there for me, I could always reach you no matter the day or the time! Thank you. You have truly been my positive supporter and friend no matter the challenge. To my wife Nakeysha thank you for becoming a part of my life as well as my children's life, you are truly ONE of a kind, once you grace someone with your presence they'll never forget you and we love you so much. To my kids my greatest treasure, you guys are truly priceless. I wish you all the luck in the world, once you achieve adult hood, my first piece of advice to you is, DON'T EVER SETTLE FOR LESS! I challenge you to be strong black men. To work through the inequalities of life, other people's prejudices yet maneuver and manipulate your way to be an outstanding successful citizen. Be an asset not a liability, use your better judgment and most importantly USE YOUR COMMON SENSE!!! Treasure your children the way I've treasured you. My last piece of advice is, no matter how bad things may get in your life don't ever give up and always hold your head up. Don't forget your past, but always look towards the future. Last but not least, I want to thank everyone who bought this book and now I challenge you to make a stand. Make a stand to better your life or better the life of someone you care about. I hope to continue to quench your thirst for knowledge, with my second novel. Please feel free to contact me at brianlking@king4lifepublications.com with any questions or comments. Or visit me at www.facebook.com/authorbrianlking.

TABLE OF CONTENTS

Chapter 1

My life abruptly changed, after a one night stand went bad, and I was forced me to move from Baltimore to San Diego. I must be honest, I have serious issues and they need to be addressed immediately or could otherwise prove to be detrimental to my life. Everybody has a dependency; some are very serious like drugs, alcohol, gambling or over eating. Others are less threatening, like being a workaholic or neat freak. My dependency is womanizing and searching for fulfillment in my empty life.

When I was two years old, my father died in a car accident and my mother took on two jobs to support my brother and myself. She never had time for personal relationships because she was always working extra hours to save up money for emergencies, and any other unforeseen expenses. So other than smut movies and penthouse magazine stories, I didn't have anything else to model a relationship after. I lost my virginity at the age of twelve and I was terrified about sticking my male member into my new female friend's small hollow cave. I was afraid of damaging her but after a few dry rugged strokes, she moistened up and I became overwhelmed with pleasure. My body began to tremor from head to toe. I jumped to my feet holding myself in my hands as it went into convulsions. A milky cream expelled from the tip. Not knowing what an orgasm was, I thought she broke my male organ. As scared as I was about the whole ordeal, I still felt a feeling so enormous that I knew I would spend the rest of my life trying to re-live that moment as many times as possible. My only alibi for such madness is abandonment of emotions and being blinded by ignorance. If only someone had taken the time and sat down to explain the birds and the bees, maybe my life and the way I treated women would have gone in a different direction.

£   £   £

As my life adjusted in an unfamiliar territory, I often walked along Mission Beach searching for direction. I sat down staring aimlessly into the water, and traced the ocean to the edge of the earth where it met face to face with the sky. The sunsets were so beautiful and the ocean was as calm as a sheet of glass. I enjoyed watching the sun set, as it allowed me to sink my troubles to the bottom of the sea. It was my only scapegoat, unselfishly casting away my sorrows and never being judged by my intentions. I have always heard that what you do in the past, will catch up to you in the future. Do I have enough time to reconstruct all the damage I have caused in various women's lives? Not to mention prevent new destruction that has yet to come. Am I only playing out the hand that life has dealt me? Is it possible to alter my course and become so much more than what I have amounted to? Was it in my destiny to settle down and have a family of my own? Or will I fall victim to my own demise, swallowed up by the same ambush that I had set for so many women? What's good for the goose isn't always good for the gander, only time will tell if I've made the right decision. My only regret is not leaving women with the illusion of meeting the perfect gentleman. The man they first laid eyes on, met and interacted with doesn't exist and they are all stuck with that fact and left with me as the evidence.

I've found temporary happiness with a woman that has stolen my attention with her beauty, her body and most of all her sophisticated attitude. Actually, Stephanie and I met by accident one Tuesday afternoon, I was supposed to be meeting a close friend of mine at Starbucks, to pick up some paperwork for a job. After I've been waiting thirty or so minutes and risking being late back to work, he calls my cell phone and tells me something came up and he'll drop off the package later at my house. At the same time, I could hear a woman breathing hard into his phone receiver and the sounds of her kissing him. I instantly became infuriated by his inconsideration for my time and stormed out of Starbucks rushing to get back to work. Still pissed off at my friend, I wasn't paying attention to the oncoming pedestrians and unintentionally knocked over a woman carrying a briefcase and a few small boxes. I helped her to her feet and picked up her belongings. When I met her beautiful brown eyes, she was stunning, dressed in a Chanel power suit, her cleavage was captivating as her breast almost blinded me as they shined, and her hair looked shiny and dangled in long tight curls. I quickly apologized for my discourtesy and offered to make her dinner to make up for any inconvenience I had caused. She graciously declined, so I offered to carry her packages to the post office, I figured it was the least I could do since I practically mauled her over on the side of the road. As we walked down Martin Luther King Blvd. to the post office, we realized that we had a lot in common. She decided to take me up on my dinner offer, following an intriguing conversation on my perspective of what women want. Terrence still teases us from time to time, about how we met. The joke being we should pay him a finders or beginners fee, I guess I do owe him a lot, if it wasn't for him, I would have never met Stephanie that day. Self-sabotaging as it may seem, I sometimes regret her attraction and feelings towards me. My thirst for infidelity I fear will tear down our foundation of trust and ruin the type of relationship I once doubted could even exist. I honestly don't know if I can return the trust and love, that she has unselfishly given me.

£   £   £

Stephanie and I struggled to catch our breath, drenched in a pool of sweat and love juices. I catch a glimpse of the clock on the nightstand, and the red light illuminates 4:20 am, we both have to be at work early in the Morning. *I can't afford to be late again!* My boss has already threatened me several times about my tardiness. Even though I'm his number one man, I don't want to push my luck. I may be one of the best financial consultants at the firm, but Mr. Shellenberger would have no problem replacing me with someone less confident and more reliable. Stephanie looks into my eyes and the moist droplets stream down her face, finally resting on the sheets below.

She exclaims, "If I never have sex again, I give you my word I will by no means be mad. You are the best damn lover I ever had."

I look passionately in her eyes, giving her my raw untainted feelings. "It's not about the physical aspect of having sex, it's about your feelings towards the person you're having sex with that makes it so intense.". Stephanie has been in only three intimate relationships prior to this one, and to be honest her sexual attentiveness was straight forward and lame. Once I broke down her walls of intimacy, reorganized and restructured her sexual terrain and taught her every position from doggy style, to riding on top, the spooning position and the proper way of giving a blowjob, Stephanie uses too much teeth and not enough suction. That was a major difference between white women and black women. White women practiced on pickles, carrots and cucumbers at an early age. They mastered the art of suction when giving head and will give blowjobs with precision and pride on demand. Most black woman on the other hand thought that it was the grossest thing, they had ever heard of. But black women learned in their young adult stages that it was more practical to engage in such an activity, because it increased the chances of their man being happy and not straying away, or so they thought. However, they became more experienced with time, but usually lacked the intensity that a white woman normally gave. It was a rare occasion to find a black woman that loves to give head or willing to go down on her man whenever he wants her to. Once Stephanie got the hang of it, she became a sexual predator making love to me every free moment she had to spare.

Like a drug user, trying to recapture that unforgettable first high, she was hooked and I was here to supply her again and again.

Whispering softly in my ear, "I forgot your birthday was coming up, is there anything special you would like?" She asked as we laid there caressing each other's body. I thought about asking for tickets to the 49ers game, but figured she already had something planned for me so I play along with her charade.

"Surprise me." I answer back, with a coy smile. I watch Stephanie fall asleep as I caress the side of her face. Deep down inside I have a special love for her. She is more woman then I am accustom to. She can be professional or personal in a moment's notice and has the wisdom to know how to use all facets of her personality, but there is still aside of me telling me not to trust her. Coming from a long past of very brief relationships that ended in turmoil and a bad marriage, I've established patterns that have taught me not to trust women. I was only willing to give them the love and attention at the extent of their own reciprocation, and even that became a challenge. I refuse to be in another relationship where I am giving more than I am receiving. In the long run, I know I may end up losing Stephanie, which is my driving force behind my drug of choice, other women. Searching for the right woman, to fulfill me and make my half a whole and make me feel like she's the only woman alive on this planet. I want a woman who can make love to me, not only physically but also emotionally and spiritually as well.

Less than four hours after closing my eyes, the sun sparkled bright warming my entire face. Turning to the side to catch a glimpse of Stephanie's all-natural profile, instead the clocked flashed back at me 8:15 am, knowing that I had to be at work by 7:45. I jumped up frantic. Damn*! I'm late again!* Stephanie was nowhere to be found, I jumped out of bed to take a quick shower and noticed a note on the dresser in Stephanie's hand writing, ***If you were thinking with your big head and not your little head, you would be at work already and not reading this letter! Thanks for this morning nasty, have a wonderful day at work. Love you Steph,*** with two heart shapes, neatly placed on each side of her name. I got myself together as fast as I could and rushed to work. I walked through the doors of DDG Investment firm, being inconspicuous like I had already been to work. Keisha sat at her desk timing how long it would be before I came through the door. I tried to crept slowly pass her desk without her noticing me, or so I thought, no sooner then I began thank my goodness and walk my normal pace she calls me out.

"Hey Jamal, another late night at the sexcapades...., damn that's the third time this week. Where do you get the strength? You must be taking fuck the shit out of me vitamins." Keisha sat there with a look of admiration on her face, but I didn't give her the satisfaction of an explanation.

I replied simply. "Good morning to you too Keisha." I continued to walk to my desk, and began setting up for Mr. Johnston's appointment. I wanted to be on point when he arrived, if I can sign him on as a new client I would meet my quota not to mention the bonus I'd receive at the end of the month. He had inherited a substantial amount of money from a car accident and wanted to make sure his family will be taken care of after he is gone.

"Oh by the way Mr. Shellenberger was looking for you earlier. I told him that you went to the bathroom then you ran out to your car to grab some papers."

"Thanks Keisha, I owe you one." I was already regretting what I said, I tried to move past her desk a little quicker.

"It's a good thing we don't punch a clock, you would be screwed." Looking in my direction seductively, she attempts but fails miserably to throw an awkwardly timed sexual innuendo Sometimes that girl just doesn't know when to quit. I turn my head, trying not to get sucked into another one of her adult conversations, "I said thanks!"

Not wanting to be annoyed especially before my meeting with a new client. I tried to put my agitation out of my mind but can't. Keisha has made it obvious on numerous occasions how bad she wants to be with me. Particularly since she found out that, I refuse to date women I work with. Almost immediately she took that as a personal challenge, to do what can't be done. Women always seem to have some of this in their nature, a notion to want what they can't have or to try and change a person that doesn't want to be changed. I have even heard through the rumor mill, that a few women here went as far as putting together a money pool to see who will be the first person to break me down, and get me to have sex with them. Every two weeks that go by that I haven't slept with one of them, they all have to put another ten dollars in the pot until one wins. Now this really sparked my interest, knowing they have a wager on having an affair with me, only excites my love for a challenge so if any of them had a chance they can really kiss it goodbye. More importantly, having sex with a woman you work with leads to disaster. The last time I had on the job sex, the sex was great, but she went crazy. One day it was a sexy lil work secret and the next thing I knew, she was telling me how she had feelings and how I should act, analyzing everything I said and how I said it. Worst of all she thought that every girl that smiled at me or talked to me, that they wanted to make out with me. This woman went as far as calling me every morning and every night, and not because she wanted to be the first and the last person that I talked to but because she wanted to know if I had other women in my bed when she wasn't around. The whole situation became very annoying and I got sick of her quickly. When it started to affect my work performance, I had to draw the line and cut off a woman who potentially offered one of the greatest sexual experiences I ever had. No doubt about it she could have had a career as a contortionist, but I never play around when it comes to the universal lubricant, money. Cutting her loose only enraged her more. As much as I loved the great city of Baltimore, I couldn't take the game playing any longer and relocated to San Diego. At that point, I vowed to never have sex with another woman that I may have even a remote possibility of doing business with.

£   £   £

After my meeting, the rest of the morning was at a standstill and I could barely keep my eyes open. At one point, I had dosed off completely at my desk, when I eventually opened my eyes I felt someone standing over me. I thought for sure that I was busted this time. I slowly turned around to see who caught me with my pants down, the first thing my eyes could focus on was this sexy short tight brown mini skirt, showing off the most gorgeous pair of legs known to man. The leg lover that I am, I looked up wondering who could be the proud owner of those prize-winning thoroughbred looking legs. Keisha was standing there with her hands on her hips laughing at me.

"What do you want?" I exclaimed. The last thing I wanted, was to be nagged by her again.

"So tell me!" Keisha asked inquisitively.

"Tell you what?" I replied, knowing she probably wants the dibs on last night's festivities.

"You know_, what she did to make you late again!" She replied with a coy smile, biting on her finger.

"Why, does my personal life interest you so much?" I asked flipping the questions to her.

"No, but.…" She stuttered.

"But, what?" I fired back.

"I just like to hear about your in-depth experiences, so I'll have a few ideas when I'm taking care of my own business." She answered as she dropped her head, but we both knew that that was a lie. I know she often had fantasies of us being together.

"Keisha, will you have lunch with me please?" I asked, changing the subject. My stomach was starting to touch my back, since I didn't have time for breakfast.

"If you drive, I'll treat." Keisha replied happily. She loves to think I'm her man, sporting her around town in my black VW Passat. In between shifting gears, she leisurely stroked the handle of my stick shift.

"Jamal, when are you going to teach me how to drive a stick?" She asked eying me up like candy. She had a way of turning any ordinary situation into something sexual. I definitely have to watch what I say.

I looked at her to see if she was serious, "Do you really want to learn how to drive a stick? Or do you like the way I power shift?" I had to throw that out there, looking down at the way she was working my handle over. She saw my expression of her toying with my stick shift and duffed me in the head.

"Can you take your head from between your legs for once? I really do want to learn how to drive a stick. And where are we going to eat anyway? I'm starving!" She exclaimed.

"Don't blame me you were the one who started the conversation, besides look at the way you're jerking on my stick!" She immediately removed her hand from the stick, placing her hands on her lap.

"Oh Jamal stop playing, you know I have this nervous twitch when I get excited or agitated. And right about now I'm feeling agitated that we're not eating!" She replied changing the topic back to food.

"Ok calm down I know this perfect little Mexican place called Alberto's, they make the best cornasatto burritos on the west coast. We're almost there." I put a little extra pressure on the gas before she became over dramatic.

"Oooh that little Mexican restaurant over on Rosecrans, I love that place! Plus there's this fine ass Mexican that works there, with muscles bulging everywhere." She explained eagerly, grabbing his imaginary muscles with her hands.

"Don't get too excited, I'd hate for you to bypass lunch, skip the foreplay and go straight into an orgasm!" I stated laughing at her imitation of being with a muscle bound man. Keisha knocked me upside my head again as she chuckled along.

"You wish! You know you would like to see this 33-25-32 fine chocolate body performing something erotic in front of you." She shot back confidently. I liked teasing Keisha and the thought of her masturbating in front of me, did turn me on to some degree. But I try not to take it too far with her, I don't think it would be worth the headache. Truthfully, I think Keisha would be the bomb in bed, hell she may be every guy's wet dream come true. But I have this fear that she could be another potential future stalker and I could not tolerate another one of those episodes in my life. Once we were inside the restaurant Keisha pulled me inside a small booth in the back corner, I already knew what was coming next. She sat down across from me and gave me this funny smirk.

"Now what are you up to?" I asked.

"You know." She said with a sexy tone to her voice.

"What does that mean?" I replied rhetorically, because I already knew where she was going with this conversation.

"It's your turn to tell me about one of your memorable love making moments, I told you about mine last week. And make it juicy!" She asked, while applying lipstick to her voluptuous lips and puckering several times to even it out.

"If you insist, but I still don't see what you get out this." I gave in instantly, because I never would have enjoyed my lunch if I had said no.

"About 3 years ago, I was shopping for some exercise equipment in Sears. A beautiful young woman walked directly in my path. She had dark brown eyes, her lips were full and heart shaped, she was about 5'9" and 146 pounds. She was wearing a light beige low V cut shirt, showing off her C- cup cleavage. With a pair of stretchy low rider jeans and coffee colored lipstick to supplement her cocoa colored skin. When she first looked at me, I felt a little intimidated, wondering why this fine ass woman was staring at me. She walked towards me and said hello my name is Jasmine you're Jamal aren't you? In a sultry voice, wait, why are you staring at me like that?"

"Sorry, you just had me so caught up in the story, now go on about this girl..."

"Okay, yeah my mouth almost hit the floor; I took a moment and got myself together. It took all my strength to reply, uh_ yes have we met before? Knowing good and damn well we hadn't, because I never would've forgotten a woman like that. She replied, well actually, you work with a good friend of mine! I had no idea who she was talking about, but she had my interest piqued. Who? I quickly asked, so I knew who to thank later for dropping my name in her ear. She replied Kimberly, I looked at her kind of strange trying to think of a Kimberly working with me. She continued on, but you probably know her as Button, I relaxed and nodded my head giving confirmation that I knew who she was talking about. She continued to talk getting all up close and personal, pulling off a piece of lint from my lapel. It was the first time in years I felt this speechless, all I could do was stand there and pay respect to her distinctively curved body. She pulled me close to her and spoke softly in my ear; Kim tells me lots of good things about you. Like for instance, I know sometimes you don't wear any underwear. Catching me entirely off guard, she slid her hand into my pants and started massaging my boys with her fingertips. And of all days, today was one of those days that I actually wasn't wearing any underwear. Jasmine looked me up and down with a devilish grin, and then whispered to me again follow me. How could I resist, she had me hypnotized by the way her hips swayed back and forth as she walked, also not to point out she had my male member sticking out far enough to salute the 82nd Air Borne Division. Ah, Keisha could you stop moaning and squirming like that? You are going to draw attention to us."

"Shout up and talk, so you got me a little hot and bothered right now." I chuckled a little and continued on.

"So she pulled me into the woman's dressing room while the attendant was assisting another customer. At first, I felt uncomfortable about being in the women's dressing room, but she knew exactly how to put my mind at ease. She started telling me about how much of a hard man I was to get a hold of, literally, without missing a beat she unzipped my pants and dropped them to the floor, she bent over without delay and swallowed as much of my rock solid member that she could stuff into her mouth, like she hadn't eaten in weeks. She tightly gripped the base of my man, making sure he wouldn't run away. Then she inhaled the tip, through her plumped luscious lips. Her hot wet tongue began to perform many acrobatic maneuvers, causing me to stand paralyzed in my place as I gripped the mirror to hold myself up. The intense sensation from the warmth and moisture of her mouth felt so erotic, I let out a moan as if I was holding my breath for a while and was about to start gasping for air. Jasmine grabbed my hand directing it down between her legs. I felt the warmness escaping from her love cavern and wanted to seek the shelter from within. I would say that her panties must have been saturated from the moisture that escaped her, but she wasn't wearing any panties as well. Her warm juices freely dripped out, while I massaged her freshly shaved sweetness. I stuck my finger deep into her waterfall, my hand was very slippery from her natural lubrication and it drove me wild to feel how wet she had become. She stood up, smiled at me with her winter cool eyes, and then she turned around wanting to integrate our love partners. I buried my sword deep behind her shield, wrapping my hand around her long black hair, giving me the extra leverage I needed to make sure she was satisfied. She started moaning more and more out loud, as her arousal heightened. I placed my right hand over her mouth to keep the other patrons from hearing her yearns." I looked up at Keisha, her eyes were closed and she was sitting there rotating her head from side to side, while she was played with her love toy through her half hiked up mini skirt. Her mouth was slightly opened, as if she was holding her breath waiting to exhale at the same exact moment her body muscles contracted and a pleasurable wave of tingling sensations moved throughout her body.

"Keisha?" I called to her. But she didn't hear me. My stallion began to swell with excitement, I was aroused, watching her masturbate before my eyes. The waiter came over to our table to give us our orders and I tried to keep the attention off of Keisha as much as possible. I told the waiter thanks for the food and ordered a medium orange slice. He looked at Keisha to see if she wanted something to drink as well. I interjected and told him to make it 2 orange sodas instead of 1. The waiter seemed preoccupied and very annoyed about something else that was on his mind and never took notice to what Keisha was doing.

When Keisha finally snapped out of her trance, I was just starting to eat my food. She took a few sips of her soda and started eating like nothing had happened. I pretended like I didn't see what she was doing, but she really had me turned on as my manhood stretched out and bulged in my pants. As much as I would have loved to seen the outcome of her little do it yourself, self-pleasuring trailer. I left well enough alone, because I knew how much she wanted me. And after that little demonstration she had just given me, it's a good thing we were somewhere in public. I don't think I would have put up too much of a resistance, at this point I was feeling weak and she was really turning me on. Thankfully we finished our lunch in peace, with the usual small talk about work and the latest gossip. Keisha opted to take a cab because she had some errands to run before she headed back in the office. I knew that was only an excuse to run home and change her damp sticky panties from her mini workout session, she wanted to freshen up before she came back to work. On my way back to the office I felt a little guilty for enjoying my gourmet lunch with Keisha, I called Stephanie to see how her day was going.

"Hello?" Stephanie whispered into her phone.

"Baby it's me, I just wanted to hear your voice. Why are you whispering?" I asked.

"I'm in training today and it's about to start back up again, besides I thought I told you not to call me at work unless it was an emergency?" She stated through clenched teeth.

"Yes but I really miss you and had to hear your voice. I wanted to see if you could meet me for lunch, but I guess another time. I'll see you at home. Love you."

"Ok bye, love you too." I cruised back through town in silence, thinking about my relationship with Stephanie. I feel like I definitely love her but I don't think I'm in love with her. She's a wonderful woman but I'm not quite convinced that I want to spend the rest of my life with her. Even though she is the most put together woman I have ever been serious with, I still feel like what if there's someone better out there for me. Unfortunately, the only way to know for sure is to interact with other women. I know what I'm getting myself into isn't right and I'm not trying to hurt Stephanie, but at the same time I really feel like there is another force more compatible for me. I know it would kill me to find her with another man, but that's different. Ok call me a hypocrite and selfish, if I'm out there with other women its ok because I have to interact with them to see if they are truly the one for me. But if Stephanie was involved with another man, then the bond between us will be destroyed and I will feel betrayed.

Chapter 2

Its Friday evening, I had just finished my 2 hour workout, now I'm taking my shower before Steph and I go out to enjoy a peaceful at the pit a nice little spot on Midway not too far from the beach. I met this fine honey there a few weeks ago, it had a nice soothing atmosphere. The way I felt after being there a few seconds, I knew it would become my new favorite place to hang out and unwind. Plus I thought Stephanie would hit it off here as well. I turn off the water and step out the shower to dry off, I sat on the toilet for a moment and thought about the fact that I wasn't getting any younger and how I want to give my mother some grandkids before it was too late. Then I thought about the few women I had encountered over the past few months, sexually they were superb and always left me wanting more. Other than the bedroom they had nothing else to offer me, other than the physical I felt no other connection. Out of nowhere Stephanie burst into the bathroom yelling.

"Damn it, Jamal! Who the fuck is this bitch sending you a text on your sidekick?"

"What! What are you talking about? I just got out the shower!" I hastily replied, buying a few seconds to get what whatever story I was about to explain to her straight.

"Your Sidekick just went off and it read 441! Now who would be sending you something like that?" Stephanie growled at me, throwing my phone in my direction. I caught the phone, dropping my towel to the floor. *Damn, I thought I told this chicken head to only text me early in the day. Some people just can't follow directions.*

"I don't know, maybe someone was trying to text somebody else and they realized they dialed the wrong number and hung up!" I explained to her, hoping that simple answer would suffice for now.

"Jamal you are so full of shit! I am not the same naive bitch that I used to be!"

"Well there are 441 numbers in the San Diego area that could have been anyone!" I exclaimed, dismissing the whole thing.

"Jamal, I am not playing these games anymore, you know I went through this shit with my last boyfriend. I'm not going through it, with you too!!!" Steph replied in disgust.

"I'm not playing games with you, that could have been anyone and stop blaming me for what your ex- boyfriend did to you. I'll never hurt you the way he did." She dismissed everything I said and stormed out the house.

"Damn!" I hurried to get dress, by the time I got outside she was nowhere in sight. *So much for our romantic night out!* I take a seat on the porch watching the neighborhood people walk back and forth to their unknown destinations. I hate the fact that I keep lying to her, but it's not like I can tell her the truth. I can only imagine how I would look telling her, *Stephanie I really have feelings for you and I can see you being my wife and the mother of my children some day in the future and just to make sure there isn't anyone better for the position, I date a few r women behind your back, to see what options I have. Thank you for being so understanding.* Don't get it twisted Stephanie is different, she has never given me any reason to not trust her. She is always fifty/ fifty with me, if I'm broke then she's broke, if my whole check is going towards bills then her whole check is going towards bills. She is slowly and surely capturing my heart, but it's hard to fully trust another woman for fear of being hurt. Most of the women that I tried to have a somewhat civilized relationship with were either trying to milk me for my money or just straight tricks with a smile. By choice or by force, I eventually learned to not trust them anymore. Instead, I employed their way of thinking and out did them at their own game. I guess you can say in my defense, I became a product of my environment and started treating women the same way they had treated me for so long. I'm not saying what I was doing is right, not by a long shot, but if women can do it for all these years, so can we! My phone went off again reading displaying the text message 441, since Stephanie left to go God knows where, I decided to hit her back *.might as well not make this evening a complete waste.* I texted Erica back, put in 10-4 letting Erica know that everything was okay. I only have women contact me by text, that way I'll never get caught up in a conversation if Stephanie ever walks in on me. This makes sure there's never a reason to act like it's one of my friends or talk in code or act like it's the wrong number, especially if they happened to call at an inappropriate time. I called my boy James to run a cover for me, I could always count on him cause he's never let me down. James is a well reserved person, he keeps a lot of things to himself. Now more than ever, since he'd been busted by two women he was dating at the same time. James had a live in girlfriend that he'd been with for about 3 years and had another girlfriend that lived north of San Diego, he was involved with her for about a year. James and the girl he had been with for about a year had a three-month-old son together and supposedly were planning on getting married one day. Little did James know, his live in girlfriend had a brother that was in prison in upstate California, doing hard time for being a habitual offender selling drugs and petty theft. While his other girlfriend had a cousin locked up in the same prison for rape of an underage girl. The technical charge was statutory rape, the fact that she looked and act legal meant nothing to the judicial court. However, I must say in his defense, they did end up getting married after she turned 18 and they're still together to this day. Back to the point, the two inmates ended up sharing the same cell while serving out their terms and being in tight quarters with another person you can't help but to be up close and personal in one another's life. I guess after talking about family and looking at pictures they thought it was odd to be talking about a guy from the same area with the same name, job and who knows what other similarities they found. All I know is after they each made a few calls it turned out to be a small world for James, he was set up and busted before he realized what happened. He's now paying child support for his son that he never sees and has lost his good paying job that his other girlfriend hooked him up. Since that incident took place, he makes any woman involved in his life suffer because he may never see his son again, but despite what has happened he's still cool people to be around. He got his life back on track, has a good job working for Homeland security, his anger towards women is still an issue but he is a loyal friend that I can always count on. I give him the run down, in case Stephanie calls him and wants to know where I am. Five minutes out the door, my cell starts ringing.

"Hey Jamal it's me Patrice, sorry to bother you so late and I know its short notice, but I was wondering if you can pick me up right now?" She asked sounding bothered by something.

"Of course, is everything okay?" I immediately replied feeling concerned for her. "I'll explain later, I just need a real friend right now."

"Sure, you know I'm always here for you." I stated whole heartedly.

"Thank you, I'll be down at the corner waiting for you."

"You're in luck I'm in the area; I'll be there in about five minutes." I stated as I cut into the far right lane to make a turn. I texted 10-22 to cancel my rendezvous, within a few blocks of picking up Patrice, Marcus hit me on my cell.

"Speak your peace!"

"My stocks are higher than ever!" Marcus yelled in the phone, already feeling the effects of whatever substance he had in his body.

"What?"

"My stocks just split 3 ways! I'm telling you I should have my own investment firm!"

"Really! What happened this time?" I asked waiting for him to sell me some kind of outlandish story.

"Well I had this one chick, pardon me I mean lady, over my crib, let's just say she was doing the business and giving me much pleasure, playing hide the nightstick." Laughing in the phone.

"So then what happened?" I asked killing time before I picked up Patrice.

"Well, she was going downtown hard on a brotha, to be honest I don't think she was breathing. She was about mid stroke about to bring me home and we heard Octavia on the stairs telling me she was home early." Marcus explained as if he was watching it right now on TV.

"What! What happened then?" I asked, swerving to stay on the road. Getting all caught up for the moment.

"The girl got scared and hid in the closet, butt naked with her drawers in her hand. But you know I was chilling, cause my stocks are higher than ever!!!" He sang into the phone.

"So where's the punch line?" I asked, so I could hurry up and end this conversation.

"Octavia came into the bedroom and asked why I was in bed so early and why was there a musty smell in the room. I told her that I was horny, waiting for her to come home. But to keep from doing the job myself, I decided to do some pushups and crunches on the floor. She gave me this funny look like she didn't believe me. Then she huffed, well can I at least take a shower first. No sooner than she closed the bathroom door, the other girl came out the closet scared as hell. She was so scared, she started to grab her clothes from under the bed and rush out the door butt naked. But I, being the man that I am, managed to talk her into finishing the job before she left. Octavia came out the shower-soaking wet, with her body piercings looking ever so beautiful. I pulled the covers back for her to jump in and then you know it was time for round two. If you were here, you would have been so proud of me." Marcus said, claiming his accomplishment for the day.

"Marcus you're doing your thing for now, but you better watch yourself. You know things have a way of backfiring on you. Look, I'll call you later I have something I need to take care of right now."

£   £   £

Octavia came back into the room from raiding the refrigerator with a hand full of snacks.

"Who was that on the phone?" She asked, as she got comfortable on the corner of the bed ready to eat.

"That was J, he was just calling to see what I was up too. And asked if I wanted to hang out tonight, but I told him that I was working on my quality time with wifey." I answered, sticking my fingers in her cherry pie and grabbing a hand full of chips with the other hand.

"Hey! What the hell is your problem, I don't know where your hands been at!" She exclaimed. "I bet you didn't even go in the bathroom to wash em! You're just a nasty ass dog, you put anything in your mouth." She continued.

"What? It's just us and you weren't complaining when I had you in my mouth now were you?" I rhetorically asked, cause she knew I was da bomb at what I do.

"Ok, ok you got that. But you know how I am with cross contamination." She laughed. "Just keep your juices over there and I'll keep mine over here."

"I love you and I'm down for whatever makes you happy." Marcus said not paying her any attention, more focused on finding something on TV.

£   £   £

I saw Patrice standing on the corner of Imperial and Euclid Ave. as I approached the corner, I turned the music down as I slowed for her to get in. I stopped at the corner and turned the stereo off, when I saw the expression on her face, I could tell she was upset, Patrice hopped in looking down at the floor. When I saw the tears running down her face. I gave her an extra minute or so to get her thoughts together.

"What's wrong?" I asked, breaking the silence in the car.

"Just drive," She said sadly, as if it took the rest of her strength to say it. Patrice and I hooked up a long time ago when I came to Oakland one year on spring break. Having a long distant relationship took a toll on us emotionally and we decided to take a chance on being good friends. Patrice was the sweetest woman that I ever dated. She always put someone else's feelings before her own, she was strong minded, articulate and her heart was always in the right place.

She also knew her destination and purpose in life, unlike some women she wasn't looking for a free ride, she paid her dues and paved her own way. I couldn't help but give her the respect she deserved. Even though we're not together, I still love her and care for her a great deal. She sighed slowly wiping the tears from her eyes, with her saturated tissue.

"Do you feel better?" I asked her, hoping she would enlighten me on the situation.

"Yes a little." She softly replied, silence filled the car once again.

"Do you want to talk now?" I asked, giving her a chance to start at the beginning.

"Sure, but can you do me a big favor first?" She asked hesitantly.

"Come on girl, anything for you, you were my first love." I answered trying to lighten her mood.

"Thank you and you know you were mine too. Look, I need you to pay for a room for me tonight. I promise I'll pay you back."

"Sure, you know I got you, anything I can do to help."

"I'm sorry I don't have any money on me at the moment, but I will pay_" I cut her off before she could finish.

"Ssshhhhh..., don't even go there, you know you're good for it, besides your money is no good with me. When I told you I got you, I meant I got you, forever. No matter what!"

"There's the Wyndham Emerald Plaza not too far from here, up on West Broadway, we can go there." She stated doubtfully.

"That hotel downtown, not that far from the zoo? That's a nice little spot, we can go there." I replied nonchalantly, not giving any thought to the price of a hotel like that. Pulling up into the parking lot, I took a nice glance at how elegant the hotel looked. They even had bell hops to meet you in the parking lot to take your bags. *Wow! Now this place is going to break a brotha, but if any woman would deserve this type of treatment, it would be her. And she deserves four stars plus!!!* I didn't let on, that this place was going to leave me rubbing two wooden nickels. I pulled up the revolving door to let Patrice out, then I scurried through the parking lot to find a place to park. I saw an empty parking space near the front entrance, right next to a beat up Grand Jeep. *I'll pass on that spot. If you don't take care of your own car, I know you won't mind knocking a few dings in mine.* After ten minutes of searching the lot, I spotted a couple pulling out of a spot on the side of the hotel. I parked the car as fast as I could and hurried in to catch up to Patrice. I rushed in the front entrance and came to an abrupt stop. It was immaculate inside, there was a bar, a restaurant, two sitting areas and the receptionist desk was off to the right side. I had all but forgotten why I was there, until I felt a light tap on my shoulder. I spun around to see who felt the need to be putting their hands on me and why. I opened my mouth about to tell this person what I would do if they ever put their hands on me again. I quickly closed my mouth as I made eye contact with the warmest honey brown eyes I ever saw.

"Jamal what's your problem? I've been sitting patiently over there for fifteen minutes waiting for you, will you come on and stop playing around." Patrice stated. We walked over to the reception desk, where a slightly thin, gray haired man was reading the paper. He neatly folded it up and stuck it in a drawer before rendering his services.

"Can I help you?" He stated with a pleasant smile on his face.

"Yes do you have any rooms available?" I asked nervously, hoping they were full and we would have to find a less expensive hotel.

"Yes we have a presidential suit with a waterbed, full screen TV, wet bar and your personal balcony for only $475.00." I had to swallow to keep from choking. Everyone knows the later you wait to check in a hotel the more expensive it is.

"What else do you have?" I said as my voice cracked.

"Well we also have single bed rooms for $219.00 plus tax and double beds for $260.00 plus tax, less the amenities." He stated in his less than favorable manner.

"Okay we'll take the double bed_" But I was swiftly cut off by Patrice.

"No." She said in a definite tone. "We'll take the single one. It's not like we've never slept together before, besides you probably won't stay all night anyway." The receptionist was shocked by Patrice's directness and started to blush. Then he gave us the keys to our room, as we stepped onto the elevator to go to 49th floor, Patrice looked into my eyes and slid her left hand down the right side of my face.

"Thank you, I owe you big time for this one." She tenderly spoke. My boys started to bulge in my pants. I mumbled to myself "Not this time. This is not a booty call guys."

I smiled back as purely as I could, "You owe me nothing, and you would have done the same for me. You can take me out to lunch one day." The doors opened up on the 49th floor. We got off and walked slowly to our room, "Here we are, room 4023." We went inside, she walked straight over to the phone to call room service and I turned on the radio to find some mellow music to calm her down a bit more. I looked out the window at the beautiful view, you could see the San Diego Bay, the pacific ocean and even Mexico on a clear night. The sunset was magnificent. It almost makes you wonder how can something as harmful as smog, contaminate our lungs and atmosphere, but make such a gorgeous sunrise and sunset, that brings out the romantic side of just about everyone. *I've always said even disadvantages have advantages.* Turn off the lights was playing on 88.7 fm. I turned around, looked at Patrice and realized that this was not the time to be romantic, I closed the drapes to the window and sat down on the bed.

"Do you want anything to eat Jamal? I'm ordering food downstairs." She whispered as she covered up the speaker part of the phone.

"No thanks." I replied, still waiting patiently for Patrice to tell me what has her so upset. I flipped through the channels to catch the last few minutes of Girlfriends, as she confirmed her order.

"Jamal I'm going to take a shower, call me when the food gets here. We'll talk then." As she headed off towards the bathroom, I exhaled then shifted to the middle of the bed, to get more comfortable, thinking I might be here for a while. Then my sidekick went off...

"Awe Shit! I know its Stephanie! She's going to kick my ass for sure!" I took a deep breath and answered the phone. We Be Clubbing by Ice Cube came screaming through the phone.

"Yo who dis?" I yelled into the phone. Feeling a little annoyed by the music almost blowing out my ear drum.

"What up Jam Mal! It's your brother." Derrick stated full of energy, he was calling from his nightclub.

"It's all good, I thought you were Stephanie hitting me up."

"Yo where you at? I tried to call you at home but no one answered! Don't tell me you guys are at it again and don't come knocking on my door early in the morning like the last time!"

"I'm out with Patrice at the moment, she had a little problem that we had to take care of." I stated nonchalantly, hoping he wouldn't start up on her again.

"So you still hitting that or what?"

"Nah, it's not like that I keep telling you. We're just close friends."

"I don't care what you say, she's got your ass whipped! Just face it, she got your dick dipped in bronze and hanging up in her jewelry box. I bet she's the first woman in California to be awarded a bronze penis, for having someone sprung the longest without giving up any booty." He laughed through the phone. When he realized I wasn't laughing with him, he changed the subject. "What are you doing later, provided that you're allowed to get away?"

"I don't know, let me see what's up with her first. I might not be able to get away for a minute. This might take a while" There was some silence on the phone as he was distracted by something, then he started laughing.

"Your boy Marcus just got here and he's trying to corner the market! When he walked in, he was talking about his stocks is at $18.00 a share, trying to holler at every woman in sight." Then Derrick continued to laugh harder. "Dat bitch is crazy, now he's yelling he's up to $23.00 a share, as he pulled two women out on the dance floor. There are plenty more hoes in here, so you better hurry up. That is, If you can finish up your business, in a respectable time frame."
"I'll try, Patrice is real upset and she may want to talk for a while."

"Well you do what you got to do, because I'm damn sure gonna put my thing down up in here tonight!" There was a knock at the door, it was room service.

"I have to go, I'll see you later if I make it to the club." We both hung up. Derrick didn't like working for other people, the thought of having someone boss him around for pennies on the dollar didn't sit well with him. He was dead set against legalized slavery, is how he explains it. He opened up a night club so he could be his own boss. He knew it would be successful, because he knew what women liked and as long as he could attract women to his club, the men without a doubt would follow. Derrick was a diehard east coast guy and never had any reason to leave Baltimore. I convinced him to come out to San Diego for a visit, because I knew there were more opportunities for him to excel. After months of convincing, he finally came to visit for a few weeks, and see what all the hype was about and got buck wild. He could not believe that San Diego was an untapped resource of fine ass single woman. Most of the guys out here couldn't see past selling or using drugs, gang banging over territory that they'll never own and the small portion that was left were gay. After his two week visit, he decided to stay permanently. He is undeniably off the hook and he takes no prisoners, he has a hard time respecting women! He wasn't always like this, he loved himself a city cat but he couldn't stand all the games that went along with the territory. So he eventually stopped believing in love and just assumed that every woman was trying to get something for nothing. Since there's such a shortage of men out here, he figured he could pretty much do whatever he wants with whomever he wants without having to commit to a relationship. The last woman he dated was so dishonest, she told him that she was pregnant and he believed her. Only to later find out, she was actually pregnant by her brother, granted it was a brother by marriage, but none the less her brother. After that incident, he swore that no other woman would ever get the best of him again. It doesn't matter how well you know a woman, you will never really **know** them until after it's too late. He now refers to himself as the gatekeeper of his own heart, he holds all the keys and controls all the exits. He's always had a good sense for business, he must have picked that up from our mother. The club is phat! It's like two clubs in one. On one side they Play hip-hop and rap, on the other side they play jazz and the blues. He figured why not attract the older and the younger crowd at the same time. Not to mention some of the younger people that feel more mature for their age or as they say, have an old soul and prefer the jazz, then you got some older folks who thought they were ageless and preferred the hip hop. Or the older men with the outdated three piece pinstriped suit, playing that sugar daddy role, with a fine, hot ass, young girl on their arm. You know the type, someone that could make them cum & go at the same time. In the middle of the two club rooms, there's another bar and some tables and in the back are a few pool tables and arcade games. There was security everywhere, cameras and metal detectors at the door, he didn't take any chances of some knuckle head tearing up his club or someone using his club as a place for drug transactions. And if you got caught doing something you weren't supposed to be doing, you would be banned for life. His club was locked down tighter than a snapper's pussy and that shit's watertight! He definitely had it going on! I wanted to be a silent partner in his club, but he wasn't trying to hear it. He had a strict no business relationship with family policy. His exact words were, blood is thicker than water, but money is thicker than blood. And I don't want to hurt you over no money! Needless to say, he borrowed the money to get his club up and running, then paid me back, but he didn't make me a partner. I opened the door, "Come in." The waiter came in and brought a plate of French fries and a country-fried steak smothered in gravy and a bottle of white wine.

"That'll be forty eight dollars and twenty seven cents sir." He stated as he looked around our room. I fumbled through my wallet trying to add up the sum of the bill. I stopped to think if there was any money in the ashtray in my car. *Damn I'mma have to pick up a part time job soon at the rate this girl is going!* I thought to myself in frustration.

"Would you like this bill on your room tab sir?" He asked, sensing that I didn't have enough money for the bill or a tip.

"Yes, please. Thank you." After the waiter left, I gave a few taps on the bathroom door.

"Patrice, your food is here!" I said through the half cracked door.

"Thanks, I'll be out in a minute. Why don't you pop open the wine so it can breathe a little?" She replied as I heard the water starting to flow down the drain.

"Okay" I replied, thinking it will still be a minute before she actually comes out the bathroom. After I popped the wine and sat it back in the ice, to stay chill, I sat back on the bed to watch some more TV, Patrice finally walked out the bathroom with an oversized maroon towel wrapped around her. She walked to the right side of the TV by the desk, turned around, looked at me and winked before she dropped her towel, to lotion up her body with cocoa butter. My mouth fell open and I dropped my glass of wine. She walked over, picked up my glass and poured me some more.

She took a sip and then asked, "Was that a good or a bad sign?" She asked cracking a half smile for the first time this evening.

"Goo...goo...good sign!" I answered, trying to clear my throat. Patrice was a dark caramel 5'8", short black hair, cut in a wavy type style. About 137 pounds and thicker than quick grits. she had a perfect number 8 frame! She took one last sip, before passing me my glass back.

"Here's your wine, try not to make a mess of yourself this time." She laughed at me.

"Thanks." I replied, trying to focus more on the TV and not the lotion being smeared all over her smooth body. Patrice looked at me trying to keep my eyes off of her and continued to chuckle to herself.

"What's your problem, you act like you never saw me naked before?" She asked me, almost sounding offended.

"I know I have… it's just that you're so beautiful and your body is shaped like a goddess. It's so perfect, like it was hand chiseled to perfection." She sat on the bed not saying a word, with her towel wrapped back around her. She began to slowly eat as she told me why she was so upset earlier.

"I found out my man was a big time drug dealer today." She started, the tears drained from her eyes.

"Say what! How did you find out?" I asked rhetorically.

"He was busted today by the feds in his studio while he was cutting a new album, he was using his studio as a front to launder his money. On top of everything else, they hit him for not paying taxes on the drugs he sold. I think he called it income tax evasion." She somberly stated.

"I'm sorry to hear that." I stated, then quickly stopped and waited for her to continue.

"He called me from jail and told me everything. I guess that was his one phone call I hear everyone talking about." Then she started crying harder.

"Sshhhh, it'll be all right." I whispered and hugged her firmly.

"Thank you; you always knew how to make me feel good. I should have never let you go, I guess you really don't miss the well until it runs dry." She tried to joke.

"Patrice I'll always be your friend; so don't ever think that I'm not here for you." She broke down and cried harder. "Patrice it'll be all right!" I said as I held her tight.

"But we were supposed to get married in 3 months!" She exclaimed, throwing her hands up in the air.

"I know this is very hard for you right now. Come on and lay down, you need to try and relax." I softly caressed her back to help her relax as she laid there with her eyes closed.

After a few minutes her muscles started to loosen up, I whispered in her ear. "I'm going to take a shower I'll be right back." When I came out of the shower, she was under the covers sleeping peacefully. I eased under the sheets so she wouldn't wake up and then slid over to her side of the bed, until I felt her warm naked silky skin against mine. She turned over, we wrapped our arms around each other.

She kissed me a couple times on my chest and whispered, "I've always felt so safe with you." I gave her another peck on her lips.

"Get some rest, you've had a long day." Before I knew it, we fell asleep in each other arms, with our legs intertwined together.

£   £   £

Marcus stumbles into me near the front entrance of the club, "Where is your brother? He was supposed to meet me here hours ago!" Marcus slurs barely keeping his balance.

"You know that lil nigga is still whipped over Patrice! They somewhere shacked up together. I don't know how Stephanie puts up with that." Derrick spit out without a second thought.

"She's one of the finest motherfuckers I ever laid my eyes on, too. If I were ever to be whipped like cream, I hope it be over someone as fine as her!" Marcus stated, seconding the motion. He started galloping around in a circle slapping himself on the ass yelling_ "Whip me baby, whip me!"

"Nigga sit your drunken ass down somewhere before you hurt yourself!" I notice two lovely ladies staring at us laughing while Marcus makes an ass clown of himself.

"Marcus, yo cut it out! You're embarrassing the both of us!" I exclaimed in frustration.

"Huh?" Marcus replied, focusing on the women that were enjoying his circus act.

"Look those women are staring at us!" I subtly stated to Marcus.

"Well what the hell are we still standing here for, let's go talk to em!" Marcus blurted out heading in their direction.

"Excuse me ladies, my Name is Derrick. And I couldn't help but to notice you staring at us." I stated jumping on the first opportunity to speak, before Marcus ruined the moment with something stupid coming out of his mouth.

"Hello my name is Rhonda and this is Yoyo. And I know who you are." She spoke seductively.

"Excuse me, my name is Marcus, a pleasure to meet you both." He interjected, getting a small portion of his fifteen minutes of fame.

"You're mad funny!" Yoyo stated still laughing at him.

"How so?" He asked, looking himself over.

"Do you always make an ass of yourself like that in public? Or are you practicing for your next gig with Ringling brothers?" Yoyo replied instantly.

"Nah it's not like that, I just love having a good time even if it's at my own expense."

"I see." Still giggling at the fact, he just made a complete ass of himself. "So you like living life to the fullest?" She mumbled.

"Actually, I normally get paid to act like that." He answered, not giving any thought to the fact she was clowning him.

"So what are you some kind of entertainer?" She continued.

"Uhh yes_ yes I am!" He answered proudly.

"Well don't quit your day job!" They both laughed harder.

"You know, I don't have to stand here and take this shit from you. I can go anywhere for that! In fact I'm going to the bar to get me another drink!" Marcus started to walk away, noticeably feeling a little insulted.

"Wait, I wasn't trying to insult you. I was just making fun conversation. I'll walk to the bar with you, can you buy me a drink?" Yoyo asked in her sexiest voice.

"Look here, first you want to insult a brother and now you want me to buy you a drink like everything's cool! Do you think you're just that fine that you can say what you want to any guy and then turn around and get whatever you want from him?"

"No, I_"

"Well it worked, girl bring your fine ass on before I sober up." Grabbing her by the hand and pulling her along, I shook my head in disgust, watching Marcus head towards the bar.

"Hey Marcus, you better make sure that's club soda and orange juice you order! Your ass is drunk enough!" I yell, after him.

"Say what? You should be happy I'm buying drinks, that's more money in your pocket!" He shot back. I look over at Rhonda who's still laughing about the whole situation.

Feeling slightly embarrassed by Marc's actions, "Please allow me to apologize for my friend. He doesn't get out often and I think he was dropped on his head a few times as a child." We both laughed to break the awkwardness between us.

"That's okay. He's out enjoying himself. Besides, you only live once and he's making sure he doesn't miss out on anything."

"I guess you're right." feeling more at ease I position myself a little closer to her so I can hear her better.

"You have to live in the moment, because tomorrow isn't promised to you." Rhonda stated as she eyed me like a lollipop on a stick.

"Oh, so now you're a philosopher?" I asked feeling her out.

"No, I'm an opportunist! I try to make the best of every situation!" She replied popping a piece of spearmint gum in her mouth. I watched her for a few seconds chewing on her gum. *Thank God, she doesn't smack on her gum. I thought I was going to have to bail out on her.*

"Oh, I see. May I get you a drink, on the house of course?"

"Yes. Thank you very much." Then I noticed a wedding ring on her finger. I motion for one of the waitresses to take her order.

"How long have you been married?" I question her, as if she was being interrogated. At first, she looked a little surprised, the waitress cuts in "May I take your order ma am?"

"Yes I'll have a melon ball please."

"And charge it to the house." I interjected.

"Yes sir."

"6 and a half years." Rhonda finally answered my question.

"Are you happy?" I followed up.

"Yes! Very why?" Throwing her hands up in the air, feeling to some extent offended.

"Most people normally go out to clubs, usually to meet other people and since you're not out with your husband_" I insinuated.

"Well I'm out with my friend!" She said defensively.

"That's cool. I guess you have another half year of happiness left." I joked.

"And just what is that supposed to mean?" She snapped.

"You mean you've never heard of the seven year itch?"

"No!" She stated putting her hands on her hips.

"It's this saying, that all marriages, presuming that they make it to seven years. That one if not both will get the urge to scratch that itch with another person outside their marriage."

"Let me tell you something I'm very happy and secure with my marriage. Sometimes I do come across nice looking men and the thought of having a one night stand has crossed my mind once or twice. But that's the extent of it, I would never take it any further. When the grass looks greener on the other side of the fence I go home and water my own grass, maybe even add some fertilizer, you feel me. A few minutes of pleasure could lead to a lifetime of pain and I'm sorry I don't want to live out the rest of my life in pain. There are diseases that you can't get rid of, psychos out there that get a little taste and become obsessive and stalk your family. Or, I could get pregnant. Could you imagine me being on the Maury show and the title is,"

"Wait, let me guess. Which guy is my baby daddy?" I cut in. we both shared a little chuckle.

"You would have to be a fool to sleep with different people at the same time and then have to guess who the baby dad is. That seems so embarrassing."

"There are a lot of men out there taking care of kids, that they think is theirs." I stated looking off in the distance, thinking what I would do if I were caught in that situation.

"Then when something happens to the child, he needs blood and after the doctor runs some tests and tells you that your blood type is not compatible, that's a fucked up way to find out your child is not yours."

"Have you ever heard of the old cliché, mommas baby! Daddy's maybe!" It didn't stick around all these years for nothing."

"I know that's right. I know of this girl, that's with some guy, she was also messing around with another guy and got pregnant. She knew it was the other guy's baby and never told her boyfriend. Here's the kicker, when they split up, she made him pay child support for a kid that wasn't his! And he's still paying till this very day."

"Now that is fucked up! Excuse my French, she should be stoned to death, for being so trifling." She paused for a second to let everything sink in and then continued. "I could never disrespect myself or my marriage like that."

"Wow an honest hoe." I mumbled, watching the expression on her face.

"What's that?"

"I said, I apologize but in a minute I have to go. I'm still running a business here."

"Oh, okay. Besides, it's getting late and I must be getting home soon myself. Derrick it was nice talking to you, it's not often I find an intelligent guy that can hold a good conversation for longer than a minute and a half these days. Before they start talking about how can they get into my pants." *It's a good thing you can't read minds*. I thought to myself.

I continued with my intellect, trying to impress her, "Sex is good and should only complement a relationship, not DEFINE it. I believe communication and trust is the sole foundation of a good healthy relationship. Without it, your relationship will eventually crumble no matter how good the sex is. The only thing good sex will do, is prolong the inevitable." I stated soundly, speaking from experience.

"Wow! With those words of wisdom I have to wonder, why aren't you married yet?" She asked in astonishment.

"To be honest with you, I'm not ready to be married. I had a friend living in Delaware and he was married to a very nice woman, but he later found out that she was screwing her brother's best friend throughout their entire marriage. I don't want to live like that, to be honest it almost turned me against marriage. While I'm single, I'm going to do what the fuck I want to do. However, if and when I get married, I will become a one woman's man, like you're a one man's woman." I stated confidently.

"I like your style. Give me your number, I have a friend you might be interested in." She said digging in her purse for paper and a pen.

"I'm sorry I don't normally do blind dates!"

"Please just this once. I just met this girl she's a little down on her luck with men. And she needs to go out with a positive man, to know there are still some good guys out there in the world that's not locked up, gay or on drugs."

"You sure have a way with words."

"So you'll do it?"

"Not so fast, what does she look like?"

"She's half Hispanic and Pilipino, A very nice person, beautiful eyes, about 5' 6", maybe one hundred and seventeen pounds. She works, has her own place and her own car_"

"So if she's all that, I have one question for you?"

"What's that?"

"What's wrong with her?" I asked curiously.

"Huh?"

"Don't stall, what's wrong with her? If she's all that you say she is, and she can't find her own date, or still single for that matter, something has to be wrong with her. Cause from this man's point of view, the last time I checked a perfectly good looking woman didn't need help finding a man."

"Okay. Well maybe she has a low self-esteem problem. But I think you will be able to handle that." Blowing it off, like it wasn't that serious. "This is against my better judgment, but here's my number." I reluctantly hand her a piece of paper with my number on it.

"Thanks, you won't regret it!" She stated in excitement.

"For some reason I feel like I already am." Honey love, by R. Kelly escaped through the speakers seeping into our ears. We both started moving to the rhythm. I turn and look at Rhonda as she started to speak.

"I tell you what, just to show you good faith. If the date doesn't go right, I'll make it up to you right now." I looked at her with a sly look on my face.

"Are you saying what I think your saying?" I said with a grin.

"No probably not, but I want you to dance with me for taking my friend out." Well, if I couldn't have sex with her, slow dancing to honey love was the next best thing. So I took her up on her offer. She presses all her curves against my body as we slow grind on the dance floor. The smell of her perfume starts to turn me on and I feel my hard on growing in my pants. *Damn, no one has given me a hard on from dancing since I was in high school.* She made me feel like I hadn't had a piece of ass in years.

"Is that Woman you're wearing?" She looked at me stunned for a second before answering.

"Yes it is you sure know your perfumes." There were two things that I had learned, that always impressed a woman. The first thing is guess their correct perfume and second bring back the right type of panty hose.

Laughing out loud, "Well I've had the pleasure of being in the company of a lot of females and they always wanted a man's point of view on how it made them feel when they smelled different types of perfume. So to say the least I had a lot of practice getting it right."

"Wait, let me get this straight. So you're trying to tell me that the type of perfume a woman wears sends out different signals to men?" She asked inquiringly.

"That's correct."

"Oh really, then what type of signal am I sending out right now?" She asked curiously, waving her wrist in front of my nose so I could get a better whiff.

"Your perfume says that, I'm a classy and sophisticated lady. So don't waste your time or mine with your weak ass game, and if you're still bold enough to step to me, you better come correct." Rhonda looked into my eyes, like we were the only two people here on the dance floor and we were making love right at that moment. Her eyes were saying go deeper I want to feel every inch of you. Clearing her throat, "I'm not going to confirm or deny that there's any truth to that. I want to thank you for the dance. It felt hard_ good... dancing again."

"No the pleasure was all mine."

"Please excuse me, I have to find my friend. It's about time for us to leave now." Rhonda stated not wanting to engage in something she may regret later. "I hope I have the opportunity of seeing you again." I said, following her as she walked off the dance floor.

"That will be nice, have a good night." she stopped and turned towards me like a starving lion hunting down her prey. "And just for the record, so there is no misunderstanding. If I was single and we had sex tonight. I would have blown your mind, physically and emotionally, without a doubt. My stuff would have tasted so sweet, that you would have complained to your dentist of a tooth ache." Rhonda was not the kind of girl that wasted time. She was very direct and to the point and left no room for error. I was slightly intimidated by her directness and as much as I didn't want to give her that much clout, especially in my own club I let her walk away feeling powerful. As I stood there astounded at her bluntness, thoughts began to swirl in my head *I can't believe I let her walk away. Married or not she should have been coming home with me and making love to me the way she just fucked me repeatedly with her eyes.* I got myself together and went to look for Marcus, I found him in the bathroom sitting in one of the stalls. Marcus was so drunk it sounded like he was having a good conversation with himself.

I knocked on the stall door, "Hey Marcus, what are you doing in there? You know if you shake it more than twice you're playing with it." He laughed along with me, as he fumbled around in the stall, then he replied.

"I don't need to jack off! I already did that before I came here, so I'm good for at least another two hours. I was just putting my clothes back on."

"Say what? What are your clothes doing off?" I asked being a bit surprised.

"I took them off to take a shit! Don't you take yours off when you shit?" He replied.

"Hell no!" I instantly responded. "Man you need some serious help and I hope you find it."

"I'm just fine, I took my clothes off to get comfortable. Nobody wants to get their clothes wrinkled up and dirty while sitting on the toilet. I think you're the one that needs to be checked out, you let that fine ass girl walk out the door."

"How do you know what did?"

"Because you're in the restroom, standing in urine while talking to me, as I'm wiping my ass. And not out there talking to her, where you should be. I'm drunk, not stupid." Marcus was right and I couldn't even fight it.

"Hurry the hell up I'm calling a cab, to take your drunken ass home." I hurried out the restroom before I passed out from the foul odor coming from the stall he was occupying. I went out front to reserve Marcus a cab to take him home, I slipped the driver a fifty and told him to keep the change. I didn't mind kicking out the extra cash to make sure he got home safe, after all he is a loyal paying customer. I stood outside soaking in some of the fresh night air, I couldn't help but to think about what had transpired between Rhonda and me. *I wonder if she is as faithful as she claims to be. Her head game was tight, and she looked like she was the type that didn't put up with any crap. Maybe if I had hooked up with her instead of some of those knuckleheads that I dealt with back in Baltimore, maybe I would feel differently about women. I hope in this case that her friend is a lot like her. You know what they say, birds of the same feather flock together.*

Chapter 3

Saturday morning I woke up around 8:30, I hadn't planned on spending the entire night with Patrice so I got up and quickly got dressed. I was supposed to be on my way to get Marcus so we could run a few basketball games. I nudged Patrice to wake up.

"Patrice, wake up. I'm about to roll out." I whisper.

"Umm, what time is it?" She asked with a scratchy voice, as morning breath emitted from her mouth.

"Its 8:35. I have to go pick up Marcus at 9, are you going to be okay today?"

"Yeah, I'll call one of my friends to come pick me up later. Thanks for everything again." She said wiping the sleep out of her eyes.

"There's a couple of dollars on the night stand for you, in case you need something." I gave her a hug, she kissed me on the cheek.

"I love you," She whispered.

"I love you too." I said as I got up to walk out the door, "Hit me later if you need me." I threw up the peace sign with my two fingers and closed the door.

"Ok." I barely heard her voice through the door. 8:57, I pulled up into Marcus's driveway pumping some ole school rap music on the radio. I turned the car off and knocked on the door. No one answered, I pulled out my spare key and walked in. I heard a TV playing in the bedroom, as I walked into the kitchen to raid their refrigerator. Octavia came out of the bedroom-soaking wet with a towel wrapped around her.

"Hi..... Jamal, I thought I heard someone out here." She said seductively, running her fingers through her hair to work the kinks out.

"Hey where's Marcus?" I asked, turning back to the fridge, taking the focus off her gorgeous half naked body.

"Oh... he's umm...., he's in the bedroom knocked out." She responded slyly.

"What! We were going to the gym this morning!" I exclaimed firmly.

"Well he kinda had his work out already today." She acted like her towel falling off was an accident, showing off her newly matching stomach ring to go with her hood piercing. I act like I didn't notice because it doesn't take much to get me excited, especially with a body like hers. I went back into the living room and sat on the couch to watch some TV.

I knew Octavia liked me for a long time and I had to give my boy Marcus mad props for having a unique girl like her. She's unique because she was the type of woman that wanted nothing to do with a man, but everything to do with a woman. Marcus wanted more for Octavia, plus he liked the challenge of trying to convert her. Over the course of a few months some persuasive language and slight manipulation, he rehabilitated her into one of his most extraordinary lovers ever. Marcus always kept it real with Octavia, but there's this one girl named Shayla that he's been seeing on the side for almost a year, and he can't get enough of her. She's an ordinary girl, with an exceptional skill of doing what it takes to make any man want more. Marcus Never took Shayla serious enough to be his only woman, but he couldn't leave her sweet sensations alone longer than a few weeks. He likes the thrill of having sex with her as often as possible. Shayla on the other hand has feelings for Marcus and wants to be his one and only, but Marcus doesn't see her that way. She gave up the cookies within a couple of days, and even though he has love for her he can't respect a woman like that. She will never be more to him than a hit it and forget it kind of girl. Octavia followed me into the room and straddled my legs.

"What the fuck are you doing?" I exclaimed, shocked by her boldness and yet turned on as the same time.

"What?" She said with a devious smile on her face, as she started kissing me around my neck, while pressing her hot tender opening down onto my swollen manhood. I knew in my mind, that I couldn't have sex with my best friend's girl, I tried my hardest to push her off of me, but my arms weren't responding. *This is a major cardinal rule you're breaking here!* I thought to myself.

"Why are you doing this?" I moaned in pleasure and at the same time wishing she would stop.

"Jamal, cut the shit! I saw you checking me out a few times, and you've known that I wanted you since before I met Marcus, now I finally have the chance, besides I heard a lot about you and it's about time to find out if everything I've heard is true." She stated as she continued to rub her pelvis even harder stimulating her clitoris.

"You know we shouldn't be doing this. No, stop!" I mumbled. "We can't be doing this!" I tried to reason.

"Damn it! The only thing you're going to break is me off a piece of that big hard dick! Besides that bulge in your pants didn't read that memo." I wanted to stay strong in my mind, but my flesh was weakening rapidly. I tried hard but couldn't resist as I gripped her firm breast with my hands licking around her supple erect nipple, counter clockwise working my way in from the outside in, switching back and forth spending approximately 8 to 10 seconds on each nipple. She ripped off my shirt and started sucking and kissing on my chest, while pinching on my right nipple. She manipulated her hands to undo my pants, with three fingers. I worked my hands around to her back door, finally copping a feel of that firm ass that I've been hearing about for so long. Octavia got very excited feeling my cold hands on her ass, being sucked this deep in the game I figured I had nothing to lose at this point, I decided to go all the way. Gradually working my middle finger completely inside her rear hole, it was uncomfortable to her at first, and then she really got into it. She moaned out "I knew you were a damn freak!" She pulled down my pants and started sucking me through my red silk boxers. Octavia unwrapped my penis like it was water and she was lost in the desert she demanded I look at her while she sucked on me, it turned her on to have me watch her while she was performed. It was hard to stay focused, the way she kept wrapping her tongue around the shaft of my dick, my eyes roll to the back of my head because of the sensation I was feeling. She eventually came up for air, kissing me every inch of the way. I couldn't take it anymore, I wanted to be inside of her right there, and the thought of this sexual act being morally wrong had completely vanished from my thoughts. At last, it's time for her to climb aboard my train, she turns around and slides down my extension, and her natural lubrication makes it easier for her to swallow me up.

She screamed, "Damn you're big! You filled me up." Octavia's creamy juices ran down over my balls saturating the couch. After a few more minutes, Octavia got up, turned around and sat back down on her pleasure zone.

"Oohhhh!!!... You know we really shouldn't be doing this. But I had to see what all the excitement was about, I can feel you in my stomach." She moaned, while continuing to rotate from side to side and up & down, in a rhythmic motion.

"It's too late now, no need to stop I'm about to cum!!!" I exhaled gripping her ass firmly.

We heard a deep voice from the opposite side of the room, "What the fuck is going on up in here!" Marcus stated, coming from the bedroom.

My heart dropped to my stomach, "Yo Mark...I'm_" I tried to plead but he interrupted me.

"How in the hell is my fiancée and best friend knocking boots, in my fucking living room! And not invite me to the party?" He exclaimed, overlooking the fact that she was having sex with someone other than himself.

"Huh_" Octavia and I said in unison, we looked at each other with a puzzled look on our faces.

"Jamal you heard me, move your damn hands so I can handle it from the back!" Octavia moaned even more as Marc and I entered simultaneously.

"So this is what it feels like to have a trios." She gasped in between taking breaths, I wanted to succumb to her as she made my body quiver like no one before. We defied the laws of nature, filling the insides of her moistened vaginal walls, massaging every inch of her with my vibrating entity. This ménage a trios went on for a good three hours. Octavia had drained almost all of the life out of my body. My reserves had kicked in, but I was still no match for her. Like a vacuum, the more I gave her, the more she was willing to suck out of me. I retained as much of my dignity as possible and gracefully bowed out.

"I hate to cut out of this 3 way dance, but I have other business to tend to." I stated aloud to no one in particular. Marcus didn't pay me any attention, all of his attention was focused on Octavia's satisfaction. She hardly managed to motion that she will call me later. I gave her a fat Owl's eye with my thumb and forefinger, while the other three stragglers pointed straight up, for the ok sign and walked out the door.

By the time I got home late in the in the afternoon, Stephanie still wasn't home yet. I decided to track her down so we could resolve our issues. I called her sister's house to see if she was willing to part with Stephanie's whereabouts.

"Hey Emily, can I speak to Stephanie please?" I asked, assuming she was there.

"She's not here Jamal, she left about 20 minutes ago, you need to get your shit together and stop putting my sister through all this drama!" She spouted through the phone with attitude.

"First of all, it's none of your business what we're going through! And another thing I'm not putting her through anything, this was a big misunderstanding. You know better than anyone, how she snaps before hearing the whole story first." I tried to reason, before losing my temper.

"Well when Stephanie has to keep running to my house to spend the night, every time you have a misunderstanding, you're making it my business. Besides that's my sister and I love her. I hate to see her torn up like this all the time. You know what she's been through already. She can't take too much more."

"Yes I know that! Let's not forget who got her counseling in the first place, to put her life back on track because of all the stuff she went through. I love Stephanie too and she's the last person I want to see unhappy, but a lot of her problems were brought into this relationship. I understand it's going to take some time for her to realize but she has it good now and things are different, I promise you this, she's in good hands I'm going to take care of her."

"Jamal, I'm sorry I snapped at you. I'm real protective of my sister." She spoke softly.

"It's okay I know you're just looking out for her, but I got this." I charmed her.

"I know you do and thank you. But please choose your words wisely, when she gets there. I love her, but I don't want her spending the whole weekend over here."

"You're welcome. And don't worry, I'll be very tactful." I warmly stated.

"Bye."

"See ya." I was on my way to the bedroom, when I heard Stephanie come in the front door.

"Where have you been?" I asked, being concerned.

"At my sister's!" She replied angrily.

"Every time we have a disagreement, you can't always run to your sisters! We need to talk things out." I said with sensitivity.

"I know, but I had to clear my head." I noticed a piece of my cell phone bill sticking partway out of her pocketbook, but that didn't bother me. I knew she didn't find anything, because there was nothing to find. A long time ago, I called my cellular provider and told them not to put anything on my bill, just what I owe every month and nothing else. That way, if she ever got a hold of my bill, there wouldn't be anything on it but the amount due. And let the truth be told, if they ain't paying my bill, then they don't need to know who I'm calling anyway.

"Stephanie look at me, just because my phone goes off doesn't mean that I'm cheating on you. Whenever I see you on the phone I don't start accusing you and saying that you're messing around do I? We both have friends, and it should be okay for us to talk to our friends freely without the other person getting offended.

If you ever think that I'm doing something or messing with someone else, you need to talk to me so we can clear the air." I reasoned gently.

"I know and I'm sorry for accusing you. I will try to work on it more, ok." She replied understandingly.

"I accept, come here and give me a kiss." After our little heart to heart, we lay in the bed together watching "Soul Food" the series, then "Sex and the City". Stephanie rolls over and begins caressing me gently, motioning that she is ready to make up not only verbally but physically as well.

"How can I make it up to you for being so mean?" She asks seductively. My hormones are to some extent already awakened, after watching Malinda Williams on "Soul Food", she knows how to work that curvaceous chocolate body in ways that I'm sure excites any man who watches her. Stephanie slides her left leg in between my legs, looking for some arousal out of my manhood.

"So what do you have in mind?" I ask stalling, thinking *how am I going to get out of this.* I can feel my man starting to harden up as the blood rushes in like a sponge soaking up water; but I know I am too sore to have sex right now.

"We could dim the lights," She whispers, kissing me on the lips a few times before continuing, "Maybe turn the TV down low and play some of those naughty games we like to play." She opens my shirt as she speaks. I want to be inside her and make everything ok, but I know I can't. My boys are in no shape to have any more recreation today.

"Steph_ I want to hold you in my arms and make you feel safe because I'm not going anywhere. I don't know what it's going to take, but I'm willing to try anything."

"Jamal?" She says as if she almost doesn't want me to hear her.

"Yeah baby_"

"Do you think we have what it takes to survive?" I lay silently for a second, honestly wondering if we could survive through anything. To be honest I believe we can survive anything, if we are both on the same page working towards the same goals together. Unfortunately, at this stage in my life I'm not sure what it's going to take, to give my whole heart and life to just one person. I turn and look at Stephanie, wanting to give her my honest opinion, but I know that it would hurt her even more and I can't bear to see any more pain in her eyes right now.

Drawing in a deep breath, "I think you already know how I feel." I try to avoid lying as much as possible, I stroked her back softly through her silk shirt. Even though it may not seem like it, I really don't like lying to her, so I try to articulate my words in such a way that answers her question without really answering her question.

"I feel you. I just don't want to be in another relationship based on lies." She pauses for a minute as if she's reflecting on something. I think about all the lies I've told her since we've been together. I wish I could come clean right now that all could be forgiven and that everything from this point forward would be right between us. Instead, I just lay here silently, leaving her with this illusion that I am the perfect gentleman.

"Hey, Steph."

"Yeah_" She answers, still looking off into nowhere.

"What's on your mind? You zoned out for a minute." I cautiously ask, not sure if I want to hear what she is thinking about.

"I just want to make you the happiest man alive and I don't ever want you to have any reason to be with anyone else. I want to be your everything and I want to take care of you, so you'll never have to do anything again."

"I'm sorry, that's just not possible." I reply.

"What?" She responds, shocked by my response.

"I care about you too much, to let you do everything for the both of us. Please don't take this personal, but I also need to hold my own, what would I be if you decided you didn't want to be with me anymore. I wouldn't have a pot to piss in or a window to throw it out of." I explain.

"Don't think like that, we'll always be together. You have to think positive in order to get positive results."

"I know, but_"

"Ssshhh! It's going to be all right. Trust in me and believe in me. I'll take care of you."

She wraps her hands tight around my neck tight and presses her body as close to me as she possibly can. "I got you." She says offering every ounce of herself in those three simple words.

"Uummm… you know what that does to me." I said closing my eyes and tilting my head back, feeling a sensation run through my entire body.

"I know, I just want to make it up to you for leaving yesterday. Relax, I got you on this one." I closed my eyes, sunk my head back into my pillow and loosened up some more as Stephanie started out by caressing my ear with her tongue. *If only my life could be this perfect all the time.* I imagine as I slip into ecstasy.

£   £   £

The following afternoon, as I am waxing my jeep in front of my house, my cell phone starts ringing. *Who in the world could this be?* I thought contemplating whether or not I should even answer it. After a few seconds of hesitating, I remembered from last night that I was expecting a call from Rhonda's friend and quickly decided.

"Hello?" I spoke into the phone out of breath.

"Hi, may I speak to Derrick please?" The sexy voiced asked.

"Speaking. Who is this?" I asked hoping this fine voice was my future date.

"This is Sharmel, Rhonda's friend."

"Ohhhh, how are you doing? You caught me off guard, I didn't think you were going to call so soon." I respond feeling excited that I would soon meet the body attached to this sexy voice.

"I apologize is this a bad time? I can call you later if you'd like."

"No, now is fine. I was just waxing my jeep." I stated as nonchalantly as possible.

"I hope you don't think I'm desperate for a date or anything like that. Rhonda told me a little about you and I would like to meet you for myself. And see if you're really the perfect gentleman as she claims."

"That's fine how's eight tonight?" I asked quickly, hoping not too sound overly anxious.

"That's fine. Do you have a place in mind?"

"How about the Indigo grill, over on India St, Their grand opening is today."

"That's good. I'm looking forward to meeting you. I'll be wearing a turquoise top and white Capri's. And I have long curly black hair."

"Okay, sounds like a winner already."

"I'll see you later then." Sharmel's replies as if she's trying to seduce me through the phone.

"See ya soon." She definitely didn't sound like a guy. I was still feeling a little leery about meeting her. *What the hell, if she turns out okay then she'll be another piece of ass to add to the list.* I showered and changed my clothes. The good news is that I know what she's wearing and she doesn't know what I look like. So if she doesn't meet my approval, I can simply leave without her ever knowing I was here. I pull into the Indigo grill parking lot hoping she is already here, while trying to find a parking space, I scan the people walking in the front door. Before I get out the car, I check to make sure that I have my mouthwash, a pack of Wrigley's spearmint gum and condoms, ribbed style of course, the three necessities for a good date. I walked in the door peaking in to see if I noticed someone of her description. She was sitting at a booth by the window.

"Wow!" I said aloud. "She is gorgeous." Her cinnamon crusted eyes flickered from the lights above, her long wavy hair was shiny and healthy looking, and her complexion resembled that of a peak sunrise on an exotic island. In that instant, it felt like we were the only two in the room, until a couple bumped into me coming in. She shouldn't have a problem ever getting a man, which made me even more leery about her being set up on a blind date. I rush over to the table and introduce myself.

"Hello, Sharmel? I'm Derrick a pleasure to meet you." I state proudly, wanting to get this date started as soon as possible.

"Yes. Uh, hello Derrick! It's nice to finally meet you too. You're even more handsome than Rhonda gave you credit for! And your body definitely fits your voice."

"Thank you. And you're even more beautiful than I thought you would be! So now we're even." we both shared a laugh releasing some of the anxiety now that we both have at least met each other's basic standards.

"Well what were you expecting, a beached whale or something?" She asks half seriously.

"No, just not someone as beautiful as you. I gotta admit, I'm a little curious as to why you're on a blind date, you should never have a problem finding someone to go out with."

"First, thank you. And second, I normally don't, but Rhonda is such a good friend that I figured I had nothing to lose if she recommended you." Not wanting to insult her by insinuating that she doesn't know how to find a man, I politely change the subject.

"Anything sound good on the menu?" I ask picking up the menu, more interested in looking between her cleavage than at the special of the day.

"I don't know, I'm not that hungry." She says picking up the cocktail menu.

"Well I'm starving and I am ready to eat!" Another five minutes the waiter comes over to take our order.

"Are you ready to order?" He nervously asked.

"Not yet, in a couple more minutes please." I respond, giving her as much time as she needs to find something. Beside I was in no hurry to end this date.

"Well can I start you off with some drinks?"

"Yes. I'll have a Coors light on tap and a glass of water with lemon."

"And you ma'am?"

"I'll have Smirnoff and cranberry juice, but I want the juice in a separate glass, a glass of ice water, with 4 lemons on the side and 3 packets of sweet and low.

"Ma'am there is sweet and low on your table." He begins to explain.

"I don't want them, I don't know how long they were on the table or who put their filthy hands on them!" She snapped.

"Yes ma'am, I will bring out some sweet and low." not wanting to cause a confrontation he moves swiftly from the table to fetch our orders.

"What was that all about? He didn't do anything wrong." I calmly ask.

"In customer service the customer is always right, he is not supposed to question what I want just do what I say." I try to change the subject and calm her down.

"Ok I see your point. So how do you and Rhonda know each other?" She watched as the waiter disappeared into the crowd before she started talking.

"I met her at the mall. We have the same exquisite taste in clothes. While in Hecht's clothing store, there was this skirt on the rack and it just happened to be the last one. Wouldn't you know it, we both looked at it and grabbed it at the same time, we started laughing. And that's how we became friends."

"That's pretty interesting. Do you have any kids?" I shot off another question, to keep her mind off the waiter.

"No, haven't been in a relationship long enough to have kids. What about you?"

"No not yet. If you don't mind me asking a personal question. Why haven't your relationships lasted long?" I asked inquisitively, hoping she might shed some light on what I'm up against. Just then, the waiter came back with our drinks.

"Here is your drink sir." He Places my drink mats on the table and then my drinks.

"Thank you."

"And here are your drinks ma'am." repeating the process with her drinks.

"This is not what I ordered!" She yelled. "I told you that I wanted my lemons on the side, not in my water. You need to pay more attention to what people order! And 2 packets of sweet n low, now what the hell I'm supposed to do with 2 packets of sweet n low!" She exclaims embarrassing the waiter and myself.

"Sorry ma'am, I will get you some more." He replies in a remorseful tone.

"And take that water back, bring me a fresh cup and four lemons on the side!"

"Yes ma'am."

"Think before you act this time!"

I couldn't take it anymore. "What is your problem? All you had to do was take your lemons out of the water." I snap at her.

"No, all he had to do was listen, to what the hell I was saying and we wouldn't have this problem! And whose side are you on anyway, pick a team!"

"I'm on nobody's side! But you don't have to treat him so mean!"

"Here is your water and lemons and your sweet and low, ma'am." She cut her eyes at him, trying to find some kind of fault with her order so she could yell at him again.

"Are you ready to order now?" I cut in quickly to give her a moment to catch her breath and settle down.

"I'll take the T bone steak, well done, with mashed potatoes, gravy and seasoned squash." I tell the poor waiter trying to apologize, I'm sorry with my eyes for Sharmels rude behavior.

"Sure. And are you ready to order ma'am?" Sharmels face is still all wrinkled up as she reads from the menu.

"Now make sure you get this right. I want the baby back ribs, steamed vegetables and the dirty rice. Now I want the special sauce on the ribs, and the vegetables need to be steamed extra-long until they are almost mushy and no seasoning on the rice. I want an apple pie and vanilla ice cream for dessert, but don't bring it out until after I have eaten my dinner. And bring me another vodka and cranberry, make it a double chased with a Molson Canadian." She was about to continue but she saw how irritated I was getting by the look on my face. "That'll be all."

It has become vividly clear why she is still single, she is a drama queen! This means she will make the worst of any situation. She continues to slam down one drink after another, by the time our food arrives she's almost too drunk to eat.

When the waiter gives us our food and I'm hoping it goes without incident. But I was asking for too much.

"Excuuuuse meeee!" She slurred out. "There's some bin wrong wiff my food! First of all the vegibowls are to mushy, do I look like a baby wiff no teeves! Where is my extra special sauce for my ribs! And what's all that shit in my rice!" She blurted out loud.

"That's the dirty rice you ordered ma'am."

"Wrong, take it back and do it again and don't take all night! Oh and bring me another vodka and blueberry juice pronto!" She ordered.

"You mean cranberry juice ma'am." He interjected to help.

"That's what I said, don't mock me ass hole!" I had to cut in, she was going way over board with this guy.

"Don't you think you had enough to drink?"

"Don't you fink you should mind your own fucking business!" She quickly snapped back as she rolled her head in my direction looking like a sloppy mess. She looked like she had just been gang banged by four professional wrestlers from extreme championship wrestling. I knew at this point, our date was over. I ate my food as quickly as I could and excused myself to the bathroom.

"Wait, before you go can we do a shot? Waiter, can I get 2 boiler makers!" She shouted across the room as everyone turned to look at her.

"No thanks, I don't want one. In case you haven't heard, too much alcohol kills the brain cells." I stated angrily. "But I guess it doesn't matter, you probably forgot what I said already.

"Come on just one shot, don't be a party pooper. You're spoiling all the fun." She laughs.

"I'm sorry. I actually like using more than five percent of my brain. And you spoiled the moment the minute you started talking with your lips between your ass cheeks! Now if you will excuse me I have to go now." I walked towards the back, looking for the rest rooms, the manager and the waiter head towards me.

"Excuse me sir, is there a problem at your table?" The manager asked.

"No it was a mistake. The girl is the problem among, other things." I stated with a frustrated look on my face.

"I just wanted to make sure, because I know he's new and I don't want any unhappy customers."

"Your waiter did nothing wrong, in fact he went out his way to make that bitch happy. Sorry excuse me, to make that girl happy."

"Are you sure?"

"Yes. To be honest with you, I don't even want to be seen with her in public any longer. Can you grab my bill please? I would like to pay for my portion of the order."

"Absolutely its right here, your total is one hundred and thirty seven dollars and seventy seven cents."

"How much is the T bone steak dinner and the Coors light?" I asked.

"That's a total of nineteen dollars and ninety nine cents. It's on special tonight."

"Look, here is twenty two dollars. Give him a tip, or you can put it in your pocket or towards the bill, either way, I don't care. All I ask is let me slip out the back door and wait about five minutes before you give her the bill. Tell her I left and to have a nice life." When I got to my car, I couldn't help but to think how disappointed I was with her. A fine piece of ass like that, reduced to drunken damaged goods. That's what happens when a girl is cursed with good looks, having guys tripping all over themselves to talk to you, or their dads want to spoil them to death, wanting to make sure the next guy is going to have to do better than what he did. And you end up becoming a misfit to society, thinking everybody owes you something. I thought about going back in there and trying to salvage what I could. *Fuck that, I ain't got the time or the patience. Rhonda you were way off base with this one, I wish you would have taken the time to get to know her first. Instead of basing things off of a few conversations on the phone.* Shortly after 2 am, my phone rang, scaring the hell out of me.

"Hello?" I mumble trying to, clear my voice.

"You ignorant ass motherfucker! Why da hell did you sneak out of the restaurant and stick me with the bill? I didn't even have the money to pay!" She yells through the phone angrily.

"Because your funky drunken ass did not act lady like and you were a real turn off. Plus I paid for my part of the bill!"

"You fuckin ass hole! You owe me a hundred dollars!"

"I don't owe you a damn thing! However, I am impressed, you're too drunk to be social but you can still count money. You ordered it so you should be able to pay for it!"

"I'm a fucking lady, I don't think I should have to pay for my food! I thought you would have been gentleman enough to pay for my meal." She responds nastily. The moaning and shuffling coming through the phone, sounds like there's a fight going on between her keys and the front door. I chuckled to myself slightly, because from the sounds of it the front door is winning.

"Thinking and thoughting comes from not knowing! Fuck what you heard! And learn some fucking manners. Biootch!!!" I yell, feeling my temper starting to rise, waking me up out of my God given sound sleep, for this nonsense.

"I'm gonna get somebody to fuck you up! And I don't ever want to talk to you again!"

"I don't think that will be a problem. And speaking of fucking me up, I was probably the first time you had oral sex in a long time, with your shitty ass attitude, so I'll take that as a compliment. And by the way make sure you savor that wet sensation in your panties before you wring em out, it'll probably be a long time before you get that stimulation again!" I said sarcastically.

"Watch your back! Just watch your back mother fucker!" She yelled, fumbling the phone, sounding like she fell half way up the stairs.

"Look, I don't know who da fuck you think you are talking to. Ain't nobody punking nobody right here! I'm a B-More brotha, so bring on the ex-one and the next one! I'm hanging the fuck up! I don't even know why I'm wasting my precious time with your drunken ass!" I slapped my cell phone shut hoping it made her ear ring, I can feel my blood pressure reaching its peak, guess I won't be going back to sleep anytime soon. *You got one coming Rhonda, hooking me up with that crazy psycho bitch!*

Chapter 4

Octavia got a call from her best friend Dawn. Dawn was bugging out because her pothead boyfriend had just beat her up again.

"Marcus, will you come with me? Dawn's man just beat her up again." She exclaims, in a panic.

"Hell no, I aint going nowhere! If her man keeps beating her ass and she's still with him, then tell him to keep beating her because she probably likes it." I state, not feeding into that domestic nonsense.

"You are so insensitive sometimes." Octavia sulks, looking at me in disgust.

"Why should I suffer and miss the game, because your friend likes getting beat on; and if she doesn't like getting beat up tell her to leave him." I huff, looking around the living room for the remote control.

"Fine! I'll go by myself and please believe I'll deal with you when I get back." She screams.

"What if it was your mom or sister being beat on?" She to mumbles as she begins to get up, acting like she's going to leave.

"Look I'm sorry. I didn't mean it like that_"

"So you'll come with me then?" She interjects, sounding hopeful.

"No, but can you grab me another beer out the fridge before you go?" Octavia looks at me with pity in her eyes, which quickly turns to rage.

"Get it your damn self, and when you're finished getting that you can work on your next nut as well. There won't be no penis between us for a minute!" She storms out slamming the door behind her. I wait until Octavia's car is out of sight then I hit Shayla on my speed dial.

"Hello!"Shayla answers with an attitude.

"Hello, what's good with you? I miss you." I recite in my most charming voice.

"I'm okay. What's up with you? I take it the bimbo isn't around, or you wouldn't be calling me." Her sarcastic tone seeps through phone.

"It ain't shit, come on it doesn't have to be like that you know how I feel about you. I was just sitting here watching the game and started thinking about you, so I called."

"Um hem. And where did Octavia go?" Not buying into my lame ass story.

"Oh she went to check on a friend about something." I calmly give into her, she obviously knows what's up.

"So what are you saying, you want to come over and do something? That seems to be the only reason you call."

"Well not necessarily in those words, but yeah." I answer perking up a little.

"Then why didn't you say that?"

"I'm saying it now! Do you want to see me or not?" Shayla pauses for a second, Oh my God Marcus, I want to see you so bad. My body throbs for your touch, but I'm tired of being your door mat. She thinks to herself.

"Give me a few minutes I gotta straighten up first."

I grab my last forty of Ole E and rushed out the door. I walk up to the front door and give a few raps on it to let her know I have arrived. No one answers, I knock a little harder, still no answer. I turn the knob to see if it was unlocked, the door opened right up and I walked in. The house was as silent as a hooker in church on Sunday morning.

"Shay I'm here." I call out, but no one answers me. I look around, then I heard the water running upstairs. Shayla must have heard me coming up her squeaky stairs.

"Baby is that you? I'm in the shower."

"Yeah, it's me." I answered walking into her room and sitting on the bed.

"I'll be out in a minute. Make yourself comfortable." I take off my socks and shoes first, and then I strip off the rest of my clothes. This smell of vanilla and cinnamon brightens the air from some scented candles burning on her nightstand. 'Giving him something he can feel' is playing on her stereo. To be honest I am a little impressed at how she's trying to set some kind of mood in here. I start sipping on my ice cold forty and sucking in the atmosphere, and right on que Shayla's coming out of the bathroom. She is soaking wet with nothing on but a pair of boy shorts panties on, small droplets of water fell to the floor from her curly hair. My eyes pierce into her body like they could make her any less clothed if stare harder. Her hair drapes just past her shoulders, her light complexion is glowing and her breasts were a mouthful and stimulated. I can see through her panties that she shaven neatly, leaving only a small landing strip pointing me in the direction of her glory. Her body mimics an hourglass perfectly, I sit there drooling not moving an inch.

"Marcus, most guys usually wait until after they get me in the bed to fuck me." She jokes, I try to play it off and start drinking my beer, but she knows she got it going on. To be quite honest I am really starting to catch feelings for her and I just hope she doesn't catch on. Perfect timing, "Between the Sheets" comes on and Shayla slides under the covers and starts kissing down my chest. I catch a whiff of her freshly shampooed hair, the mixtures of smells are so erotic, I can't help but to want to enter her right there on the spot.

"I'm going to make you feel real special." She whispered to me in her sexiest tone. She is trying to make love to me, and I am not going for that. I need to keep this strictly at a booty call status. After Shayla lubricated my working tool with her mouth, I roll her over on her back; I put her left leg over my shoulder and keep the right leg down. Start out slow, first, sliding my man a quarter of the way in and pulling it out. She is astoundingly wet and moaning like she's enjoying every inch of what she's feeling. I gradually go deeper and harder. Her moans turn into screams, but I don't care. I want her to know that this is not a make love session, no, this is a no frills straight fucking session. I flip her back into the doggy style pose, grabbed my forty and took long sip while I dig as deep as I could inside of her. I know I'm hitting it right, because her love canal winces every time I pack my 9 1/2 inches inside her. Shayla is out of breath, panting like she's about to pass out from a lack of oxygen. Unable to talk, she motions with her hands for me to stop. Instead, I turn my head maintained my stroke and finished off my beer, shortly thereafter I feel my load boiling with pleasure to the tip until I erupt on her back and partly in her hair. I wasn't about to risk the chance of slowing down for her and not finishing what I came here to do. I look at Shayla, the tears rolled down her cheeks, I feel sorry for her, and she had no idea that this relationship will never go any further than this bedroom. I wanted to apologize for my actions, yet instead I flip her back over and began spooning her. We lay there breathing hard as hell, sweat expelling from every pore of our bodies. Shayla turns to me, with a repulsed look.

"What da fuck was that all about?" She yells in between breaths.

"What?" I asked with a blank expression on my face.

"I went through all this extra trouble to make this a nice and romantic atmosphere for us and you turn it into an all-out fuck frenzy! What were you trying to prove? I already know you can fuck. And look, look at my panties all torn up." She holds the evidence in the air, torn in two pieces. "These were brand new and now I can't even wear em anymore."

"Well what did you think I was coming over here for? It's not like we're a family playing house up in here." I blurt out, then instantly regret saying it.

"I'm starting to wonder that myself, I know we're not family but I thought that's what we were working on. I should've known you were never going to leave her." She mumbles, then pauses for a second thinking over the whole scenario and then starts backing up, "Then you had the nerve to disrespect me and drink your beer while we were being intimate. So what am I now, your storage bin to drop your loads in?"

"Look this shit is old, you never complained before. Why you making such a big fuss now!" I reply trying to squash the whole thing.

"Before there weren't any feelings, now it's about me and you together, working on a future. Oh excuse me, that's what I was doing."

"Wait slow down, I didn't say nothing about me and you together, you assumed that on your own." I reply defensively.

"So all that shit about you leaving her, was just a lie to get my goodies." She asks her eyes starting to swell. How can I tell her it will be nothing more than just sex, and that the only reason I'm still around is that I can't leave her alone. I feel like a deer caught in headlights. I don't want to make this situation worse nor am I trying to make her feel bad it is what it is.

"Now come on, you know it's going to take some time to do that. It's a process. I can't just leave her overnight." I state apologetically.

"Why not, you can just come fuck me over night, I guess I'm the stupid one huh. I can't see the forest, for the trees." She spouts in disbelief.

"What's that supposed to mean?"

"It means you won't be getting the milk for free anymore, next time you'll have to buy the cow."

"So it's like that now, well, I've been thinking about this for a minute and now is about a good time as any, I think we need to slow things down for a little bit anyways." I grab my clothes off the floor and head towards the door, not daring to wait for her reaction. "I'll call you sometime."

"Don't bother, I'm sure you can find other bitches you can fuck."

I sit in my car and thought about what had just taken place. It hurts me more than I thought it would. Behind this six foot four, two hundred and twenty pound solid exterior I'm a crushed man. I don't want to show my real feelings towards Shayla, because it'll make me look soft. I don't want to lose my relationship with her, but I know it can't go any farther. I look at Shayla's house one last time put the car in gear and went home. Not long after I return, Octavia comes through the door.

"Hey baby did you get everything straight at Dawn's?" I ask, hoping this conversation goes smooth so I can get my mind off Shayla.

"Yeah it's all cool, for now. By the time I got there, they were sitting on the couch together watching a movie eating popcorn like nothing happened. I told her she was a damn fool for putting up with him. Then he had the nerve to get smart with me, telling me that if someone had slapped me around a little bit, I wouldn't have such a smart ass mouth. And Marcus honey just for the record, don't you ever plan on putting your hands on me, because the fourth of July will come twice the year you do." She states matter of factly.

"I know I don't have to hit on you, all I have to do is put this dick on you." I joke, but she fails to see the humor in my statement.

"Ha, ha, that was so funny." She says mockingly. "So anyway, who won the game?"

"I don't know I was too busy trying to get that nut by myself that I missed it." I state smartly.

"Marcus you can be a real ass hole sometimes. Are you ever gonna grow up? I am getting real tired of your immature shit. You need to work on your communication skills if you want this relationship to go any further." She storms off to the bedroom and I'm left sitting there thinking about the argument with Shay and the conversation with her. I know Octavia doesn't mean what she said, but I don't want to push my luck any more than I already have. Not to mention I'm not trying to set any records for losing the most women in a single day. *I hated to hear her whining and complaining all the time and I'll even admit I do need to work on my communication skills more. I love Octavia and it's safe to say that I have never loved anyone as much as I did her. I'm not sure how long she's going to keep putting up with my stuff. I can see Octavia being my wife and the mother of my children someday. But right now is not the time to bring kids into this world. There is too much violence and crime going on everywhere. And my greatest fear is what if I wasn't there when they really needed me. How could I ever live with that?*

£   £   £

I ran nearly tripping up the stairs into the house from sitting on front steps to get the phone. Completely out of breath I grab the phone, "Hello?"

"This is a collect call from the California county jail." The automated phone voice stated. *Quentin what do you want? Right now is a little too late for apologies.* I contemplate not answering the phone.

"Will you accept the charges?" The automated voice continues. I stand there frozen, not sure, if answering the phone will give me closure or make matters worse. *It's been at least three weeks since I heard from you.* "Uh, yes I'll accept the charges." I state nervously.

"Hey baby." He speaks, as if nothing is wrong and we're still together making plans for a wedding.

"Hey, but don't baby me! You're lucky I even accepted your call."

"I'm sorry. I never meant to hurt you, I'll tell you as many…"

I cut him off. "It's always the people you love and trust the most, who always seem to screw you over in the end! You were supposed to be here with me. Our marriage, our relationship everything, it's all ruined!" I begin to sob uncontrollably.

"Hey boo, stop crying. I still love you and want to do all the things that I promised you."

"Stop, don't make promises you know you can't keep. Look at you, your broke busted and disgusted!" I yell.

"Just give me a chance to make everything right…"

"I'm sorry but you've used all your life lines with me mister."

"I can't change the past, but I can make a better future for you and me. Baby, please don't deny me that. I can make this better." He pleas.

"I don't think so. I don't want to spend the rest of my life with a drug dealer, wondering if you're in jail, at work or even worse…dead!" I can feel the intensity of my emotions rising in me as I'm talking.

"But I did it for us!" I paused for a second to regain my composure, before I switched to my alternate terminology throwing in a few choice words of my own.

"How can you say you did it for us? I never asked you to sell drugs for me nor did I ever say we had to have some big elaborate wedding! You know I'm not materialistic, those things mean nothing to me. All I wanted was a real man with strong personal values, someone to be there with me to help raise a family and be my back bone. I don't want to raise kids alone lying to them about where you are and what you're doing. Kids deserve to know their father, not know you through a bunch of memories and pictures. You say you want to do things for me, for us, and look at you know! You're living in a 10' x 15' cell with another man. They tell you when to go to bed, when to get up, when to eat, what clothes to wear and how to wear them. Hell, you can't even take a shit without getting permission! Now tell me how da hell you gonna do something for me!"

Quentin became quiet… "Yeah I know my shit is fucked up right now. I was just trying to save us a few bucks, so we could have a nice wedding, and not get stuck paying back a lot of credit cards at a high interest rate. I just wanted everything to be special." He remorsefully recalls his thinking at the time, *I'll just get in and get out real simple.*

My anger is beginning to grow again, "Do you realize that I could have lost everything because of you? Not to mention, the danger you put me in when we were out in public together! Now if that's what you call love, you need to look it up in the dictionary and reevaluate your definition."

"Listen, I'm going to change things when I get out. I promise everything will be on the up and up. I just need you to stand by me and be the strong one. Like I was the strong one and held you up. Patrice please don't abandon me right now!" Quentin began to break down and sob a little. I felt his pain and wanted to reach out and be there for him, but I stood my ground. *I promised myself I would never be anyone's carpet to walk over, nor will I ever settle for less.*

"Bravo, bravo. That was good you almost had me. You've only been in prison for three weeks and you got that jailhouse talk down already! It's amazing how you can make shit look like shine, just from having too much time on your hands and room to think. The only thing left for you to do is make things right with God!"

The operator cut in, "You have one minute remaining on this call."

"I only have a minute left and I just want to tell you how much I care about you and miss you." He tries to rationalize.

"Don't bother!" I snapped, "Why don't you go find Bubba and tell him how much you care about him, I'm sure he'll be more than willing to listen. I hope that one day you get yourself together and make money the honest way and don't bother calling me anymore!" I slam the phone down before the operator cuts us off, dive into my bed and cry myself to sleep.

£   £   £

My phone goes off just before my two o'clock meeting. It's Patrice I can tell she's been crying by the sound of her voice. We agree to meet after work, at the Miramar café. By the time I walk into the cafe, Patrice is already there.

"Hey sweet pea how are you doing?" I asked and I kiss her on the forehead.

"Not too well…" She answers somberly, her voice sounding scratchy as though she has been crying for days.

"I'm sorry to hear that, what's on your mind?" After a few moments of staring into her half-filled coffee cup, she looks up towards me, "He called me yesterday."

"What! Finally. How did it go?"

"Well, he called me and can you believe that Negro called collect! He was talking about how he wanted to make up for what he did and right his wrong. It was hard, but I didn't give in. When I heard his voice, I got so angry inside and it brought back all the feelings that I've been suppressing. It really confused me."

"And now that you've had time to think about it, how do you feel?"

"Well_ I know I did the right thing, but I don't feel like I did the right thing."

"Why is that?"

"I feel like I owe him so much because of our history. Everybody makes mistakes and people need to be forgiven sometimes."

"I can understand that, it's going to be hard to move on with your life. But it can be done, you have to be true to yourself first." I explain.

"Thank you so much Jamal for listening to me, you are truly the best friend I always wanted but never had. Everything would have been perfect, if Quentin was more like you."

"Don't mention it, you're always good to me too and I am truly grateful to be a part of your life. If it makes you feel any better, I've never had a good solid relationship since we stopped seeing each other. And don't say it because I already know most of that is due to me." I say trying to make her laugh.

"My relationships pretty much have sucked after you too. I want you to know that I appreciate having you as a good friend and I'll never take our friendship for granted." She chuckles…"Besides you're the only man I could ever talk about anything with and not feel like I had to hold back out of fear of being ridiculed or used."

"You know I feel the same way about you." I reply thoughtfully.

"Thanks for being a good friend, now take your butt home and convince Stephanie that you're a good man before she leaves you." Patrice cutely scolds me with her gracious smile.

"It's nice to see that pretty smile on your face again, I'll call you later and let you know how things go." I leave out of the café feeling real good about myself.

£   £   £

Bright Sunday morning and all I can think is with the week I had, I need to go to church and feed my hungry soul, with some good news. I grab my phone and made a few calls to see if someone will go with me.

"Derrick, I'm heading out to church in about an hour, you think you might want to tag along?"

"Yo dawg, I just rolled in from last night and the only place I'm heading to is them sheets. But since today is Sunday, the least I can do is pray from the time it takes me to get undress, slip under my sheets and hit my pillow." He says in a sarcastic tone.

"Suit yourself, I'll hit you up later_" Before I could even finish my statement, he had already hung up on me. I call James next, he definitely needs some Jesus in his life. I hit #6 on my speed dial.

"Hello?" A groggy voice rumbles in the phone.

"James get up, it's me. I'm calling to see if you want to go to church with me today?" I ask.

"Man I was sound asleep! Yo I was having this phat dream. I was about to have_"

"Look, do you want to go with me or not?" I interject.

"I do like all those honey's at that church, particularly the deacon's daughter, she is a fine ass bronze looking honey." He pauses for a second thinking of how there were more women than men there, which increased his odds of hooking up with someone. Then his other line beeps in.

"Hold on, that's my other line." Two minutes later, he clicks back over.

"Look here I won't be able to go with you, something came up and I need to take care of it as soon as I can." His tone sounded more serious than before he clicked over.

"Is everything ok? You sound real different right now."

"Everything is cool, it's just something that can't wait. Thanks for thinking about me, I appreciate that and I would appreciate it even more if you prayed for me when you get there." He states anxiously.

"You got it, holler at me if you need me." I hang up the phone, wondering what had transpired on the other line that suddenly changed his attitude, but quickly switch my focus back to getting to church. *You know what, I know it's meant for me to go, so I'll just rock it solo. I'm not going to miss out on my blessing today.* I take a nice warm shower, throw on my Sunday's best and get on my way Steph had already left to go to work, she normally uses Sunday's to finish up on paper work she didn't get a chance to finish from the past week and prepare for the upcoming week. I arrive at church just in time for morning worship. Standing on the front steps of the church were some of the most beautiful woman God ever created. Junior starts coming to life, but I am on a mission with God this time and nothing is going to stand in my way. I am here to listen to the word of God and repent for my sins. I did however chuckle to myself, thinking of the possibility of talking to a few of them after church. *I've always saw myself living out the rest of my days with a God fearing woman. I feel bad about double dipping on Stephanie, God I hope me coming to church today will give me some extra credit for all the wrong that I have done. All I'm asking for is someone who will complete me emotionally and spiritually.* Another woman walks ahead of me into the church, with a dress that's almost too short and too tight for a place of worship. *Let me get up in this church and repent, quick fast and in a hurry!* I think to myself as I watch her hips sway back and forth like they are fighting to get out of that skirt.

"God is good ladies...." I announce, as I start up the steps.

They all turn around, "Praise the Lord, brother Jamal, it's nice to see you again." They all said in almost perfect unison.

"It's very nice to see you ladies too." I reply, "I can tell the blessings are plentiful in your neighborhood." I mumble as I walk through the doors. The church was just about full, I find an open seat in one of the pews towards the front, and I need to be as close as possible to make sure I hear every word clearly. The sun shines so bright, right through the decorated stained glass and the choir sings gloriously and with modern twist on an old hymnal "A little Talk with Jesus". I allow the rhythm to move in my spirit and I am reassured that this morning I am where I am supposed to be. Listening to the harmonious sounds. I feel a weight lifting off me as I sit there inhaling the gospel. I look around at all the people in the church It's almost like going back in time. Mother Scott still passing out peppermint candy to the kids in the pew behind her, somebody's baby yelling louder than the choir, the same group of women sitting in the back of the church talking about everyone and what they have and have not done. I call these women the W. G. G. S., the weekly gospel gossip section. Oh and I can't forget those wanna be player pimps, the type that think they can come to church, find a nice wholesome woman then guide her and mold her into the type of person they believe will worship them forever, before the streets corrupt their innocent minds. Real players knew better though, because some of those women that you find in church are worse than the ones on the street. Let's not forget about the kids that steal out of the collection plates. They hold their palms in a fist facing down, when it's their turn to drop their change into the collection plate they open their hand to drop change in, just enough to make that jingling sound and then quickly scoop more money out and walk away. It's not perfect but Lord knows I'd be lost without this place and so would the rest of the people decorating these pews, I guess that's one of the ties that bind us all here together makes us family and call this church our home.

Pastor Robinson begins his sermon talking about relationships. He speaks about how a man is supposed to act and how he is supposed to treat his wife. I look around as a lot of the women shout out, confirming what the pastor just said, he continues his sermon moving into the woman's role in a marriage and how she's supposed to carry herself. A couple the men shout out, but they sounded weaker than the women because they were simply out numbered. The Pastor says something that catches my attention. He starts talking about the ratio of women to men in the church and why the women outnumber the men five to one. Women were much more humble then men and God can use you when you are humble. A woman is more likely to let her husband win an argument even if she's right, just to make him happy or feel like he's in charge. A woman will submit to her husband, cook and clean for him, even if she worked a hard 8 hour shift just as he had. She may want to sit down and relax but she knows she can't because she has **wifely duties** to tend to. She will appreciate her man, even when there is nothing to appreciate him for. The men on the other hand have too much pride and God can't use you if pride is in the way. A man can be too stubborn to receive free food to help take care of his family, for fear he may look feeble to other people. A man would rather drive an extra hour and waste time and gas, before finally stopping and asking for directions. Just to make it look like he knew where he was going. Pastor Robinson finished up by saying, he wish he knew how to purge men of too much pride, then maybe he would be able to get them to attend services with their family, instead of sitting in their living rooms in front of a big screen TV, watching a football game.

After the sermon, I congratulated him for his deliverance.

"That was an excellent sermon pastor Robinson. I found it enlightening and uplifting. I felt as though you were talking directly to me."

"Thank you very much and God bless you, it's nice to know that I at least touched the heart of one person today. It's been awhile since I saw your face peeking out from the pews and I hope to see you on a more permanent basis. By the way we've just started a new male ministry program where the men get together every Sunday morning before church, for about an hour to talk about different issues. Sometimes men just can't talk to their significant others or they don't have anyone to talk to at all. The purpose of the ministry is to offer men a platform to vent and discuss events that are affecting their everyday lives, without being made to feel wrong. The ministry will be a place for young men looking for an unbiased opinion and solution to their problems."

"I'm thankful that I've been blessed enough to make it back into the house of the lord one more time. I will keep your male ministry in mind." I answer Pastor Robinson, only because I think that's what he wants to hear, but deep down I know the kind of stuff I want to talk about can't be talked about in that type of ministry.

"Well brother Jamal you know you're always welcome, all you have to do is make that choice and there's always an open spot in the choir if you decide you want it back."

"Yes sir I know, but I don't think I did the choir any justice. Besides I thought the object was to get people to come into the church, not chase them out. Now, on a more personal note, Pastor I know you're a busy man and I don't want to hold you up too much longer, but is it possible to speak to you privately?"

"Of course you can, why don't you go into my office and have a seat. I'll be there shortly." He answers placing a fatherly hand on my shoulder.

"Thank you so much pastor."

"Don't thank me, it's my duty to serve." I walk down to the Pastors office and sit on his plush couch, waiting for him to arrive, I can't help but notice how well things have been going for him. His brand new Dell computer, complimenting his newly remodeled office, complete with surround sound and a CD burner. *I wonder what kind of apps come on a computer like this.* I tapped on one of the keyboard keys so the desktop icons would pop up. The pastor had it going on, he had a picture of the choir for wallpaper with music notes floating from their mouths, several other icons stuck out, like AOL, pinball, windows media, Microsoft and fresh bucks. Fresh Bucks was an unfamiliar icon to me, I thought it was another one of those multi-level marketing programs. I never believed in that stuff, because they tell you how rich you're going to get by following their program. When all you get is more in debt from paying for membership dues, paying for supplies, training and shipping & handling fees. When in reality all you received was an education in how to be a fool, I didn't think it would hurt to take a quick peek at the program while I waited, I doubled clicked on the icon. I was speechless, I fell back into his oversized leather chair. My eyes grew as child pornography filled the screen. The pastor had hundreds of pictures of nude little kids and pictures of him with kids in compromising positions.

"That sick bastard! How in the hell can he walk around here and call himself a man of the cloth, doing this kind of shit!" I spoke out in anger.

"Please forgive me father for swearing on holy ground." I opened the door to storm out his office, Pastor Robinson was coming in at that same moment.

"Hey where's the fire? I thought you needed to speak with me?" He asked concernedly.

"Not anymore I don't!" I hastily replied.

"You never gave me a chance._" Hey replied looking a bit confused.

"A chance isn't what you need!" I growled, as I looked him up and down.

"I beg your pardon?"

"Pastor when was the last time you broke your knees to pray and repent for your sins?"

"Huh?" He asked with a perplexed look.

"Pastor, do you confess for your sins and ask God to forgive you? Do you practice what you preach?" I drilled him.

"Where's all this coming from?"

"I know pastor, I know." I responded with disappointment in my voice.

"You know what?" He asked looking for more clarification.

"I know enough to know that you shouldn't be a pastor!" a few people had gathered around, to see what the commotion was all about.

"Now wait a minute, you're going too far!" He raised his voice.

"No you wait! Before you put both feet in your mouth, turn around and look at your computer. How could you? Everyone trusted you and believed in you. And you've betrayed everybody!" The pastor pushed me back into his office and closed the door. Feeling the embarrassment of being busted he put his hands over his face as he started crying.

"I know I need help, but what should I do?"

"You can start by giving up your ministry!"

"What!"

"Yeah you heard me."

"But what will I do, there must be another way?"

"Then you start to make big rocks into little rocks, and little rocks into pebbles and pebbles into sand. Cause that's the only occupation you'll be qualified for once the people find out what kind of man you are. Or should I say the man you ain't."

"I can change all this I just have to look deep within to find a way..."

"Pastor when the soul is damaged, the last place you need to look is deep within. You should know that, you taught it 2 years ago in bible study."

"Please don't turn me in!" He pleaded.

"It's too late."

"It's never too late, doesn't the good book say forbearing one another, and forgiving one another. If any man have a quarrel against any, even as Christ forgave you, so also do ye. Colossians 3:13

"Yes pastor it does, but the bible also says Behold, all souls are mine, as the soul of the father, so also the soul of the son is mine: the soul that sinneth, it shall die. Ezekiel 18:4. Pastor your time has come to past." I stormed out of his office, slamming the door behind me. Having a sudden loss of appetite, I went straight home to think things through. Stephanie wasn't home yet so it gave me time to dwell on what had transpired without any outside influence. Sadly enough before I had a chance to decide on whether I was going to turn him in, I saw on the evening news that Pastor Robinson locked himself in the bathroom of his three story home and committed suicide by wrapping an extension cord around his neck. His oldest son broke into the bathroom and found him lying on the floor with a letter next to him asking for forgiveness of all the parents and children that were involved. He said he never meant to hurt anyone and hoped that his death will take away some of the pain and grief that they may feel. The letter concluded with, "I hope that all the children involved will receive all proper guidance and counseling that they need to break this vicious cycle and live to become model citizens and role models for other people to look up to." A few days afterward, his records were unsealed from a physiatrist he had seen in the past. His records had indicated that he hated his father with a passion and he was abused as well as a child. Furthermore, his father beat him mercilessly and then he would sit there laughing in his face while his drunken brother would sodomize him. Sometimes he would join in, but he mostly liked to watch. His mother knew what was going on, but she never said a word nor did she try to stop it. He quickly lost all respect for his mother for allowing it to go on. Later on, Pastor Robinson realized that his mother was also afraid of him, because of the way he used to beat her. He realized she wanted to help, but she didn't want the attention brought back on her. She lost two kids because of how he beat and kicked her in the stomach. Because of the trauma he caused her, her doctor told her that she would never carry another baby full term. He never understood why his mother stayed with his father for so long, because of the way he treated her. He guessed that his dad had broken down her self-esteem so much, she thought that she would never be able to find another man that would love her and her kids, he made her feel less than human. His grandfather was also a wino and molested his father when he was a child. Despite his upbringing, he became a pastor to counsel and correct the sick and the weak. Instead, he became the monster he tried so badly to destroy.

Chapter 5

In the kitchen putting my culinary skills to the test, in hopes of coming to a truce between Stephanie and myself. I whip up the perfect meal, everything but the gravy is made from scratch.

"Damn, I'm tired of this gravy getting all lumped up." my frustration rises knowing Stephanie will be home soon, and I need this to be on point. I pull out my cell phone in desperation, *Maybe Derrick knows how to make homemade gravy.*

"Hello?" Derrick answered as if he had been sleep for hours.

"Yo Derrick wake up! I got a question for you."

"What's going on?" He states groggily.

"What's going on, with you? I haven't heard from you in a few days now!"

"Yeah, I guess we were making moves at different times." He slowly replies.

"Yeah I guess so, but anyways do you know how to make homemade gravy?"

"Make what! Why?"

"I'm trying to cook Stephanie a nice dinner tonight."

"Oh yeah."

"Yeah, she's working late tonight and I want to surprise her by having dinner ready when she gets home."

"What are you making?"

"I made baked macaroni and cheese, collard greens, yellow rice, and baked chicken smothered in gravy with mushrooms and a chilled bottle of White Zinfandel."

"Damn dog, you ain't making dinner! You're planning a hostile takeover! Shit, you about to sink her battleship and she didn't even pull da motherfucker off the docks yet. What you need to do, is take her ass to McDonalds and get her a value meal and supper size dat shit! You already got in house pussy, what the hell you still trying to impress her for?"

"I'm raising the white flag between us, just trying to make things more comfortable in our relationship."

"Comfortable? It looks like your raising the red white and blue flag on that ass!"

"Come on now, there's been some tension between us lately and_."

"And what you need to do is relieve that tension the old fashion way, by laying some pipe to dat ass! Nigga don't tell me you fucked around and lost your way, sitting in that townhouse on the hill. Oh shit we got another lost brother in the world! All I'm going to say is I wish you luck, personally I don't think any woman is worth that much trouble! I can tell you how to lay pipe all day long, but I can't tell you how to make gravy." *That went about as well as black man hosting a Klan meeting.* I toss my phone on the table. 30 minutes later, Steph slowly walks through the door, much to her surprise she sees a table set for two and candles lit and me standing there ready to cater to her every need.

"Jamal? What is all this?" She asks obviously not feeling the mood.

"This is for you. To let you know how much I care about you and appreciate having you around." I explain.

"Well you shouldn't have… I grabbed a bite earlier, besides you should have checked with me first." She snaps.

"What! It's a surprise. I was trying to make things better between us and relieve some of the tension between us." Steph cuts her eyes at me and replies, "You're normally out hanging with your home boys anyway! So what makes tonight so different?"

"Well I wasn't, I was slaving over this hot stove trying to do something nice for you! And you're welcome! This is the thanks I get for wanting to spend some quality time with you." She looks around the room, taking in all the trouble I went through to make this a wonderful evening, "Just give me a little, cause I'm not hungry." Stephanie sat at the table quietly rubbing her temples, waiting for her food. She is silent I can see that something is bothering her.

"How was work?" I ask, breaking the tension in the air.

"It was work." Her answers are short indicating that she doesn't want to talk.

"Did you get to complete all the paper work that you needed to?" I continue, hoping that if she would release some of her anger, she may feel better.

"Yeah, why?"

"Excuse me! I was just trying to have a conversation with you while we were eating! Damn I could have just had dinner by myself."

"I guess you could've… I didn't ask for this anyway!"

"Okay let's just drop it and eat." I say, trying to get ahold of the conversation, before my temper gets the best of me.

"Jamal did you cut the grass today, like I asked you to?"

"No, I didn't get time. I planned on doing that tomorrow."

"Well did you at least fix the patio sliding door?"

"No, not yet." I answer feeling irritated.

Steph snaps at me, "Well then I'll do it, it seems like I'm the only one around here that does anything anyway!"

"I had other things going on my mind; I'll get to it as soon as I can. What is your problem tonight?"

"Nothing, just nothing… I'm finish; I'm going to take a shower." She pushes her nearly full plate of food away from her.

"Well, with that attitude, it seems a whole lot like something!"

"Whatever." Stephanie mumbles as she walks away. She takes a long shower, while I cleaned up the kitchen and take out the trash. I go into the bedroom and cut on the TV. Flipping through the stations, I exhale a hundred and sixty seven channels and nothing good to watch. Boxing is on HBO, I reluctantly begin watch that over the Brady Bunch marathon. Shortly thereafter, Steph comes out of the bathroom, her eyes puffy like she may have been crying.

My anger instantly diminishes, "What's wrong?" I ask feeling concerned *I just want things to be right, when will enough be enough for her.*

"Jamal, I'm sorry for the way I have been snapping on you. It's just that I have been really stressed out lately and I know I should have talked to you, but we were kinda on the outs so I haven't wanted to bother you. I am sorry if I have been taking it out on you."

"It's okay, but what can I do to make you feel better now?" I caress her back with my fingers. She sits there with a blank look on her face. "Well do you want to talk about it?"

Letting out a sigh she just lets it go. "It's my boss. There's a new position at work and it could mean a big promotion for me, but_" She pauses for a moment.

"But what?" I ask, waiting for her to continue.

"But my boss wants to give it to someone who works hard for it, or should I say **works him hard for it**. I really bust my ass for that company and I deserve the promotion more than anyone!"

"Well do you think there's a chance that you might get it anyway?"

"No, he's been hitting it off good with some bulimic, bleach blonde bitch up the hall. They've been buddy, buddy ever since the position became available."

"Steph, try not to worry about it. We still make a decent amount of money between us. So it's not that big of deal."

"You ass hole!"

"Now what! What did I say this time?" I exclaimed.

"Jamal, you sound just like those other asses out there! You guys always talk about how you want an independent woman, someone who knows how to take control and then when you get one, you can't handle it! You start complaining that they're too demanding, too bossy or they have a chip on their shoulder! I bet if it was your ass in the same situation at work you'd come home having a shit fit too, where is my support?"

"Wait slow down… we're on the same team! Look, all I was saying is that you don't need to stress yourself over it. We have everything we need right here. Maybe it's not meant for you to get this one…"

"What! How dare you."

"Now hear me out. Maybe it's not meant for you to get this promotion right now, because there's something greater waiting for you down the road. You just have to wait your turn."

With a look that says I may have gotten through to her she replies, "Maybe your right, I don't know but I have to get my rest so I can go into work to play house nigger tomorrow. While some bulimic, bleach blonde bimbo gets to have cocktails and nooners with the boss during working hours as she steals my promotion."

The next few days, went smoother around the house between Stephanie and I. Not too much new at the office. I couldn't help but to wonder how the pastor's family was dealing with his death, especially in view of the fact that it's been in the media every day, since it happened. No sooner than I complete my portfolio that was due at the end of the day. I checked out all the new penny stocks that were coming on the market. I actually put away a nice nest egg for retirement because of these stocks. I walk back to my desk from using the restroom and getting a bag of greasy chips out of the snack machine, I feel my phone vibrating in my jacket.

"Hello?"

"Hey…"

"Patrice? _" I asked unsure if it was her.

"Yeah." I look around to see if anyone noticed me on the phone and dipped into the break room for more privacy.

"Hey baby, what's good? I take it everything is well, I haven't heard from you in a while."

"I'm hanging in there. Look I know it's been a minute since we talked and there is a lot I need to feel you in on." She responds solemnly.

"Is everything okay?" I ask.

"I really don't know…" She answers hesitantly.

"Well I tell you what_ hang on for a second." I click to the other line and clicked back as soon as I could. "Hello, sorry I had to take that call. That was a new client of mine he was thanking for the advice I gave him the other day, it really paid off and now he wants to have dinner and talk about some annuities. Please continue." I say, reverting my full attention back to Patrice.

"That's okay. Like I was about to say, I'll be off in a few hours. Lets meet at On the Border down on Camino De La Reina for a drink and I can tell you all about my situation."

"Okay sounds good. How about 4ish?" I suggest.

"Better make it four thirty, with all the traffic."

"That's cool."

"See you then." I hear her phone disconnect, and head back to my office. Man I hope everything is all right with her. I just don't know how much more she can take.

"Hey there birthday boy, I really look forward to downing a couple of shots at your party!" a coworker yelled down the hall.

"Thank you, I really look forward to it as well. I need to unwind and get loose." I replied. Everyone else was whispering behind my back, about what their getting me for my birthday. Finally this workday is over, time to head to On the Border to see what this girl is talking about, I shoot Stephanie a quick text to let her know I am working late to finish up a few last minute details on the Childress Barton portfolio and preparing it for presentation, so she wouldn't call me and interrupt Patrice and I, while we are talking. I find a parking spot near the front of the restaurant and park. I reach into my glove box and pop a piece of Double Mint gum in my mouth. I walk through the door in search of a familiar face.

"Hello. May I help you sir?" The waiter pleasantly asks.

"Yes can I have a table for uh_, never mind. I see my party has already arrived."

"Hey Jamal," She jumps up, gives me a hug and a kiss. "I hope you don't mind I ordered your soda for you."

"Well I hope it was a_"

"Yes I know you only drink clear sodas, because the dark colored sodas are harder on your kidneys." She interjects.

"That's my girl." I say with a smile as I sit down.

"Well I started to order your favorite drink, a buttery nipple. But I figured since you have such long nights an alcoholic beverage might be a bit too much to handle this time of the day."

"Once again you are correct."

"Well I should be, I paid attention while I was with you. Besides I'm not just a beauty, without any brains" We share a laugh and no sooner than our smiles fade she drops her head and zones off.

"Patrice! Hello…" I say as I snap my fingers a few times in front of her.

"Huh." She looks up as if she has forgotten I was there.

"What's up? You were right here with me and then you went planet hopping. What's on your mind?" I ask intently.

Giving me a half smile, "When I was with you, things were so simple. Everything just fell into place, I really had no worries." Pausing for a second and looking off to the right, "Don't get me wrong, I'm not a home wrecker but lately I have to question our judgment, when we decided to just be good friends."

"Well we had a really good friendship and neither one of us wanted to risk losing it, if something went wrong in our relationship. And at the time the distance, really put a strain on us."

"But if we had such a good relationship and we communicated very well, then it should have survived anything we went through." She counters.

"So where is all this coming from?"

"Right now, I am so confused." Patrice looks at me no tears in her eyes but somehow it looks like she's crying to me.

"Okay, I'm listening to you. What's going on?"

"There's a reason why you haven't heard from me in a while."

"And that would be?"

"I was in the hospital."

"Come again?" I ask, wanting to make sure I heard her right the first time.

"I was in the hospital." She exhaled, tears slowly trickle down her face. It kind of scared me, not knowing what she was going to say next.

"What happened?"

"I had a nervous breakdown and lost it. It's not like me to do something like this, but I wanted to get over Quentin as fast as I could. Then I met this guy. He was a nice person, but I knew it was going to take some time to allow myself to get close to him. I wasn't trying to rush into anything. I really wanted to get to know him. We took it slow and he was the ideal gentleman. I guess that was a sign right there huh, everything went to smooth. We really connected, he could relate to me on different levels. He was really nice to be around and we had so much fun."

"Then what happened? I haven't heard anything wrong yet." I cut in hoping she'd get to the point.

"We crossed the line and went from friends to lovers. I just knew I was doing the right thing."

"Yeah, then?" Waving my arms in the air, for her to continue to the point.

"Then I saw him in the grocery store kissing and carrying on the way he shouldn't have been."

"Damn, he had another woman!" I blurted out.

"No, worse."

"Awe Shit! Not with another man…. Damn!" I exclaim, shaking my head from side to side.

"Yes."

"Are you sure?" She looks up at me with daggers for eyes, piercing right through me.

"I was so shocked, I got light headed and almost passed out. I didn't know what else to do. So I approached him while they were carrying on. At first, he was shocked to see me and since he knew he was already busted he just played it off like, we were only friends. He told his man, woman or whatever it was, that we were just friends and that I tried to get with him, but he turned me down. Then his, whatever you want to call it, started yelling at me about how he got his man trained and he would never want me, when he has all of him. And I couldn't do for him like he could. I was so humiliated, I was in tears. When I looked at him all I could say to him was, I know who's the dominate one in your relationship! Then his significant other jumped all up in my face yelling, that's right bitch! And there is no need to cry, just check the front of his drawers for track marks next time and you won't have this problem again honey! I was so upset I just ran out the store and went to the nearest bar to knock the edge off. You know I don't drink, so it didn't take long to get drunk."

"I know, but the only dilemma is when people with problems drink to get rid of them, they only become drunks with problems."

"I found that out the hard way. And to make things worse_"

"It gets worse?"

"Yes, while I was at the bar trying to drown my sorrows. I figured what harm could it be to talk to someone else to relieve some anger. There just so happened to be a woman sitting next to me so I just started rambling, like I had diarrhea of the mouth. Surprisingly she was real attentive to what I had to say. At one moment, she even cried with me. It was a relief, to have someone listen to me and not pass their opinion. Then she made a move on me, she started rubbing her hand on my shoulder and telling me how I have to be strong and hang in there. Then she told me about how she was seeing a married man for about 23 years and how he promised her so much and one day they were going to have kids, right when he divorces his wife. Later he told her that when his kids get older, he was going to leave his wife. Then, when they were older, he said that he had a lot of real estate and other assets that he would lose if he left her. That's when she realized that he was never leaving his wife, he was only telling her what she wanted to hear so that he could keep on getting what he wanted. He even went as far to say that every time he has sex with his wife, he imagines her. She gave up her family and friends and never had a family of her own. Then her hand slowly drifted towards the small of my back. She whispered softly into my ear. How about you and me go and get to know each other better? I know how to make you feel good. Then she had the nerve to reach in to kiss me."

"Damn!"

"I kind of lost it after that and that's how I ended up in the hospital for about a week and a half."

"This is unbelievable!" I sit there basically in shock.

"Jamal, I swear I don't know what's going on! Do I have a sign on my back that says come and get it? No experience necessary! Get it while it lasts…"

"Patrice I can truly understand why you're up set and I can only imagine what you're going through."

"Jamal I think I just need to get a way for a while."

"Huh, what's that supposed to mean?"

"I have been checking out a few places on the east coast."

"The east coast?" I question with a puzzled look on my face.

"Yes, you heard me. I am looking at three cities right now. Atlanta, Georgia, Lake City, Pennsylvania and Jersey City, New Jersey."

"Why there, what's so special about them places?"

"Well other than the fact that it's thousands of miles from here. I thought about Atlanta, because the land is cheap, and the job market is booming right now and I love being around my people. Second was Lake City Pennsylvania, because Lake City is a small town in a big state and it's just off of Lake Erie. You know how much I love the water, plus No one knows me there and it's a great place to start over. Last, but not least Jersey City. Looking out at the statue of liberty every day seems like a change I could welcome. Not to mention that's a strong image of a woman standing tall and with determination, now that may be just the motivation I need to get my life back on track."

"So your mind is pretty much made up?"

"Yup, but don't worry we'll keep in touch, as long as you have time to answer your phone."

"So when is this move thing supposed to take place?" I ask a little salty, thinking of my one true friend moving so far away from me.

"It's not a move thing! It's my life, my sanity I really need to do this." She replies defensively.

"I apologize. I wasn't trying to down play you. And you know that I'm always here for you." I humbly state.

"And that's all I need, don't take that away from me. Sometimes I just want your ear, to listen to me and nothing else."

"I'm sorry." I stated again apologetically. She pauses for a second, "The day after tomorrow."

"Wow! Isn't that a bit sudden?" I exclaim.

"No, in fact it's long overdue!"

"But_" I try to interject looking for a way to reason with her frantically searching my mind for the words to make her change her mind.

"Look my mind is made up, there's nothing anyone can say right now to change my mind." She says in a tone that tells me I have lost this battle before even really having a chance to fight.

"Well where did you decide to move?"

"I'll let you know when I get there." She states with a slight smile her tears slowing down as she talks.

"Patrice, look at me. I don't like the way you're going about this! It's too dangerous out there. Maybe you should give it a little more time to think this through. Wait at least until this weekend I'll go with you. Help you get settled in."

"No, but I appreciate the gesture. My mind is made up and I'm leaving. Don't worry, I'm a big girl now. I have you to thank for that. You've taught me how to be independent and take care of my own business. You've made me a survivor and I'll never forget that. Besides you have a sweet someone to care for right here." She somberly states.

"But what if you_"

"And if I fail… I hope I can count on you to get me back on track. You know you're my guardian angel." She says as she winks at me.

"You know you can always count on me."

"Jamal, do you remember what you said to me prior to us dating?"

"Yeeesssss."

"Tell me again…" I took a deep breath and exhaled, "I said that we were great friends and we have the potential of being great lovers. But if it doesn't work out, it is always better to try and fail, than to have never tried at all and wonder for the rest of your life."

"So let me try, no one ever said it was going to be easy. This is a new experience for me, yes I'm afraid and excited at the same time."

"But I still worry about you."

"I know and I'm truly thankful to have a person like you in my life. You give me the strength and power to continue. You're a real inspiration." She said whole heartedly.

"Patrice just remember if things get hectic and you're going through hell-"

"I know, I know… then keep going until you get to the other side. You were a great teacher in all aspects of my life. And I love you dearly for your words of wisdom."

"Take care of yourself and don't accept any wooden nickels." I joke.

"I love you too."

I stand up and give her the biggest hug that I can muster my eyes flood with water. As much as I need to let her go, I am afraid that, I may never see her again.

£   £   £

Thursday evening after work, I hit the weights in my garage, stress testing 245 lbs. on my bench set, that's all I could do to take my mind off Patrice moving so far away. Fifteen minutes into my routine, Stephanie walks in the garage on her tippy toes pretending to be looking for a screwdriver holding down her breast with her left forearm trying to keep them from running amuck. She wore nothing but a light blue pair of satin lingerie panties that stretched perfectly around that nice plump ass, she knows the quickest way to get me turned on is to parade around in sexy underwear. I sit my weights back on the rack and stare at her panties merging into the crack of her ass while she purposely bends over looking in the toolbox.

"Can I help you?" I ask, feeling aroused by the sight of her bent over in barely anything.

"Yes you can, but only if that hard thing in your shorts is a screwdriver." She came over to the bench and massaged my manhood before she pulled down my shorts and jerked me with her warm hands a few times as if she is warming me up before the big game. Not able to resist temptation, I rip her panties off, bend her over the weight bar and enter her from the back, my big black balls rapidly banging against her clit.

"Oooohhhhhh! Jamal!!!" She yells! "Slow down! I don't want to cum so soon." But it was too late it was just about over before it started, the second I saw the skimpy outfit she was parading around in I might as well have looked down and been limp because I wasn't holding anything back this time., The closer she came to climaxing the closer I came to my orgasmic bliss. I love the way it feels when we climax at the same time, feeling her pulsating on my already ejaculating penis. This is the only time I can truly say we are unified as one.

"Oh yes... Jamal I can feel it!!!" She reaches between her legs to feel my balls banging against her now saturated crevice. The moment she grabs my balls I began to burst.

"Steph!!! I'm Cumming." Her legs started shaking in every direction like she was having spasms.

"Oh shit, I'm Cumming too!!!!!" Exhaustedly, we both fell to the bench seat breathless, our sweat streamed together dripping rapidly to the garage floor.

"Damn we did it again." I mumble softly. A few seconds later, my cell phone rang again. *Now who in the heck would be calling at a time like this!* I thought as my phone kept ringing. I picked it up and saw Patrice name show up on the caller ID.

"Now see Jamal, who the hell is that? You might as well answer it, it must be important the way they keep calling." Stephanie exclaims, picking up her panties from the floor and heading back into the house.

"Will you calm down its Derrick calling me back! He said hello." I lie, covering up the mouth piece, so Patrice won't hear what's going on.

"Well he sure picks the perfect time when he calls. I'm going to take a shower."

"Okay honey, I'll be there in a sec."

"And tell your brother to get a real job." Stephanie taunts as she closes the door. I wait a few more seconds, just to make sure she is completely out of ear shot.

"Hello_" I excitedly answer.

"Hey, Jamal it's me Patrice. I was about to hang up, I thought we might have had a bad connection or something."

"How are you doing? I didn't expect to hear from you so soon. How did everything go with the move?"

"It went fine, a lot better than I thought. Are you busy, you sound like you're out of breath?"

"Nah, I was just working out in my garage. You know it takes a lot of energy to be me." I laugh.

"Yeah well I'm going to leave that one alone."

"So stop holding out, where did you move to?" I ask anxiously.

"You sure don't waste any time. I miss talking to you too." She chuckled, stalling a few more seconds.

"Stop stalling, I just spoke to you a few days ago."

"Okay then, let's skip over all the pleasantries of life. And just get to the meat and potatoes."

"Time is a terrible thing to waste, give me the juice."

"Okay, okay. I decided to move to Lake City." She says in excitement.

"So how is it up there, any pretty women?" I ask curiously.

"You know, the same shit, just a different ass its coming out of. But nothing I can't handle. And no, there's no women for you mister almost married. You better learn to behave yourself, you were never like that with me. Were you?"

"Ok I'll cool it. I can't believe you just asked me that, there's was no room in my life for anyone else when I was with you. As strange as this may sound, even when we were apart, you consumed my every waking moment."

"Awe, that was so sweet of you." She spoke as her voice cracked.

"What's all that noise in the background?" I ask, upset that it broke into the short moment we were having together.

"Oh, I stopped in this hole in the wall bar, around the corner from my new apartment. They make some awesome fried chicken in this place. As a matter of fact the place really reminds me a lot of home. SO, I'm sitting at the bar watching some trying to be players attempt to pimp some unsuspecting girls. Smelling like discounted aftershave from Kmart and aged smoke, one guy wearing a du-rag around his neck waits until he sees a woman. Excuse me, I mean a girl that he wants to hook up with and puts the rag around her neck to mark her as his property. I don't understand how these women can stoop so low and allow someone else to mark them as their possession. And these women are the first ones to get mad, when someone calls them a bitch or hoe. I will admit though watching these busters does make me miss you a lot."

"What! Was that supposed to be a compliment?" his feeling is insulted.

"Well I didn't mean to call you a buster_,"

"What did you mean?" I follow up, defensively.

Barely being able to control her laughter she tries to explain "What I meant to say is watching these guys trying to run game on these girls, reminds me a lot of you. You know, you've had more than your fair share of girls, but at least in your case, you didn't resort to using whack lines to pick them up. You were smooth and made them feel like ladies, even if it was bullshit you were feeding them."

"I wouldn't go that far." I reply letting her off the hook, with that weak excuse.

"Tell the truth, you've had at least … I'd say more than a hundred women?"

"Damn! You up in my business like that?" I ask, stalling on whether I should give her an accurate count or not.

"No, just concerned about you. How many girls do you think you were with? Be truthful." She asks more seriously.

"Well, uhh… I'm not sure. I stopped counting because I kept losing track. But for what it's worth, I never cheated on you."

"Why so many girls?"

"After you, I never found another woman that was as complete a package as you. So I had to take a few girls here and a few there to equal you. I know it's not right but it's the truth, Stephanie is as close to a whole you that I've ever had, but there's something different about her that makes me not commit to her completely." I answer truthfully.

"That was so sweet of you. But I really want the truth, why?"

"That was the truth, and_" I pause, reflecting back on some of the relationships I've had.

"And what?" She asks, breaking my chain of thought.

"I came to the conclusion that there are no more honest women in the world. Their either after your money, they want to use you to take care of them and their 5 point 3 kids, their spending habits or they're just plain fidelity challenged. So why should I keep putting myself through all the hassles of trying to find that perfect one and setting myself up for disappointment." I state solemnly.

"Isn't that a bit negative, I mean no one is perfect." She reasons.

"You were." I reply.

"Thanks, but I'm not perfect either Jamal, and from it how I'm feeling right now."

"You were perfect for me."

"What about Stephanie? You guys have been doing pretty well together."

"Yes we have, but look at the damage I've done since we've been together! Besides it doesn't matter how long you've been with someone, you still don't really know what you're getting into, until after it's too late."

"That's true, B this is all a part of the love and learn process, you're going to have to have faith in the other person, to be happy. You can't be happy with someone and not trust them at the same time. Jamal you should consider this with Stephanie."

"I guess you're right. She does deserve more than what I have been giving her. Speaking of which, she's getting out of the shower now. So I will have to call you later."

"Okay, I understand. Take care of your woman and keep in touch. I hope you get a chance to come out and visit someday."

"I hope everything works out for you and you know I'm just a phone call away, I love you."

"I love you too, Jamal."

"Good bye." I made it into the bedroom, just as Stephanie was hanging up the phone.

"What took you so long? I was about to call in the Calvary for you." She states in a snooty tone.

"My brother has some serious issues. I hope we don't ever have the problems he has in his relationships, well there not really relationships, so let's just say encounters." I state as I sit on the bed and slide over to Stephanie's side to cuddle with her. She immediately gives me the cold shoulder and gets up to go wrap her hair.

"Is something wrong, did I do something or say something to offend you?" I ask.

"No." She answers, not giving our conversation anymore thought.

"Was it something someone said to you on the phone that changed your mood?" She cut her eyes at me in the mirror, surprised that I noticed her on the phone.

"No." She calmly responds, but her expression through the reflection on the mirror tells another story. *Oh, I see where back to playing charades!* I think as I feel my anger start to grow.

"So I guess you're not feeling a certain kind of way right now about something?" I ask, trying to connect with her one last time.

"Nope, it just seems like we're heading in two different directions in this relationship." I am not feeling this answer and the expression on my face must have told her so. "It's just that I'm more focused on making career moves and you're more focused on hanging with the boys." She sneers, holding up her hands bending her two fingers, making quotations. Then she walks into the bathroom to brush her teeth. *That's a nice way to end a conversation.* I sit there with my arms folded, mad as hell. I turn my head debating on whether I should go in there and finish our conversation or leave well enough alone. I see her cell phone sitting on the nightstand. *If you won't tell me anything, maybe your cell phone will!* I think reaching over to pick it up. I look through her phone and find nothing, she just erased her call log and messages.

"Damn!" I exclaim, feeling like she is a step ahead of me.

"Say what?" She asks from the bathroom.

"Nothing, I was talking to myself." I get undressed and turn the light off before I get under the covers to go to sleep. I don't even bother to wait for her to come out the bathroom. Stephanie eventually comes out and sits on the bed for a minute, eventually she gets under the covers her body close to mine. "Jamal I hope you weren't offended by what I said?"

"Nope." I reply with a one word answer trying to avoiding talking to her at all at this point. She continues to ramble on for a few more minutes about who knows what, whatever she is talking about, I'm really not interested in hearing it anymore.

"Jamal I really want to know what you think about that." *Huh?* I think to myself, about what. I play it off as if I was listening, "You know what I'm thinking, I'm just a man." she lays there a few minutes in silence.

"Jamal, do you sometimes start off listening to me, zone off midway through the conversation and then wonder what I was actually talking about?" She asks earnestly.

"Nope." I reply from under the covers, with my back still turned to her. I can feel her eyes looking through me. Then she takes a deep breath and exhales, slides under the covers and appears to have fallen asleep.

Chapter 6

I strolled in the house around 7:45 from getting my haircut.

"Marcus, I'm glad your home." Octavia states, sitting on the end of the couch looking pitiful.

"Hey, why are you sitting here in the dark?" I ask delicately.

"I've been thinking about some things that we need to talk about."

"Is everything alright?" I ask, trying to think back on what I may have done wrong.

"No everything is fine, it's just that we've been together for almost four years now and besides living together our relationship hasn't progressed anywhere." I can hear how sad she is in her voice.

"Stop, I think I know where you're going with this. Yo I ain't gonna front, to be honest I have been thinking the same way. I think it's time we settle down, start our own family and get married. That's if you don't have a problem with it?" Octavia looks at me surprised, tears trickle out of her eyes.

"I'm so happy that you feel this way too! I was afraid that if I mentioned this to you, it would push you away." sounding relieved, I see her body language change and watch as the comfort flows back into her limbs.

"I can understand you feeling that way, we all know the quickest way to get rid of a man, is to mention EPT or marriage. Most men are afraid to commit, for one reason or another. I haven't exactly been the best man in the world to deal with and I'm not afraid to go on record telling you that. However, I am willing to give it my all to make you happy. I want to hold you and console you and let you know that I am yours forever. And with having said that, Octavia will you marry me?" For the first time in our four year relationship, I speak with pure sincerity; I feel my eyes swell up with water and my emotions get the best of me.

"Yes, yes I will marry you…" She answers, getting all choked up.

"Just to let you know how serious I am about this, you know that next week is our 4 year anniversary together. How about we set the date two years from that day?" I say, feeling all excited about this marriage thing.

"Yes, that will be fine and don't worry about the ring. We can pick one out later." She says trying, not to seem materialistic.

"Then I guess I'll have to take this one back to the store." I Pull out a small box from my pocket and wave it around in the air. Octavia turns around to see the jewelry box I'm holding in my hand. She opens it and is in awe, stuck looking at the beauty and clarity of a one and a half carrot princess cut diamond ring. Her tears flow freely down her cheeks, she wraps her arms tight around my neck.

"You have truly made this the happiest day of my life." Her voice splinters up so bad I can hardly understand what she is saying.

"I figure that two years will be enough time to save up some money and pay for the wedding. I don't want to be like other people, living beyond my means."

"That's fine, I can't believe that you actually want to marry me. You have made me the happiest woman in the entire state of California. I promise to make you the happiest man alive, all your desires will be fulfilled. You will never have to want for anything." She yells, jumping up and down.

"I love you … come give me a kiss." The phone starts ringing, interrupting our few seconds of passion. Octavia rushes to answer the phone.

"Hello?"

"Hello, this is Dr. Shaw. May I speak to Marcus Barnes please?" I watched Octavia expression change from a blissful look to this eerie impression on her face.

She looks at the phone funny then at me, "There's a doctor on the phone and she wants to speak to you."

"For me?" I asked rhetorically, grabbing the phone.

"Hello?" I answered curiously.

"Hello this is Dr. Shaw from Alvarado Hospital. We have your mother Bernice Barnes in the emergency room, we found your number in her cell phone. Can you come to the emergency room as soon as possible?" My heart drops, as the sound of the female's voice transmitted from the phone to my eardrum.

"Yes I'm on my way. Uh_, can you tell me what happened?"

"It appears that she had a heart attack, that's all I can tell you for now."

"What! Oh my God, okay I'm leaving now." I drop the phone on the floor and run towards the door, Octavia yells to me in a panic, "What happened!"

"It's my mother, she had a heart attack. I'm going to the hospital." I yell back half way out the door.

"Wait, I'm coming with you." I barely heard her behind me. Lost in my thoughts we are speeding down Central Avenue. *I owe everything to her, she is the person that taught me everything. She taught me how to stand on my own two feet and not depend on anyone for anything. I will be lost without her.* I am nearly blinded by the traffic lights and the water in my eyes. Weaving in and out of cars running through intersections with no regards to traffic lights and stop signs, or speed limits. I'd almost forgotten that Octavia is in the car with me until she screams for me to stop. I slam on my breaks and come within 3 inches of hitting a kid crossing the street on his bike. I put my hands over my eyes and try to focus, but I feel the pressure of my whole world caving in around me.

"Marcus, it's going to be alright, just hang in there. Slide over and let me take over the driving. I'll get you there." Octavia coaxed me, rubbing my leg. She drove us as fast and safe as she could, the rest of the way to the hospital. When we got to the emergency room, they told me she was in stable condition and I would be able to see her in about another hour. We waited just under an hour but it felt like days before they came out to get us.

"Mr. Barnes." I pop up immediately.

"Yes, I'm right here." I stand up, heart heavy like its pumping ten gallons a second.

"You can go back to see her briefly, she's very tired and needs to rest." Octavia stands up to walk in with me.

"I'm sorry ma'am, but only immediate family." I spoke up, cutting him off and grabbing Octavia's hand, "She is immediate family, this is my wife." She looked at me so proudly, as we walk into the room together, the lights are dim and an array of machines are beeping, making all kinds of noises and tubes seem to be falling out of her nose. I fall to my knees at the sight of my mother in this condition. Octavia grabs me before I fall to the floor. We stood next to the bed in shock looking down at my helpless mother. My voice split as I try to speak to her.

"Mom?" she partially opens her eyes and tries to focus on me. Opening her mouth to speak but she is obviously far too weak.

"Yes it's me, try and relax you're in the hospital, you had a heart attack."

"How did you know I was here?" She scarcely garbled out.

"They got my number out of your cell phone and called me."

"How did they know which number to call?" She whispered.

"Because I put ice in your cell phone." Bernice was weak but not stupid. She gave me a look, as if I knew better and had more sense than to put ice in a cell phone.

"Calm down mom. I.C.E. stands for in case of emergency. That way anyone can contact me if something happened to you." The charge nurse walks in, "I'm sorry but it's time for you to leave now, so she can get some rest. We're going to keep her for a few more days to run some more test and observe her progress. You can come back tomorrow during regular visiting hours." She talks to us without eye contact her focus is my mother's vitals and fixing the sheets on her bed.

"Okay thank you. I love you mom I'll see you tomorrow morning. Nurse, call me if there's any changes." I walk outside the door, something keeps telling me not to leave her. I stand paralyzed looking back at the door. And I feel Octavia's hand grab mine.

"Come on she needs her rest, she'll be better tomorrow when we come see her. I'll take a personal day and we can come back first thing in the morning.

£   £   £

It was exactly 12 midnight on August 24th.

"Happy 31st birthday Jamal!" Stephanie whispers in my ear.

"Thank you." I reply, rolling over to get more comfortable with my pillow.

"Now get up!" She stated, shaking my body.

"Huh? What are you doing I was sleeping."

"I said get up!" She demanded.

"For what?"

"I have a surprise downstairs for you, and it can't wait till morning either." She said with a big grin on her face.

"Okay, let's go." I drag myself out of bed and head downstairs following behind Stephanie to the dining room. She has red candles lit all around to accent the dining room.

"Sit here and put on this blind fold, I'll be right back. And no peeking!" She commands, running out the room for a few minutes.

"Give me your right hand," She asks then impatiently takes my arm, she ties a scarf around it and secures it to the chair. Then she does the same with the left arm. She starts kissing me around my ears and pulls off my blind fold. She was wearing a white see through 2-piece lingerie set. I can feel the blood already starting to flow between my legs. She turns on the CD player, *If This World Were Mine* by Luther Vandross escapes from the speakers. She does her best to give me a strip tease followed by a lap dance. Stephanie has really blown my mind this time. After she removed her top, she began to play with her breast, she watches me as I get more turned on by the second. When she turns around, she pulls down the bottom half of her nighty, giving me full view of her beautifully round booty. She plants her firm ass on my hard penis, she slowly rotates her hips from side to side, as if I had spilled something in my lap and she was trying to clean it up. Stephanie wraps her hands around her ankles and stands straight up.

"Ummmmm, it's a perfect night for a full moon!" I let out. She glides her hands up her body until they touch her breasts and covers them. Then she slowly turns around, rotating her body like a belly dancer. I see something flicker as she turns. At first, I thought I was seeing things, and then I realize that she had gotten her stomach pierced. My mouth fell open, drool escaped from my bottom lip like I had a hole or something.

"Do you like it? I know how much you like gold, so I got this cute design for you to play with." I am speechless, she has out done herself this time. I can see the silhouette of a candle burning behind me, glaring off her bare ass as she turns about. I become more aroused watching her play with herself and all I can do is watch. I can see that Stephanie loves the way I'm more responsive to her every move, she straddles me and initiates a game of tongue tag. She places the blind fold over my eyes again and walks her lips all the way down to the tip of my twig. Then the song juicy fruit starts playing. I can feel her hot breath hovering around my boys. She begins to suck on my chocolate milk balls, like she wants them to melt in her mouth.

"Mmmmmm, that feels so good," I moan. All of a sudden, I feel another pair of lips starting to kiss me on the back of my neck. At first, my body tensed up from the surprise of another person joining in on the action. I was surprised because this was way out of character for Stephanie, so I thought. The reality of this manage trios, was turning me on more than ever at this point. All of a sudden, I felt another pair of lips licking my lips. I couldn't believe Steph had turned my birthday surprise into an all-out freak show, I swear I never saw this day coming when she would willingly share me with another woman. I could never top this.

"Damn!" I knew I was about to blow my gasket any second. Someone untied my hands and spoke seductively in my ear, "I heard you were good with your hands, it would be a shame to keep one of your greatest assets tied up." The voice seemed familiar, but I couldn't quite place it. I stretched my hands out to get a feel of what I was working with. My left hand landed on someone's jungle watering hole. I maneuver my hand between her legs and stick my middle finger deep into her damp closet.

"Ohhhh!!!!" She moaned out.

"Ooohh!!!" I replied turned on by the sound of her moaning and the mystery of who she is. Someone else had just sat on me and decided to take a ride the third person lock her lips on my bottom lip, I could taste strawberries from her lip gloss. The suspense is killing me. I had to know who the other women were.

"Please take my blind fold off, I want to watch you take care of your business." I beg, the blind fold came flying off. I am flabbergasted at the sight of two of Stephanie's coworkers, Denise and Amber all over me. I was completely shocked!!! I've never been with a white girl before, and now I have two. Stephanie has officially opened up Pandora's Box, because I'm definitely tasting some vanilla latte tonight. Amber started kissing Stephanie, I was taken aback to see Stephanie engaged in any type of lesbian action. It put me in a trance for a brief moment. Denise quickly stole my attention by inserting her fingers into her vagina and licking them clean. She picked up and opened a banana flavored condom. Then she inserted the condom into her mouth, knelt down between my legs and unrolled it onto my over grown penis using only her lips and tongue. Amber proceeded to bend over a chair.

"Cum get your birthday present!" She teased smacking herself softly on her butt cheeks. I couldn't resist her any longer looking at her evenly tanned ass and those savory pussy lips peeking out the back door. I smacked my piece in Amber, penetrating my dart all the way to the base as fast as I could.

"Whoa! Don't hurt it." She moans. "Do you have something wrapped around that thing?"

"Yeah a hundred and ninety-five pounds of pure chocolate!" I continue to bombard her relentlessly. Denise moans louder as she is dripping from attending to her own sexual needs, kneels down between my legs and start licking my boys midway between strokes. Stephanie is engaged in self pleasuring 101 as she looks on in excitement. *This is the best birthday surprise I could have ever gotten!!!* I think to myself, looking at all the naked women surrounding me.

"Oh shit!! Amber you got me Cumming already!" Amber and Denise both promptly began to clean up the mess in a very sensual way, as I try to contain my eruption. I look at Stephanie and whisper, "This is the best birthday ever!" I didn't think I had the strength to satisfy three women all night long by myself, but I managed, completely exhausting my reserves.

£   £   £

My phone starts ringing, startling me out of my recap of last night's festivities. I roll over to look at the time, it was 9:02 in the morning.

"Shoot, I'm late again!" I yell before answering my phone. "Hello?"

"I knew you wouldn't make it to work on time on your birthday, if you were going to show up at all!" Keisha states cheerfully through the phone.

"Keisha? What are you doing calling me?" I snap.

"To wish you a happy birthday and tell you that I've taken the liberty of getting you the day off today. I know if you're late again this month, you'll be placed on 90 days probation, or possibly even fired."

"I doubt that he would fire me, I'm too much of an asset to the company right now. He'll just make things uncomfortable for me. But good looking out, I owe you one!" I hang up the phone and roll over to go back to sleep. I definitely need to get my energy back. The phone rang again. *Awe man! Can a brotha buy some sleep this morning!*

"Hello?"

"Get your bitch ass up!" Derrick yells in the phone, with his music playing even louder.

"What up broham." I reply as if I was already up and about.

"Are you ready?" He asked.

"Ready for what?"

"To get some liquor for your party tonight!" He exclaims.

"How did you know I was home?" I asked curiously.

"I ran into Keisha yesterday and she told me that she got you the day off today. Yo, that is one fine honey you're working with there. I don't know why you ain't bust them panties yet!"

"Stop playing, what store do you want to go to?" I ask, changing the subject before he went off on a tangent.

"Meet me at .... ABC Liquor in 1 hour!"

"Cool, I'm out." I hung up the phone and try to get at least two more minutes of solid sleep, before I have to get up, take a shower, and head to the liquor store. Standing outside the store waiting for Derrick to arrive, some kid walks up to me yelling, "I know you! You're a famous person aren't you? Can I have your autograph?" I look around to see who he is talking to, but there is no one else in the vicinity. I open my mouth, but before I had a chance to respond, I hear a woman's voice speaking behind me.

"He's famous alright, but you're too young to know about that!" Octavia had just walked out the liquor store, with a bottle of wine.

"Hey honey, how are you?" I greet her, as I give her a hug and kiss on the cheek.

"So why haven't I been invited to your party tonight?" She asks obviously, feeling a certain kind of way about it.

"What! You were invited." I try to explain. "You didn't get your invitation! That damn Marcus! I gave him a personal invitation especially for you! I wanted to hand deliver it to you, but he said he would take care of it so I gave it to him. That's the last time I get him to deliver something important for me!"

"Well I thought that you had forgotten all about me." She replies poking her bottom lip out.

"Trust me there's no way I could ever forget about you." I state firmly. "Especially the way you tried to suck the marrow out of my bone a week ago!" I continue to mumble.

"I just aim to be the best at what I do." She responds, obviously picking up on what I had mumbled.

Derrick walks up at the tail end of our conversation. "Yo G, you ready to do this," he says, pulling off his sun glasses to get a better look at Octavia.

She gives me another hug, "I'll see you tonight! Oh and by the way, Marcus's mother had a heart attack two days ago. She's doing somewhat better, but she's still in the hospital. He's out there visiting her right now."

"Give him my condolences and I'll understand if he doesn't make it to the party tonight. Tell him to take care of moms first."

"We'll make it, now that we know she's going to pull through." Octavia pinches my ass before she walks away. Derrick gives me a look that says 'you got it like that!'

"Ain't that Marcus's girl, what's up with dat?" He asks, checking her out as she strolls away.

"Long story leave it alone." I say, turning around to walk in the store.

"Man everything is a long story with you." He laughs, following me into the store. The party is being held in the ballroom at the Hilton San Diego Resort at 8 pm. It was already 8:33, and Stephanie is still in the bathroom getting ready for the party.

"Steph, will you hurry up please! I'm late for my own party…" I state for the umpteenth time. That girl is going to be late to her own funeral. I think to myself, looking at my watch again.

"I don't know why you're in such a hurry, you have the main attraction with you already!" Stephanie stated coming out of the bathroom, looking even more gorgeous than even I could have imagined.

"Your right, but I don't want my party kicking off without me." I stand in the bedroom doorway watching Stephanie put on her earrings. "By the way, I kinda have a little bad news and there's really no good time to bring it up. But then there's never a good time for bad news."

"What is it now Jamal? You've got more shit going on with you than the city's sewage system." Stephanie scowls at me, like she knows what I am about to tell her.

"Calm down, it's not really that bad if you hear me out before you react." I can see Stephanie's blood beginning to boil and her nostrils flare up.

"Just say what you're trying to say." She snap.

"Okay I got a letter in the mail today for a paternity test." I start to explain.

"You what, Oh hell no_, we don't even have any kids together and you're out planting your seeds in the next bitch!" Stephanie starts pacing back and forth, with her arms flailing in the air at me.

"Just hold on let me finish. The letter was addressed from the Child Support Enforcement Agency in Baltimore."

"When was the last time you were in Baltimore?" She yells.

"A few years ago, the child is five now." Stephanie folds her arms, thinking back to see if I was accurate about what I said.

"So who is this person taking you to court?" She asks tapping her foot heavily on the floor.

"Some girl I got involved with before I moved out here to San Diego." Steph was starting to calm down a little, but she was still heated.

"I don't know about all this, I might have a kid and paying child support shit! Jamal, give it to me straight. Do you think it's yours?"

"To be honest no I don't think so. I always take extra precaution and only use my own rubbers." I reason with her.

"I bet you do, just like you have them rubbers taped up in your glove box." I was surprised to hear her mention those rubbers in the car. I didn't think anyone would ever find them, because they were hidden so well.

"Stephanie, those things have been in there for years, I forgot I even had those. Look, these women are too damn devious nowadays. Plus knowing how much that girl loves money, if it was mine she would have sued me a long time ago." I yell, turning the focus back on the girl and not the rubbers in the car.

"And when is all this supposed to take place?"

"In two weeks. We'll talk more about this later. Are you ready to go?" Trying to blow it off and not make it as serious as it is, I go to grab her hand and lead her out the door.

"Jamal you're starting to become more of a liability than an asset. Let's go before I change my mind all together about you." 9:15 pm Stephanie and I enter the party. The room is just about full, people are everywhere, dancing, drinking and doing what they do best, just cutting up and eating free food. Marcus walks up to me swaggering hard, he seems to be more drunk than he would usually allow himself.

"About time you got here nigga, with me being second in command I was about to start running things!" He slurs out, the aroma of alcohol slaps me in the face.

"Well I had to wait on Steph, you know how women can be sometimes." I reply, looking around the room throwing a few head nods to people.

"Yeah right, you know you were somewhere trying to get one last shot in before the party!"

"What you need to do is stop worrying about me so much and slow down on them drinks, the night is still young."

"Did you tell Stephanie about the paternity test yet?" He asks, blatantly putting my business on Front Street.

"Yeah, I told her right before we came here." I answer, dropping my head down.

"Man I bet she took it hard, I'm surprised she still came to the party with you." He blurts out.

"You know Stephanie, it wasn't pretty, but we managed to make it here in one piece." Octavia snuck up behind Marcus trying to ease drop on our conversation. This girl knew everything about everything when it came to the gossip chain, she could find dirt in the middle of a sandstorm. I couldn't help but to notice her, she looked gorgeous, I couldn't take my eyes off her. She is wearing a skintight, black one-piece cat suit and matching ankle strapped sandals.

"Marcus can you go get me another drink please?" Octavia asks, never taking her eyes off me.

"Sure, would you like a new car to go with that as well?" He sarcastically answers.

"I said please."

"Okay I'll be right back mas 'sir!" Marcus walks away mumbling something, I yell after him, "And get some food to soak up some of that alcohol."

"So how are you Jamal?" I was staring at how good she looked in her outfit. "I said hello!" She states again, waving her hands in my face to get my attention.

"Oh... uh_ hi, you look very lovely tonight."

"Thank you, I bought this outfit just for your party. By the way I have your present out there, but you'll have to come get it." I look around for Stephanie, she is talking to some friends and drinking Champaign.

"I guess I'm all yours for the moment." Octavia grabs my hand and rushes me off, we end up in a secluded corner of the club near the coatroom. She walks in looking around as if she is actually looking for something.

"I know I left it over here somewhere." She mumbles, bending over looking behind some coats.

"Maybe someone put it near the back. By the way you need to keep an eye on your man tonight, I don't want him tearing up the place." I say.
She moves further into the coatroom and looks behind a rack, she bends over in my direction, so I can see that she isn't wearing any panties underneath her outfit.

"Here it is..." She yells out, I walk closer to see what she is grabbing at and to get a closer look at that well developed body of hers.

"Where's it at?" I ask, looking in the direction she's grabbing. She turns around wearing a bow on her shoulder.

"Happy birthday!"

"I thought you...." Before I had a chance to comment about the bow on her shoulder, she was whipping junior out of my pants and swallowing it up, like it was tonight's main course. The more my manhood raised the further down she went. I had to admit, the girl really knew how to blow my mind. I was a little nervous to know that Steph was so close and yet got a rush from the thought being caught at the same time, the whole situation had me extremely turned on. She looked up at me every once in a while, to make sure I was enjoying my present. When my throbbing volcano erupted, she made sure there were no traces for anyone to find.

Getting up to leave she whispers in my ear, "Save a dance for me." wiping the side of her mouth with her finger, she walks out. I take a few breaths and walk out a few minutes after her. Stephanie grabs me by the arm, I try to think of a quick lie.

"There you are, everyone is waiting for you to make a speech." I close my mouth and went along with game. Well if it ain't broke, don't try to fix it. I thought walking over to the DJ's booth. I grab the mic and give it a few taps, as the DJ cuts the music,

"Hello everyone... First, I would like to thank our God because without him our existence would be none. I would like to thank everyone for coming out here to help me celebrate yet another birthday." Marcus's drunk ass yelled out over top of me, "I didn't come here to help you celebrate shit!!! I came for the free food!" Everyone chuckles, and I continue.

"This really means a lot to me. I hope that everyone is having a good time, so eat and drink as much as you possibly can." The DJ cuts in with Atomic Dog by George Clinton and the crowd goes off. I try to mingle for the rest of the night, but I can tell that Stephanie is getting a little pissed off at the other women hanging all over me. The party ends around 4:30 in the morning, I say my goodbyes and give out a couple of hugs to the last few people standing in the parking lot. Stephanie and I get in the car to drive home.

"Steph... I am worn out!" I sigh and yawn as I'm talking to her.

Stephanie places her left hand on my inner thigh and softly says, "What do I need to do, to help you stay up so we can get home safely?" She speaks seductively, as she rubs my pistol through the crotch of my pants. I pull out of the parking lot, with my zipper coming down and my sword swinging in her hand. By the time I made it to the end of the block, my boys were in heaven from the heat of her mouth. She mentions that they feel cold and she wants to warm them up a little. Steph slowly licks up and down my lollipop giving much needed attention around the head. Before I know it, we we're parked in our drive way, the windows were fogged up from the steam and Stephanie is riding me like she just invented a new sport called stick horseracing. It felt so good that I couldn't resist any longer knowing I was about to debut my finale, Steph wasted no time going back down to plug up the hole in my pipe. After she cleared away all the precipitation, she came up for air laying her body on mine. We fall asleep quickly from over exhaustion. The next morning I wake up to the sun in my eyes, a very bad headache and some older Filipino woman bamming on my car window yelling.

"You nasty! You nasty! You nasty! Yous no clothes on!" I realize that Stephanie and I had forgotten to go in the house this morning and fell asleep in the car completely naked.

"Hey Steph, wake up! We forgot to go in the house." I state shaking her to wake up.

"All man, what time is it? And why is that lady yelling so loud?"

"Well it's almost 8:30 in the morning and she is yelling because we're both sleep in the car with no clothes on."

"Shit!" She yells, coming to the realization, that anybody passing by could have seen her completely exposed.

"Well Steph it's not like you have anything to be embarrassed about, so let's go in the house and make some breakfast…" I nonchalantly state.

"Yeah right, so you just want to get out the car in the nude and walk into the house in front of all these people!"

"Yes, it's our house, why can't we? Besides with your body I don't think anyone will object." Stephanie looked at me like I was crazy as she twisted up her lips.

"Well if it's so easy to do, then you go right ahead and lead by example." I shoot Steph a look that expresses my willingness to do just that. Since there's no shame in my game, I grab my clothes, swing the door wide open and get out the car with my twigs and berries swinging in the wind.

"Come on Steph it's your turn to cook breakfast!" I yell over my shoulder laughing, leaving the car door open and her completely exposed to the neighborhood. Two teenage kids riding their bikes down the street crash into each other after getting an eye full of Stephanie's abundant urbanized womanly body. I know Stephanie is mad by the look she has on her face, as she scrambles to put her clothes on. The old lady caught a good glimpse of me walking into the house, she looks at Stephanie with a big smile on her face, showing a mouth half full of teeth.

"You veddy lucky lady... him big dick fella!" Stephanie looks at her in disgust, shakes her head and storms into the house.

Chapter 7

It has almost been a month since my mother's heart attack. She appears to be getting her strength back, I usually prepare a healthy Sunday meal for her, but this Sunday I've decided to bring her some baked turkey, mashed potatoes, cabbage, string beans and rolls. *I know she shouldn't be eating this kind of food just yet, but I figure if she is going to die then I may as well let her die happy*, I half-heartedly joke to myself pulling up to her house. I arrive at her house early so I can do some light cleaning for her while she eats. I could have used my key, but feeling a little lazy, instead I ring the doorbell, she never answers, So I end up using my key.

"Mom, I have your dinner ready." I yell, but there is no answer. I start to wonder where she could be. She usually calls me if she goes out somewhere. I sit her plate of food on the table and start to leave. As I'm walking out the front door I stop an overwhelming feeling that comes over me, I turn around and walk upstairs towards her bedroom she isn't there. I notice the light left on in the bathroom, I go to push the door open and turn the light off but run into the door. Something is blocking it from the other side, I push even harder and manage to get it open, I look on the floor and can't believe my eyes. My heart drops when I see my mother lying on the floor unconscious. I call the ambulance on my cell phone and start CPR. The ambulance arrives about seven to ten minutes but even that was too long for me. I am tired and my arms burning from doing CPR chest compressions, but there is no way I am about to stop. The paramedics take over and immediately rush her to the hospital. I don't hesitate to hop in the back of the ambulance with her. When we arrive at the hospital, they rush her straight into the emergency room. I call Octavia on her cell phone, the first chance I get to let her know what has happened.

"Hey baby I was just thinking about you?" Octavia states softly.

"She's gone! I think she's gone this time! I lost her!" I yelled franticly into the phone.

"Marcus calm down, I don't understand what you're saying. What's happened?" She yells, beginning to panic herself.

"My mother, she's not breathing! I found her on the floor in the bathroom not breathing! I tried to revive her but she wouldn't wake up! I tried, I really tried! Why wouldn't she wake up? Oh my God she can't leave me like this, she didn't even get a chance to eat her dinner." I break down and start sobbing. Octavia is crying as well, but trying to hold it together for the both of us.

"Baby where are you?"

"I'm at the hospital now, they have her in the back."

"Try to calm down baby, I'm on my way." Octavia exclaimed, grabbing her keys and pocketbook off the table and running out the door. As scared as she was for Marcus, she tried to remain calm and stayed focused on driving to the hospital. Whizzing past other cars on the road, her mind kept shifting back to Marcus and what he must be going through. She was driving twenty miles per hour over the speed limit, a police officer clocked her speeding as she whizzed through an intersection, while driving recklessly and pulled her over.

"Ma'am I stopped you because you were going 65 mph in a 45 mile an hour zone and while driving recklessly. Can I see your license and registration please? Octavia put her hands over her face and took a deep breath to get it together and then quickly handed him all the necessary documentation. While looking over her information he asked, "Is there a reason you were driving so careless ma'am?"

She cleared her throat as best she could, "Yes, my mother just had a heart attack and I was going to the hospital to be with her." Seeing my sincerity and the tears running down my face. With my information correct and no priors or warrants. He decided to cut her a break.

"Ma'am I decided not to give you a ticket. If I were in the same situation, I would probably do the same thing. I can't allow you to be speeding through the streets though. But what I will do is escort you to the hospital to make sure you get there quickly and safely." I looked at him with a surprise look.

"Thank you so much." I said whole heartedly, I was shocked that a white cop was rendering his assistance to me, a black woman. The cop turned on his lights and sirens and we were at the hospital in no time. The cop pulled alongside of my car wished my mother well and drove off. Up until that point, I hated cops. I thought that a cop was nothing more than a white person who traded in his white sheet for a blue uniform and a shiny badge and was only around to harass black people. Now I am forced to believe that not all cops are bad people, or at least there's a little good in everyone. I took the first available parking space open and rushed inside to find Marcus pacing back and forth in the waiting area.}

"Hey baby I'm here, you okay. Do you want to sit down?" She rushes over to me.

"NO_ I can't sit down more than a few seconds."

"Have the doctors told you anything yet?"

"No not yet. I keep asking, but they keep telling me they'll let me know something as soon as they can. Why did I get to her house so late? If I had gotten there sooner I probably could have saved her. I knew I should have talked her into moving in with us, how could I have been so stupid." Smacking myself on the head I can do nothing but bury my face in my hands and cry.

"Marcus don't beat yourself up over it. I'm sure you did everything that you could possibly do."

"You don't understand, my mother was there for me my whole life and the one time she needed me I wasn't there for her." I explain.

"But baby this is not your fault." She tries to reason, and as much as I want to feel like she is right I can't help but be mad at myself.

"I guess you're right, but I still just feel so bad and helpless. It's like I let her down."

"It's going to be okay." Two and a half hours have gone by before someone comes out to talk to me.

"Is there a Marcus Barnes here?" A lady with a white lab coat on, over her clothes looks around the room as she speaks.

"Yes I'm over here." I state, walking towards her.

"Can I have a word with you in my office please?" She guides me towards her door with her hand.

"Sure." I reply nervously.

"And you are ma'am?" She asks Octavia, abruptly stopping her at the door.

"I'm his wife." She replies confidently, I nod confirming her statement and reach for her hand.

"Sorry, please have a seat. My name is Dr. Hamilton and this is Willis Tremmel our Chaplain on duty." I start to lose it, knowing there's only one reason they want me to talk to a Chaplain.

"No, no, no. This isn't supposed to be happening!" Octavia tries to comfort me, hoping it will help keep me under control.

"I got you baby. We're going to get through this." She mumbles.

Dr. Hamilton continues to talk, "Your mother suffered a massive heart attack and we've done everything we could to save her." He explains calmly.

"No God! You've made a mistake. She wasn't supposed to die yet." I yell out looking towards the ceiling.

"She was pronounced dead at 7:22 pm. I'm deeply sorry, our chaplain is here for you in your time of need." I am at a loss for words. The little bit of energy I have, drains when I view her body. Derrick, James_, Stephanie and Jamal all rushed to the hospital to help console Marcus _in his time of mourning. The next few days he was a total wreck while we made funeral arrangements and packed up all of his mother's belongings. The funeral was on Friday at 11:00 am.

£   £   £

I am stretching in the garage from my 2 mile run, sweating out all the junk food, I've been eating in the past week.

Stephanie opens the door to the garage, "Jamal when you're finished I need to talk to you." She closes the door without waiting for me to acknowledge her.

"I'll be there in a minute." I yell, realizing I'm not talking to anyone. Damn, what does she want now? I try to think if I had done something wrong lately, and I need to really think before I talk to her, but I am drawing a blank.

"Hey honey what's up?" I ask cautiously, trying to sound calm like nothing is up.

"Like you don't know!" She snaps at me. I stand there dumbfounded not having a clue as to what she could be talking about.

"Now what did I do?" I shoot back, tired of her always yelling at me.

"Hello! Excuse me, don't you have a court date next week that we haven't talked about yet!" Stephanie exclaims.

"Oh yeah that." I mumble and lower my head.

"Yes that. What are your planning on doing about that?"

"I decided to drive up there the day after the funeral."

"Drive! Are you crazy? Do you know how long it will take you to drive all the way up there? Plus it is just too dangerous."

"I'll be fine. It only takes three days to drive, plus I could use the time to get some fresh air and clear my head." I reply. *And it'll give us some time apart, I need to figure out if I want to continue to invest in this relationship or cut my losses and move on.* I think to myself listening to her squeaky nagging voice.

"You can do what you want, but I'm against it."

"Look don't worry, I've drawn up an itinerary of which route I'm taking and where I'm going to stop off for the night. So you'll always know where I am."

£   £   £

The funeral was very beautiful and they made her up so nice, it looked like she was taking an afternoon nap. Marcus held it together as best he could, but once or twice, the burden of losing his mother was too much for him to handle. He was glad that she's in a better place, but mad that he'll never be able to talk to her again. He regrets most not giving her any grandchildren before she died.

Marcus pulls Derrick, James and myself to the side, "I want to thank you guys for being here for me."

He forces himself to smile, "you're the only family I have left, I guess you're stuck with me whether you like it or not."

I speak first, my eyes feeling heavy with tears I look at my friend hopeful we can make it through this.

"I'm sorry about your loss, just let me know if there is anything that I can do and if you ever need to get something off your mind, I'll always listen."

"Thanks." Marcus says as he gave me a big bear hug.

Derrick gave him a hug as well, "Yeah the same goes for me too. As much as I hate to say it, we're all born dying. These bodies are only being loaned to us, they're not for keeps."

Marcus half chuckles, "That might be a good thing for you then, because your body has been through some wear and tear." We all shared a laugh at this comment.

James steps up next, "Marcus I'm here for you day or night, call me anytime. I love you man." He states as his eyes water up. Marcus looks at him with a funny look. "Listen at mister always missing in action, trying to be all sentimental all of a sudden. I should call you road runner, because nobody can catch up with your ass." We all looked at each other then burst out laughing again. It feels good breaking the tension of the funeral, and it was better to see Marcus laugh, because now I know he will eventually be all right. The last few days have been really tough, but we are boys and together we'll make it through anything.

Friday just after midnight, I'm ready to start on my journey across the states. Stephanie doesn't bother to get up and wish me off, so I throw my last bag in the trunk and head on my voyage cross-country. I am on 8 East in no time. This takes me straight into Interstate 10. I could have gone north to pick up I 40, to save time but I can't resist going to New Orleans, Louisiana and hitting Bourbon St. the home of the Mardi Gras. *Life just isn't worth it, if you don't stop to look around every once and a while.* I think to myself as I hop on I 10 East. I made it through Arizona and New Mexico in about 6 hours. When I hit Texas, I thought I was going to die. It took forever to drive through that state. I filled up twice in Texas, once at the beginning and then before I left out to hit Louisiana. *Gas is the highest it's ever been, at two thirty-five a gallon, I should be able to write this off on my taxes.*

About half way through Texas just pass Ozona I have to pee badly and but don't want to stop. I don't see one black person anywhere in the crowd and no one looks friendly. I pull over to the side of the highway and grab an empty Gatorade bottle with the big mouth. I use this in case of emergencies, to pee when there is no other place to go. It really comes in handy at times like this. I am almost finished peeing when a state trooper pulls up behind me and flashes his lights to get my attention. He catches me mid-stream and I can't stop, so I look back at him., he gives me a thumbs up sign to see if I am okay or need help, I barely pinch it off with one hand, give him a thumbs up with the other and nod that I was am okay.

"Please God, don't let him get out of his car and catch me like this." I mumble. I grab my cell phone with my free hand and, raise it up to make it look like I pulled over to use my phone. Another minute or so and he pulls off waving at me as he passes. *It's funny how life works sometimes, if I had really needed help this time, I bet that cop would have never pulled up as fast as he did. At least he didn't catch me with my pants down*, I chuckle to myself.

After driving through Texas for almost a whole day I was wore out and ready to take a nap, but I swore I was not resting until I made it to New Orleans. Every weekend was Mardi Gras weekend. I had been on the road roughly about 30 hours, minus the two naps I took at rest stops. There was nowhere to take a shower, but I used some wet naps that sufficed for the time being. As tired as I was feeling, when I saw a sign New Orleans 72 miles, I immediately perked up and kicked it into high gear. Not expecting my cell phone to go off, I jumped when I heard it ring.

"Hello?"

"Hey baby how are you doing? Sorry it took so long for me to call you and check on you." Stephanie states cheerfully.

"I am tired as hell. I'm not too far from my hotel and I'm glad it only took you a little over a day to finally call especially since you didn't even get up to see me off." I want to cuss her out for not seeing me off and then waiting a whole day and some change to finally call and check on me, but I don't have the strength and need to focus on being safe.

"Sorry, I was just too pissed off at you and this whole situation." She replies, still sounding a little irritated.

I really don't want to argue, at least not right now, "How are you feeling?" I ask flipping the subject.

"I'm hanging in there." I hear some kind of noise in the background, as if someone is whispering in her ear.

"Stephanie, what was that noise?"

"What noise? I don't hear anything but the TV."

"And when did you start watching TV. I can't pay you to watch TV when I'm home."

"Well I watch it when you're not here and you only watch sports anyway!" She snaps defensively.

"When the cats away the mice will play." I say sarcastically, hoping she catches my drift.

"Whatever! I just called to see if you were okay, not for a third degree. And since you want to act like that, I'll talk to you later." She hangs up the phone abruptly. Too tired to concern myself, I toss my phone over on the passenger seat, *I don't have time to worry about her, I was more concerned about keeping my car on the road.*

I finally make it into New Orleans. People are drunk and partying everywhere. I check into my hotel and go straight to my room lying across the bed completely exhausted, my body wanting to rest, but my mind was ready to see the town.

"I must be a glutton for punishment." I mumbled, hopping up off the bed, I knew I could never get a proper amount of sleep, if I didn't have at least one beer and get my party on for a few minutes. *I didn't come this far just to sleep, I can do that anywhere,* I think to myself, hopping out the shower throwing on something dressy but still casual. I thought about heading to that bar on the corner as I closed my room door behind me. Four and a half hours and too many beers later, the sun began to creep over the buildings, I knew I had stayed to long.

"Sorry ladies, the party is over for me. I'm not as young as you may think I am, I have to get some sleep."

One of the girls starts frowning, "Well can you have breakfast with us first? Maybe I could tuck you in afterwards." I glance over her beautiful native Indian body and her matching smile. Her hair is wavy and streamed half way down her back. Her light brown eyes are full of energy. Her breasts look firm, they have to be at least a full C. I continue to my gaze down the rest of her body, I couldn't miss the fact that she had a wash board stomach with a blinging belly ring. I was going to hate myself tomorrow, but I had to decline. If I took her back to my room I would have never been able to keep my hands off her and my body was on autopilot from sleep deprivation.

"I appreciate the gesture but I can't do it. I'll take you up on that offer at a later date." I say exhausted, my body ready to topple over on the next flat surface I see.

"I hardly doubt there will be a later date." She replies, kisses me on the cheek and whispers in my ear, "Your loss, not mine." I look back at her one last time, to burn a visual image of her in my memory. By the time, I made it back to my room the sun was up and I thought that I would have a problem going to sleep. But the truth is, I was sleep before my head hit the pillow. I was three sheets to the wind, dreaming about drunken girls running through the streets, flashing their breast for beads and pulling down their pants for sheer entertainment. Images of people having sex in the streets, and hookers walking up and down trying to find horny drunk men to hustle, all danced in my mind as I slept peacefully in the big easy. Before I know it, my alarm clock is ringing in my ear. It was 7:15 that evening, I feel like I have only been a sleep for about twenty minutes. I get up brush my teeth and take my shower. I check my cell phone for any missed calls. Stephanie had called me three times.

"I'll never hear the end of that." I mumble. I start to call her back, but quickly decide against it. We would just get into another argument anyway. So I might as well save them all up, just have one big argument and get it out the way later. I need to hit the road but I have to get something to eat and do a little sightseeing first. About 9:30 Sunday evening, I get back on route 10 heading east. I love t nighttime driving, it is cooler, the air is fresher, and there is less traffic on the road. I hit Mobile, Alabama with the quickness. After Mobile, I got on interstate 65 North towards Montgomery, then onto 85 towards Atlanta, Georgia. I have to stop in Atlanta, to see where the players play. No self-respecting man can call himself a pimp or a player, without surviving a night stomping with the big dawgs in the ATL. I make it to the out skirts of Atlanta on 285 and the traffic is horrible. Every direction I look is gridlocked. It takes me forever to get to my hotel, when it should have only been a 30 minute ride from where the traffic first jammed. *I should pull my car to the side and walk the rest of the way to my hotel.* I definitely would have saved some time. After sitting in traffic for three and a half hours, I finally make it into the parking lot of the hotel. My blood pressure is up and my tolerance level for any annoyances is very low coming off a serious case of road rage. All I want to do is take a cold shower and go to sleep. I call room service to wake me up at 8:00 pm so I will be well rested and full of energy for my night on the town in chocolate city. By 9:30, I am dressed to impress and ready to club hop, I thought about James and Marcus, wishing they were here with me on this momentous occasion. I guess that sometimes you have to roll solo and make moves together when you can. I went to the southwest section of town and found a club playing some reggae music. I pay ten dollars at the door to get in and I can't believe my eyes, all the nearly naked women out there popping their coochies on the dance floor. The club is packed and mainly women litter the dance floor and tables.

"Wow look at the crowd." I exclaim. The attendant at the door responds, "Yeah I know it's a slow night, we have twice this crowd on Thursdays."
After about two hours of getting my freak on, I decide I want something more up close and personal, I hop in a cab out front. "Please take me to the other side of town where the strip clubs are." I order with excitement.

"You're not from around here are you?" The cab driver asks.

"Actually I'm not, how did you know?"

"Other than your accent, you would never pay twenty dollars to go clear across town, when you could have walked to the best strip joints in town three blocks away."

"Thanks for the insight. Good looking out partna." The cab driver charged me two dollars and fifty-five cents for fare, but I give him a ten and tell him to keep the change. I tip him big, because he was more interested in my satisfaction then making a few extra bucks. And I appreciate that. Most drivers would have taken the money without a second thought.

I walk in the front door of the strip club across the street, I can't believe how big it is inside. It looks like a small city within a big city. First, I walk past the champagne room. Men were sitting in chairs receiving lap dances from topless dancers. Then I walk pass the Cadillac room. Men are situated in semi-private booths and the dancers are completely nude giving lap dances. The last couple of rooms were called Pure Ecstasy. The rooms that were being occupied are closed with a red light on above the door and a bouncer standing outside. I guess it's self-explanatory what was going on behind those closed doors. Smirking at the bouncer standing at the door I move past the many different rooms to find the best seat in the house. I finally make it to a section of the club called the rendezvous room. There's a bar going around three quarters of the room, a large stage in the center, and it is separated in the middle by a thick cloth. On one side male dancers entertain the women and on the other side female dancers entertain the men of the establishment. By the time I sat down, there were two dancers on stage giving an Oscar award winning performance. One girl was lying on her back covered in candy. While the other girl performed alongside, licking all her sweet spots. I was seriously enjoying the show.

The guy sitting next to me asks, "Have you ever been here before?" Not once taking his eyes off the action on the stage.

"No." I reply shortly. Now is not the time to strike up a conversation.

Then the guy nudges me his eyes never leaving the stage, "Watch this." The girl on the floor vaults her butt into the air, spreads her legs and yells heads or tails. Two people yell heads and three yell tales. I was flabbergasted at what I saw next. The girl spits out two quarters on heads and three quarters on tails. Another person yells out, "I need change for a dollar!" She spit four quarters on his table, everyone is clapping and throwing money on stage. For the entertainment I was getting tonight I should have gave the cab driver the whole twenty. 6 am rolled around a lot sooner than I had anticipated and I was about to head back to my hotel room, when a dancer grabs me by the arm.

"Hey where's the fire?" She asks, pulling me back. I turn and look at her for a few seconds. She was gorgeous, too gorgeous to be working in a strip club, but I was happy that she was here to grace me with her presence.

"I'm sorry, it's late and I have some business I have to attend to tomorrow, or should I say in a few hours."

"Awe, I've been checking you out all night and I was hoping we could spend a little time together before you go." She starts to massage my inner thigh with her hand.

Getting excited, "Well what do you have in mind uh_ uh_" I realize I didn't even know her name yet.

The girl interrupts me, "Winter but my friends call me Destiny." She spoke in a sensual almost hypnotic tone.

"Destiny, you sound like your way to expensive." I point to her tattoo above her right breast that read Fulfill your Destiny.

She starts to laugh, "I like you, you have a good sense of humor. How about we get better acquainted in the_, well I would suggest the Cadillac room. But you look like a man who's been in ecstasy once or twice."

"And just how much will it cost me to go into ecstasy a third time?" Destiny pauses for a brief moment as she stares into my eyes with a sexy smile, She gently bites on her bottom lip contemplating a suitable price for me.

"Since I like you so much, I'll give you my special client rate of only three hundred and forty five dollars."

"Three hundred and forty five dollars!!!" I blurted, losing interest fast. "What the hell is regular price?"

"Four twenty five. I promise it will be worth it."

"Winter, Destiny, Fortune, by the looks of you I bet you're worth every penny. Right now, I don't have the time or money. How about you take that gentleman over there into ecstasy, because he seems more ready and willing then I'll ever be. You have a good night." I stated, as I broke break free of her arm grip and exited out the door.

9 am sharp I was checking out of my room. I didn't want to drive during the daytime but I didn't have too much of a choice. It's going to take me at least ten hours to get to Baltimore from here and I have to be in court first thing Wednesday morning. After fighting traffic to get back on 85 North for two hours, I finally broke free and started cruising at a normal speed. The only time I had planned on stopping was to get gas and eat. I had to laugh while telling James about the Indian girl I met in New Orleans, he said that he still be there because someone that fine he just wouldn't have been able to leave behind, and all

Derrick talked about was how he would have turned that strip club out in the ATL. He said Destiny would have been a memory and they would have had to change the name pure ecstasy into the boom, boom room. I made it to Richmond Virginia and merged onto 95 North in about five hours and change, I should be seeing the Domino Sugar sign and Baltimore skyline. Being on the road all this time has given me a good opportunity to reflect on my relationship with Stephanie and what I am really looking for in her. By the looks of things, it doesn't look too good for her and I. Absence makes the heart grow fonder, is what I always heard, but for me I am actually starting to enjoy her not being around. I felt bad for thinking that, because she really hasn't done anything to make me feel this way. I guess in this instance, it's really not her it's me! It feels good to have hit the home stretch, I should be in Baltimore in the next few hours. Within two hours, I am crossing the Potomac River out of Virginia and into DC. I'll never miss the congestion in Northern Virginia! I can feel the electricity in the air, shortly after 10:00 pm I am getting off the highway on exit 55 heading into downtown Baltimore. There's no better feeling, than being in my old stomping ground. I drive down Baltimore Street, I look at the strip clubs and keep driving because I know none of these clubs could ever compare to what I saw in the A T L. I drove to my mother's house hoping to get a good home cooked meal. The lights were out, I figured she was probably is still at church, not that there is anything wrong with it, but she spends so much time at church she might as well put an apartment in the basement. I head inside, and situate myself in my old bedroom. I start to call Stephanie and let her know I made it here safely, but the way we've been vibing I decide to call her later, don't want to make my night any worse so instead I go to sleep.

Chapter 8

Wednesday morning I wake up to the smell of scrambled eggs, sautéed onions, sausage, bacon, grits and English muffins with butter.

"Good morning mom, I made it home before you got in from church last night." I say as I pick her up, swing her around, and give her a kiss on the cheek.

"Ohhh, there's my baby. I knew you were here, because you took my parking space in front of the door! Next time, park across the street, ya hear." *Even though it's public parking out front, people are serious about their parking spaces in front of their doors, you would think they paid for them*, I chuckle to myself.

"Now tell momma all about your trip?" She replies over loading my plate with grits.

"It was long and tiring, but I enjoyed it. I stopped off a few places and went sightseeing, to make it more interesting though."

"So when you say you went sightseeing, you mean you went out had a few drinks and showed your behind." She asked cutting her eyes my way.

"Yes ma'am, boy you still don't miss a beat." I laugh.

"Momma may be getting older, but I ain't getting dumber. Here's your breakfast, eat it while it's hot. Chile you never could resist the smell of my cooking. Even when you were young with rows of peas on your lil nappy head, you were always the first one up looking around for food. You used to eat so much when you was younger, you almost made me shamed."

"Come on mom I haven't had peas in my head for years now. Plus I was a growing boy back then" I said, stroking my wavy hair with my hand.

"It still seemed like it was yesterday to me. Speaking of which, what kinda trouble you done went and got yourself into?" She asks seriously.

"I'm not in no kind of trouble, just some chicken head claiming that I got her pregnant a few years ago and looking to get paid. I'm just here to claim my innocence." I state proudly.

"I know I raised you better than that, in this white man's world you're guilty until proven innocent. This would have never happened if you would have kept your little boys wrapped up in some plastic." She scolds me.

"But I did listen to you and I'll prove it when this is all over. Now if you will excuse me I have some business to tend to."

I made it to the courthouse early enough, to make sure no business was being taken care of without my presence. The judge calls the case to order promptly at nine thirty.

"Ma'am please state your full name." The Judge looks over some papers gathered in front of her.

"Sabrina Lynn Brown."

"And sir can you please state your full name for the record." He asks me.

"Jamal Christopher Edwards, your honor."

"And this petition is for proof of paternity and child support. Do you both agree?"

Sabrina and I both state in unison, "Yes." Then we both turned towards each other and give each other an evil look.

"Do you Sabrina, have anything to say to support your case?"

"Yes, for the last five years I have been raising our daughter all on my own. Struggling, trying to make ends meet for the both of us, he never sent any money, he never even called her, it's like he thinks if he ignores her she doesn't exist." Sabrina starts to shed a few tears. "Plus he was the only person I was with around the time I got pregnant. I don't care if he doesn't like me, but why did he abandon our daughter like that."

I mumble to myself, "This crazy bitch is good, she almost got me convinced it's mine."

The judge was definitely buying everything she said hook, line, and sinker. The judge snaps at me changing the tone of his voice, "Mr. Edwards is there any good reason you have for abandoning your daughter and not bothering to help support her?"

"Well, your honor first of all, the first I have ever heard of having a daughter was when I was slapped with this paternity law suit a few weeks ago, and the dates don't match the time frame we were messing around, there's at least a seven month difference." I explain.

"Is your name on the birth certificate?"

"I don't think so." I answer throwing my hands in the air.

Sabrina interjects, "Yes, yes his name is on there, I have a copy if you want to see it." She yells out.

"It a shame that this poor young lady has been traumatized the past few years trying to make ends meet for her and her daughter. While you were out there, free to do as you will, running amuck and girl hopping. You should be ashamed of yourself."

"Your honor, it hasn't been proven that she's my daughter YET and if you're just going to take her side over mine then why am I even here?" It didn't matter what I said. I am guilty until proven innocent. My mother was right again.

"Don't you ever talk to me in that tone in my own courtroom; I'll fine you in contempt of court. Is that understood?" The Judge voiced out, at me. It bout killed me to answer him, I was hotter than the devil's toe nails, but for now, my fate and future was in his hands, so I had to play it cool until I got out of there.

"Yes your honor." I answer him through half clinched teeth.

"Ms. Brown how much are you asking for in child support?" Sabrina's eyes glistened over, as the tears dried up and a big smile instantly grew upon her face.

"Um_ three hundred fifty dollars, your honor," she replies excitedly. The judge scribbles something down on a piece of paper, and then after a few seconds, he looks at Sabrina and asks, "Is that all? The max for one child at his pay salary is six hundred fifteen dollars; it could always be reduced later if you like." Sabrina was smiling as if she had just hit the 10 million dollar jackpot. I can't believe this crap! I thought as I watch the two work together to do me in.

"When do you want this support to go into effect?"

"Today!" She immediately yells out.

"Well, you could go as far back to the day you first filed a petition." I mumble under my breath, "Damn judge why don't you tie the Neuse and put it around my neck for her." I was getting so mad I could feel the steam rising off my body and my hands were shaking as if I was having a seizure.

"Is there any last words you have Mr. Edwards?" The Judge taunts me, as if I am about to be executed.

"Yes I do. With all, do respect your honor. It's a crime, when a mother has to raise kids on their own without help from the BIOLOGICAL father, but it's also a crime when a man is stuck paying the price for something he did not create. On the other hand, when he does try to be a good father, he gets screwed over by the mother, because she doesn't like who he's with or if something doesn't go her way. When is the day going to come when women are prosecuted for filing false claims or using their kids as pawns to get a few extra dollars? Good guys always finish last!" I state firmly, holding my head up as high as I can.

"Mr. Edwards I totally understand what you're trying to say."

"Thank you, sir."

"When the results come back positive, I'm ordering you to pay five hundred and seventy five dollars a month in child support and you will be three thousand, six hundred and forty dollars in arrears, which you'll pay back at a rate of an additional sixty dollars a month, until it is caught up." I turn white as a ghost. It felt like somebody had taken that long cold hard flagpole from out front and rammed it up my ass as far as it could go. We received our mouth swabs and this concluded the day, we had to return to court the next morning for the results. I returned back home and went straight to bed, I didn't want to talk or see anybody, all I wanted was for the Judge to read the results and clear my name. I lay there thinking about how that so called Judge disrespected me, I would think being a male himself, he would have had some kind of understanding for how I felt. This judicial system really needs to be revamped.

Thursday morning, I was back at the court house by 8 am prompt. The Judge calls court back into session and reads the results. There was no way that her daughter could be mine and but I was sweating bullets. The Judge read from a piece of paper, "When it comes to five year old Jessica. Jamal you are not the father.

"Yes!" I exhale loudly. I look at Sabrina as the smile glued to her face, disintegrated into a shocking and petrified look.

"Mr. Edwards, here's your chance to do something good and contribute back to society. Would you like to voluntarily pay child support for this girl?" I look at Sabrina and she looks at me with her water filled eyes, hoping I would say yes. Damn am I the only sane person in this court room.

"Your honor, if I was in the child's life, I wouldn't have a problem raising her or paying child support. And I applaud every man who is willing to take care of another man's child and it's about time they be recognized for it."

"So does that mean you'll do it?" Sabrina's frown began to turn up.

"Hell no, your honor! After what you just put me through. Who's going to pay me for the time I took off and the money I spent to come from the west coast!"

"That's it Mr. Edwards. I am holding you in contempt of court. Your fine will be seventy five dollars."

"That's fine by me your honor, if that's the price I have to pay for freedom!" Sabrina tried to apologize to me in the hallway, but when she saw the expression on my face, she realized now was not a good time to talk to me and went back inside the courtroom until I was gone. She also had one of the security guards escort her to her car. I drove through the projects on the way back to my mother's house, so I could calm down from the injustice that was almost forced upon my quality of life. A kid skipping down the street singing, caught my attention, he was singing the theme song to the Jefferson's TV show. I pulled over as the kid skips pass my car singing,

"As long as I live, it's you and me baby. Ain't nothing wrong with dat!"
It choked me up and brought tears to my eyes, to see a child that had old dirty clothes on, living in an area well below the poverty level could have so much joy in his heart he had to skip down the street to express himself. I imagined how life would be for him if he kept his heart pure and full of joy throughout the rest of his adolescent years. Reality slowly set in as I pulled off and drove pass some teenagers with their pants hanging down so low you see their whole pair of boxers sticking out in the back while they drank forties of malt liquor beer hanging on the corner. By the time I got to my mother's house she was sitting on the front porch waiting for me.

"How did it go? Is it yours? What happened?" She stood there asking, anticipating an answer.

"Slow down, everything is fine. I told you it wasn't mine." I coolly state.

"I'm so happy for you." She replies clapping her hands together.

"Mom the judge treated me like I was a criminal and then after it was all over with, he had the nerve to ask me if I still wanted to pay child support."

"You didn't accept it did you?"

"No, I got a seventy five dollar fine instead."

"I told everyone that you're in town. There are a few people who want you to come over and visit when you get a chance."

"Mom you mean I drove two thousand seven hundred and sixteen miles and they can't drive five minutes across town to see me, then they ain't worth seeing, I'm going in the house to wash up for dinner and then I'm going to bed. I have a long trip back to San Diego."

"Jamal, now that you're doing fine out there in California. Don't forget where you came from. There are people out there that need your wisdom and your direction."

"Mom, I empathize with a lot of people living in poverty. Some don't think they can do better, some don't know how to do better and a few others that just won't do better. I didn't forget that used to be me in the projects at one time and I want to give back. Give someone else a chance, like I got a chance. I'll be the first to admit, I'm not perfect. But I have never been in trouble with the law and I never sold drugs to make a living. And if I can show kids that selling drugs is not the next step on the ladder after high school, then maybe they can broaden their horizons and look beyond the projects and discover there's a whole world to conquer out here."

"Baby I am so proud of what you have done with your life and I was so afraid for you."

"Why?"

"I was afraid, that if you not had done the right thing. I was going to have to knock your head off." We both start laughing. "Now go wash your hands so we can eat, before this food gets cold." Before I sat down to eat, I run back out to the car and grab an envelope from out the glove box.

"Mom look I have a surprise for you." I spoke coming back inside the door.

"Oh baby you shouldn't have, uh don't just stand there like a lump on a log, give it to me," signaling with her hands for me, to give her the envelope. She tears open the envelope and pulls out two tickets to a Patty Labelle concert.

"Thank you so much, I've wanted to see her in concert for so long."

"I read that she was going on tour and one of her stops is right here in Baltimore. I figured I would do something nice for you, since you've done such a wonderful job raising me." I state proudly.

"That wasn't necessary, a mother is supposed to take care of her kids not expecting any type of reward. The first reward was making you and the second reward is you making something of yourself. But I'll keep the tickets anyway, since you went through the trouble of getting them."

"Now momma behave." I reply laughing.

"Jamal sit down I want to talk to you." She says id as she put our plates on the table. "I know it's not any of my business, but what's going on with you and Stephanie? I talked to your brother and he's been telling me all kinds of crazy stuff about you been sleeping on his couch and carrying on. And look at you, I see you're here alone and you haven't mentioned her once."

"I know, mom Steph and I are complicated. She's a good girl and I know she means well, but I'm just not sure if she's the one I want to spend the rest of my life with. How do I know if she's the one or there's someone better for me." I question the only woman I have ever fully trusted.

"You should have thought about that before you guys shacked up together. Now I know you're not a saint by a long shot, but don't lead her on. If you don't want to be there, you need to let her know and break it off. Personally I never cared for her, but it's not my relationship."

"I do love her, but how do I know she's the one?"

"Son, when you first lay eyes on that special someone, all the rules and stipulations you have about your ideal mate will go right out the window. You haven't really lived until you've found that special someone to die for."

"Mom, why didn't you and dad, I mean Lawrence get married?" I ask curiously.

"Oh I wanted to get married, I wanted to marry your dad before I had your brother. But the timing was never right with him. It was always one excuse or another why he couldn't. Then one day, I think you were about, six months old, he waltzed right up in here with a younger woman, told me that the kids and I were tying him down too much and he needed a break. He packed his clothes and that was the last I had ever heard of him. A few days later I heard he died in a car accident, I'm sorry you never got to know him."

"Well I want to be the first to thank you, for not running out on us too. I can't think of one day that you weren't here for me." I say whole heartedly.

"Now there were times when you guys drove me crazy and I longed for the day that you two would be out on your own. But I allowed myself to get pregnant so it was my responsibility to make sure you were taken care of until you could take care of yourself."

"Mom when I finally do decide to have kids, I'm gonna make sure that I am a father to my kids far better than he ever was!" I promise her and myself.

"And I wouldn't expect anything less of you. But you need to get yourself in order first, before you do anything else. Then you will see everything else will start to fall in place."

"But mom I_"

"Listen, boy listen. I've raised you. I think I know my own son. You need to stop all that game running with women, hopping in and out bed with this one and that one. Everything you do will come back full circle before you die. Be careful how you treat women, because the same thing may come back to haunt you. I remember grand mom Sarah used to always tell me, be careful how you treat people climbing up the ladder, because you'll run into them same people on your way back down."

"Ok mom, I'll get myself together, I promise, mom in my defense I never meant to hurt anyone, I just didn't see the need to waste so much time talking to one person at a time. I figured I would cover more ground in less time if I talked to multiple people at once, that's all."

"Now Jamal Christopher Edwards, you know you don't make any sense at all! Think about it this way, how would you feel if you found Stephanie had been dating another man the whole time she was seeing you? Wouldn't you be upset?" I sat there with my mouth wide open, she was right, I never looked at the big picture and saw things from another perspective. I'm going to try my best to patch things up with Stephanie when I get back home."

"Baby close your mouth and come help momma do the dishes."

On my way back to San Diego, I took the least scenic route possible. I only stopped to rest for a few hours here and there, gas and a quick bite to eat. I tried calling Stephanie several times on the way, but I only got her voice mail and the house phone just kept ringing. Once I crossed into Arizona, I decided to call her one last time. Her cell went straight to her voice mail again, this time I left her a message.

"Hey Steph, I've been calling you the past 2 days. You're not answering your phone or returning any of my messages. I love you and can't wait to see you and I hope you're ok. By the way, I just crossed into Arizona, I'll be home in a few hours." I made it into San Diego late in the evening, I pulled up to the house hoping to see Stephanie's car in the drive way. I was ready to put everything behind us and start a new life with her. Everything that my mother said to me really seeped in on the drive back home. I'm getting older and it's time to put all that running women behind me, I don't want to miss the opportunity like Marcus had with his mother. I want to give her some grandkids for her to spoil before it's too late.

It was great to be back home, I left all my stuff in the car and rushed in the house. I can unpack tomorrow morning.

"Stephanie I'm home." I say walking in the front door, there's nothing but an empty echo there to greet me. The house was a wreck and the air smelled stale, like Stephanie hadn't been here all week. The same dirty dishes were in the sink that was there when I left. This is not like her. I was too tired to complain at this point, so I went to bed. I tried waiting up for her as long as I could, but the fatigue got the best of me and I went straight to sleep. I have no idea what time Steph even came in. Monday morning Stephanie was getting ready for work and must have been annoyed at the fact that I didn't have to get up and go to work as well. She was making all kinds of noises knocking and banging on everything.

I've had enough, "Stephanie is there a problem?" I shout in angst, yanking back the covers.

"No. why?" She snaps back.

"Cause your making a lot of noise, while I'm trying to sleep. What's been up with you lately? You've been real some timey." I state.

"Oh, I figured you got plenty of sleep, since you didn't have time to talk to me!" She replies with much hostility in her voice.

"Most of the trip I didn't have a signal. The few times I did talk to you, you seemed too preoccupied with something. Or someone?" Steph turns towards me with a shocked look on her face.

"What are you trying to say?" She asks cautiously.

"For starters, the house looked like it hadn't been touched since I left. Then I called your cell phone quite a few times and it went straight to your voice mail. You never turn your cell off! You've been acting real strange lately, like you have a different life or something."

"I don't know what you're trying to insinuate, but I don't have time for this. I'm gonna be late for work." Looking embarrassed, Stephanie rushed out the room, slamming the door behind her. That was a big red flag; she was too much of an opportunist to let me get away with sly remarks of that magnitude. Normally she would have stayed here all morning until she was satisfied that she had won the argument or removed all doubt of my allegations. Now that I was up and couldn't go back to sleep, I started cleaning up the house. I wasn't due back at work until Monday, so I just relaxed around the house for the next few days. Stephanie worked later than usual the next few days and even though I was missing her like crazy, we avoided each other most of the time and only talked to each other when it was necessary. I made it a point to go to bed a few hours after her, to ensure there was no leeway for pillow talk. Thursday night, I called Derrick to see if he was coming over to watch wrestling, since James seemed to be too busy and hardly had time to talk. Some girl answered the phone.

"Hello?" I look at my phone at first to see if I had the right number.

"Uh, hi is this Derrick's place?" I ask, sounding a little uncertain.

"Yes it is." She answers, sounding very chipper.

"Is he home?"

"Sure, hold on." After a few seconds, Derrick grabs the phone.

"Hello?"

"Well I guess wrestling is out tonight?"

"What up J!!! Glad you made it back home safe." He replies, with a better than normal attitude.

"Who was that girl?"

"You wouldn't believe me if I told you, then again you might. Last night after I left the club, I went past that reggae spot, over on the Southwest side. It wasn't jumping so after two drinks I left. On my way home it started to rain, I was reaching under my seat to grab my Lucy Pearl CD while I was driving. Just as I was reaching under my seat, I sneezed, accidentally pressing the gas pedal to hard and bumped into this Audi 5000 in front of me. The car sped out of control and rolled into a ditch. I ran over to the car to see if any one was hurt, she was a little startled, but okay. I helped her out the car, introduced myself to her and told her how sorry I was for hitting her. She understood and empathized with me that accidents happen. Then she introduced herself as Veronica. Since her car had gone into a ditch and my jeep was fine. I felt bad and asked her if she wanted to call the cops, she said no because she doesn't have any insurance. We exchanged information and since my place was closer she asked if I could give her a ride to my place so she could make a few calls."

"But she could have used your cell phone."

"As luck would have it, my cell went dead right after the accident. By the time, we got back to my place it was lighting and thundering pretty bad and the electric had already went out in my neighborhood. I told her my phone was off because of the storm. She cut me off and asked if I would mind if she spend the night and left in the morning. Of course, I didn't have a problem with that. So we were sitting on the couch by candle light, I was telling her about how I accidentally ran into her and I sneezed again. When I sneezed my right hand that was laid across the top of the couch behind her head, wrapped around her and pulled her closer towards me. I started to remove my arm and apologized, but she stopped me as a bright streak of lightening lit up the living room. She held my arm so tight and told me that she felt safer with my arm around her."

"You always be trying to be a smooth operator, that shit doesn't work anymore Billy D."

"No it really was an accident this time." He laughs.

"Yeah okay, let me guess, you end up spending the rest of the night really getting to know her. I guess you tore that ass up like a true champ!"

"Well she's still here, ain't she?" He states with confidence.

"Look, don't be calling me later, crying that you've caught the bug from someone." I joked. "But anyway, have you talked to James lately?" "No, I don't think I've talked to him since you left two weeks ago." He answers, obviously not caring one way or the other if he had or hadn't.

"I have been trying to catch up with him, these past few days. I guess he's got something going on right now." I exhale.

"Well maybe he's been working some extra hours or something."

"No, he hasn't been working. I can't explain it, but it's almost as if he's avoiding me or something. This ain't like him, he's acting funny. I didn't even get a chance to talk to him at the Funeral. As quick as he came he was gone." I state pondering over the situation in my head.

"Well call Marcus to see if he wants to come over? I have to get back to my guest."

"I did, he's feeling reclusive right now, he's still mourning over his mother. Somehow, we gotta break him out of it."

"I tell you what, how about you figure out what James is up to first. And I'm going to take care of some business right now, call me if you hear anything, just not tonight! Oh and Jamal just one more thing don't get kicked out tonight cause you can't come over here."

"Alright I got you." I laugh before we hang up.

Chapter 9

Sitting at my desk, counting down the seconds as usual until quitting time, 5, 4, 3, 2, 1. 4:15 the clock turns, and it's time to clock out.

"Hey Jamal do you mind giving me a ride home today? My car is in the shop, I finally added that surround sound DVD system for the family." This deep voice streams over my shoulder.

"Hey it's my man Tony." Tony was a coworker from the other side of the firm. He is a mogul when it comes to networking. I wouldn't be surprised if he owns this company in a few years.

"Well of course I'll hook you up with a ride." I reply gladly, grabbing the rest of my stuff out of my drawer.

"Thanks I'll give you gas money." He replies reaching into his pocket.

"Don't worry about that, it's on my way home. So I hear you up for another promotion?" I ask making small talk.

"That's what I heard, I saved the company almost a quarter of a million dollars last quarter alone." He answers, tooting his own horn.

"How did you do that?" I ask, hoping to get a tip or two to boost my sales.

"First I took it upon myself to learn everything about this company as well as other companies that we deal with, things that no one else was willing to learn, when it came time to renegotiate contracts, I simply showed them the areas we should stop investing in and other areas we could afford to take bigger risks in, and it paid off big time. Right now I'm so important; they can't afford to fire me."

"You'll be taking over the company soon and those fools are paying you to do it."

"That's right, or I'll start my own business and run this one in the ground. I'm just counting the days until I walk in the boss's office and kick him out of his own seat and slap my name plate on his desk." Then he pauses for a minute as if he was imagining himself actually walking in there and doing just that. With a sly smirk on his face he continues, "That fat ole fossil might have a heart attack and die, not being able to comprehend that a nigga has just taken over his company." We both look at each other and start cracking up.

"Don't forget about us little allies that work with you; make sure you pave the way for us too." We get about 6 blocks from Tony's house and his phone goes off with a text.

"Damn _" Tony moaned. "It's Shonda, she's a good personal friend of mine."

"Huh? What's that?" I ask, not sure I heard what I thought I did.

"She's a friend of mine from back in the day, let's just say we go way back." He stated winking at me. Damn does everybody have a private stash on the side? I thought to myself chuckling.

"Uh... do you mind running me pass there for a few minutes?"

"Well Steph and I..." He cut me off, before I could finish.

"I promise it will be worth your wait." He gave me this little smirk and patted me on the leg. Oh, what the hell, it won't be the first time I was late coming home from work. Another ten minutes and we are pulling in front of Shonda's house. Tony knocks on the door, and a 5'9" dark cherry complexioned woman with the most gorgeous light green eyes and her long dark brown hair, barely covering her nipples through her see through Teddy, opens the door.

"Hello_, oh I didn't know you were bringing reinforcement with you..." Looking me up and down, I was about to turn around and catch him later. Before I opened my mouth, Shonda grabs me by my pants and yanks me in continuing her conversation, "Two's company, but threes a crowd and I like an audience, the more the merrier." She pushes me down on the couch and wastes no time with introductions. Instead she pulls down my pants and kneels down in front of me. I look at Tony with a questionable expression on my face, wondering what in the hell did he just get me into. Tony looks at me and threw his hands up in the air as if he didn't know this was going to happen and continues to laugh. Shonda looks at me and says, "There are only two types of people that don't wear underwear... stone cold freaks or people that don't know how to do their own laundry???" She massaged her cold hands on my dick, quickly bringing it to life.

"I just so happened to not like wearing underwear, I hate feeling like I'm constrained." I reply, rocking and maneuvering to get my pants off to get more comfy as she stimulates me.

Shonda responds in between licking and stroking, "I'm betting more on you being the freaky type." She continues to strokes my dick, with a circular twist of her wrist and licking the tip of it with her hot wet tongue, sending a tingling feeling through my body. Never missing a stroke Shonda peaks up at me hoping I am enjoying my unexpected blow job, she starts deep throating me, moving her hand up and down in unison with her mouth, while rotating her hand around the upright of my dick. The screwdriver motion is driving me insane. Tony joined in the action, sticking a 12-inch double-headed dildo up her back door while playing with her pearl tongue with a lubed up vibrator. The more he blazed her, the more intense she works me, it was like we were playing dominos. The more she got turned on from him, the more she did to pleasure me. It wasn't long before I couldn't contain my load. Shonda didn't seem to care to much she was right there to catch every drop, continuing to rotate my dick with her hand. I'm not sure what she did that was so different, but that was the best I ever had.

Tony stood up and stated, "Now it's my turn."
Hopping up on the couch waiting to be pleasured, Shonda turns towards him and starts giving him the imperial oral treatment. Now it's my turn to gratify her from the flipside. I went straight to the pink gold, which is the quickest way to make a woman have an orgasm. The clitoral area has hundreds of nerve endings, all in that 1/2" strip waiting to be stimulated. My mission is to inspire every single one of them, after all, that is the least I could do after her outstanding supporting role. I turn the vibrator on high, rubbing her pearl with a downward twisting motion. She begins to moan immediately. Just listening to her moan in pleasure gives me another rise, I thought about what she said earlier about me being a stone cold freak. Her comment made it my duty to not disappoint her; you never get a second chance for a first dick session. I grab my pipe slide it into her love hole to get it nice and lubed, then while marinated in her juices, I pack it in her rear entrance. I drill her like a jackhammer driving through a piece of concrete. The harder I slam my dick in her danger zone the more she likes it. My balls slapping against her pussy and I gave Tony a signal, which says I am hitting her right, in the back. Reaching her euphoria Shonda starts yelling, "Fuck me faster I'm cumming, I'm cumming!!!" She fell on top of Tony pinning him on the couch, while she tries to catch her breath. Tony looks a little disappointed due to his abrupt loss of pleasure.

Shonda gradually looks at me with an exhausted look on her face and says, "You must truly be the freak of all freaks, no one has never made me cum from giving it to me in the back door." She looks at me seductively. Tony grins and shakes his head, he knew I had to capitalize on that. I couldn't have someone walking around giving me a bad name. Forty minutes after leaving Shonda's house, I walk in the door.

Stephanie is waiting at the door starting on me already, "Where the fuck was you this time? And you smell horrible!"

"Just calm down, I can explain. When I clocked out at work, some girl from the office brought her baby in for everyone to see. We were all sitting around talking, passing the baby and lost track of time. Just before I was about to leave, I picked up the baby to say good bye, the baby shit out of its pamper all over me. See, I still have some on my shirt, I thought I cleaned it all off." I explain showing her a small brown stain on my shirt.

"What kind of fool do you think I am!!! Do I look that dense to you?" She walks off, leaving me standing there looking stupid. Then she yelled from the other room, "Hurry up and get your ass ready for dinner I'm starving." *She bought it,* I smirk, then my facial expression turned to sadness. *I need to get my ass in check! This is not how I want to live my life, I need to chill out for a while and figure this thing out before someone gets hurt bad. Starting with myself and maybe everything will get better.* I was starting to feel bad about all the women I had been with and all the games that I had played with Stephanie. She made sure that I had lunch to eat, she kept the house clean, did the laundry and didn't mind spending quality time with me, when I was around.

£   £   £

I took Stephanie to her favorite Italian restaurant called Trattoria La Strada, I hoped taking her there would brighten her mood. After we sampled a couple of wines and made our selection, the waiter goes to retrieve our drinks, while we wait for him to return, we browse over the menus.

"Look Stephanie, over these past few months our relationship has gotten off track. I want to know what I can do to make it right again?" I ask delicately, Stephanie looks at me with a funny look. "Granted I know I'm partly to blame in this, I'm willing to step up and do my part. What I want to know is, are you with me?" Stephanie opens her mouth to speak, but is interrupted by the waiter bringing us our drinks. She then orders a short tour of Italy, which consists of a small portion of lasagna, chicken parmesan, and garlic bread sticks. I order spicy pasta with sausage and a Caesar salad. After the waiter left from taking our order, I try to get to the bottom of things.

"Stephanie what's going on with you, you haven't said one word to me since we left the house."

"What is there to say, everything is out of my hands." She states looking down at her cell phone for the tenth time.

"What is that supposed to mean? And why do you keep checking your cell, you expecting a call." I exclaim feeling my anger build.

"Jamal please don't even go there, our relationship is in shambles because of you. I'm tired of your games and your bullshit!" she blurts out firmly.

"Stephanie I'm going to be honest with you, I may not have been the perfect person to share a life with, but I want to call a truce between us. I'm ready to do whatever it takes, to move this relationship to the next level." Stephanie looks at me, unmoved by my statement.

"Forgive me if I'm not jumping for joy. Your mouth is saying one thing and your actions say something completely different. I need something more than your word to make me believe everything is going to be ok." I am caught off guard and surprised Stephanie is coming at me this way.

"What are you saying that I've been less than honest in this relationship?" I snap, "If I'm such a bad person to be with, then why are you still with me? Maybe you're too paranoid to know when someone is treating you good. Tell me, what proof do you have to even insinuate that I've done anything wrong in this relationship?" I state nervously, not really knowing what she knew or was about to say. Stephanie stared at me in pity, as if I had some kind of disease, then she spoke her eyes overflowed releasing streams of water.

"Jamal, you never could see the big picture. You think everything is about you and nothing can exist outside of your world. I can't confirm anything right now, but I want to leave you with a piece of advice. Just because I didn't see certain things happening, doesn't mean that they don't exist.

"What in the hell does_" I'm interrupted by the waiter bringing us our food.

The waiter sits our food on the table, Stephanie asks, "Can you bring me a box for my food please?" Then she looks directly at me and continues, "I suddenly lost my appetite." The waiter looks to see if she is serious, then he turns towards me to see if I want a box as well.

"I'll be right back with your box ma am." He states then walks off.

"Thank you." She responds, her eyes pierce a hole through me as I start to nibble on my food. I contemplate on whether or not I should push her buttons and see if she has anything on me. I opt against it.

"I don't know what you think you know and I'm not a mind reader. So be up front with me, do you want to work on our relationship or not?" I ask, trying to control my attitude. She pretends as if she doesn't hear me and continues to stare at me. We sit there in silence, while I eat the rest of my food. A few feet away from the car, I unlock the doors with the keyless entry. Stephanie stands by the door and waits for me to open it like I normally do. I ignore her hopping in the driver side and start the car up. I pop in a mix CD and turn it up as loud as I can stand it. Stephanie finally gets in the car, disappointed that I'm not acting like a gentleman, but I don't pay her any mind. Normally having my music up this loud annoyed the hell out of me, but I was doing anything I can to get up under her skin.

"Jamal, Jamal! Can you turn the music down some? Please!" She asks, now it is my turn to ignore her, I continue to bob my head up and down to the rhythm of the bass kicking out from the speakers. *I bet what's good for the goose, isn't good for the gander!* I think looking over at Stephanie sitting there with her arms folded and her lip poked out. As soon as I pull into the drive way, Steph jumps out before I come to a complete stop, runs into the house and gets straight in the shower. Not wanting to feel the awkward air between us, I stay downstairs flip on the TV and call Derrick to tell him about the girl I encountered earlier today with Tony. I figure that at this point, I really have nothing more to lose in this relationship.

"Hello?" He answers, groggily.

"Yo dawg, what's going on?" I state, still amped from the music I was playing in the car.

"What do you want, I was sleep and I don't feel so good." He mumbles.

"Well you can be sick later, I have to tell you about this fine ass girl I boned a few hours ago."

"Speaking of which, what's about 1 inch long and hangs down?" He asked.

"That's easy a vampire bat." I answer.

"What has a 9 inch dick and hangs up?" I thought about it and couldn't come up with a single animal that has a penis that big and hangs up.

"I don't know what?" I ask, expecting him to tell me about some exotic animal he saw on the animal planet channel. But instead, he hangs up the phone. The phone rang again.

"Yo that was ig-nant. Why did you hang up on me?"

"What! Hey this is James." He replied, sounding a bit confused.

"What's going on? I thought you fell off the map! You don't have time for your boy anymore?" I ask.

"It's not like that, I was taking care of some personal business. You know how it is sometimes." He answers nonchalantly.

"Damn, it was that personal that you couldn't call me and at least say kiss my ass!" I respond.

"I told you I had something to take care of. You know I'm always here for you. I'm sorry to call you so late, but we have to talk later."

"Is everything okay?" I ask, switching to a serious note.

"Yeah_ um, everything is fine. But we'll talk later."

"Well I'm on the phone now, I know you didn't call me this late to just to tell me you'll talk to me later." I exclaim.

"Hold on I got another call coming in." I got real annoyed being on hold for a couple of minutes, just about to hang up then he clicks back over. "Jamal sorry about that, look I really need to take this call, plus what I need to say should be done in person not over the phone." He states sounding a little hostile.

"Alright, whatever! You know where to find me." I reply and hang up on him. *It's not like we've been all that tight lately, I don't care if he don't ever call I don't need anything but my sanity.* I think aloud to myself, I probably didn't mean that but need a place to take my frustration out since I am not taking it out on Stephanie.

£   £   £

The next week everything has died down between Stephanie and I, it's as if nothing ever happened. Thursday evening after work, Stephanie walks in the door, happy as can be, she leans over the couch and gives me a big kiss, like she hasn't seen me in years. I look at her strangely wondering how she went out of her way to avoid me, and now suddenly seem so overjoyed to see me. Not to mention, she has barely said five words to me since the incident in the restaurant. If I didn't know her so well, I would swear she was either bipolar or on some kind of hallucination causing drug.

"Jamal I'm so sorry for the way I've been acting these past few weeks, I think I'm going through menopause or something. I want to make it up to you, can I take you out to eat and maybe a movie?" I look at her like she is crazy, but reluctantly accept her apology and agree to go out this evening. *I'm not sure how many good days we have left together, but I might as well enjoy them as much as I can.*

"Ok, but I need to shower and change first." As Stephanie drives to her restaurant of choice, all I can think about is the restaurants alcohol selection. I plan on getting tore up, just in case she decides to act a fool like she did last week. Stephanie makes a left, pulling into Olive Garden. *Does every restaurant she picks have to be Italian!* I am not going to complain since she is treating; instead I follow the host and immediately order a drink. I start with a shot of Tequila and a screwdriver, because it always gets me in the mood for an eventful night. Stephanie orders a sex on the beach, it helps her knock the edge off and relaxes her. After we eat, we are laughing, carrying on and having a good time, like two drunken sailors on a liberty pass. Standing at the counter waiting for her to pay for our food, Steph is about a 1/2 inch away from my face staring right into my eyes, I can feel her warm breath escaping from her nostrils. I know she has had too much to drink when she begins to rub my manhood through my pants, those Lemon drop shots are taking a toll on her. After having quite a few drinks myself, I am down for whatever naughtiness she wants to get into.

The cashier asks, "How will you be paying for this today sir?"

"Plastic…" I answer, never taking my eyes off Stephanie. I nonchalantly unzip my pants and pull out my staff for Steph to play with. I slip the visa out of my back pocket and give it to the cashier giving her a friendly smile all the while my manhood is coming alive. Stephanie's eyes are fully dilated, she is excited to see how hard my Mister had gotten from her playfulness.

"Damn I can't wait to get you home." She whispers in my ear.

"Nope, sorry you're on punishment. You have been a very bad girl." I whisper back.

"Awe, don't do this to me. Can't you just spank me?" She states a little too loud, grabbing the attention of the waitress she looks up from behind the counter and gives us a funny look, we all start chuckling.

"I can't do that, because I would be letting you off easy. You have to do hard time." The lady behind the counter hands me a copy of the receipt to sign and another copy to keep. Just then another couple walks up behind us, Stephanie tucks my boys back inside their cubby hole, with a finesse that turned me on slightly.

"We'll definitely continue this later." She teases kissing me on the cheek. I had so much fun with Stephanie tonight that I don't even care I ended up paying the bill. As we walk to the car I grab her waist and she playfully pulls away never dropping her eyes letting me know that she was in control tonight. *I truly wish every night could be this much fun between us, we haven't had this much fun together in months.* I think looking at Stephanie, wondering when all this will come to an end. Later that night while I am banging out my chest on the bench, I overhear Stephanie telling one of her friends about her almost embarrassing moment at Olive Garden, her friend must have replied, about us being so nasty and wanting to see the movie, because Stephanie yells, something about us not making any movies. I start laughing to myself. The next day I am sitting at my desk, trying to be more productive then I had been for the past couple of days. As I drew up a portfolio for a new investor, I notice Keisha walking in my direction.

"Hey Keisha, what's good?" I take a moment to look up from my work to talk with her but instead she just walks by barely mumbling.

"Hello." like I am some stranger, never even looking back at me. Strangely enticed by her disregard of my presence, I get up from my desk and head out of my office to where Keisha is normally sitting and waiting for me with several overtly sexual comments prepared.

"What's going on? You ain't never just walked pass this fine ass brother and not had a come on line." I ask, pressing down the lapels of my suit waiting for her to take notice, smile, comment, something.

Instead Keisha replies, "Nothing is going on…" She keeps looking at her computer screen as if I am not even there. But I know better than that, there is definitely something wrong. Keisha pretty much avoids me and everyone else the rest of the day.

About a few minutes to four, I call Steph on her job, "Hey sweet thing, how was work today?" I ask her.

"It was so, so. But I'm not complaining. What's up with you?" I hear her shuffling some papers around.

"I was just calling you to tell you that I love you and that I will be working a little late, so don't rush home."

"That's fine with me, a few girls want to go out after work, so maybe I'll tag along."

"That sounds good, have fun and I'll see you later."

"Ok, love you."

"Love you too." I reply before I hang up the phone. I sit there taking a minute to reflect on how good I feel about our relationship. It isn't anything close to what it used to be, but at least we have been talking. Now with that out the way and the building just about empty I turn my focus to taking care of some work hoping to double up my productivity since I didn't have to be side tracked with the normal office antics I have to combat during normal business hours. Shortly after seven, I feel myself getting hungry and begin packing up my things to head home. I gather all my belongings and start to head towards the door, I notice Keisha still sitting at her desk looking depressed. I look at the door and think about leaving, despite the fact that my stomach is touching my back, leaving her here like this wouldn't be the moral thing to do. *I can't believe I'm about to play mister sensitivity, what da hell is wrong with me lately?*

I walked over to her desk, "Hey what's wrong? Do you feel like talking?" I ask softly, rubbing her on the shoulder.

"Nothing is wrong, I told you earlier." She replies. "I'm just trying to finish typing up this report." I look at her computer monitor, the screen is in standby mode from being in idle too long.

"Keisha look at your computer, it's in standby, you can talk to me it's just us here." I state compassionately. She puts her head down into her hands and took a moment obviously trying not to cry.

"Well... I go on vacation tomorrow and I don't have anywhere to go or anyone to spend it with." She exhales.

"That's the reason you're all depressed?" I blurt out, unsympathetically.

"Yes!!!" She wines. "I understand you and Stephanie aren't getting along that well, but at least you have someone to argue with." She exclaims.

"Sorry, I didn't mean to say it like that. Think of it as a blessing in disguise. There's no attitude to deal with, no conflict of interest, no deciding on what and where to eat and most importantly, you don't have to worry about no one else's attitude but yours."

"You see that's what I want! I want the rivalry and comradely, I want to wake up in the morning chilly and mad because someone stole all the covers from me. I want to wrestle and pillow fight in bed, in the middle of the night. And I also want someone to hold me and whisper in my ear to relax, because everything is going to be all right." the water now flows freely from her eyes for the first time. I suddenly feel warmth and love for Keisha like I have never felt before. Her words touch and engage me in a way that draws me toward her. She is no longer just another coworker; she is a warm blooded person full of emotions and affection. Somehow this intimate view of her makes me feel connected to her if in no other way than a primal duty that a man has to a woman, and I would have felt less of a man, if I allowed her to feel like less of a woman.

"I think I can help you." I said, hoping I won't regret what I'm about to do, later.

"How can you help? You already have a girlfriend and you got FUCKING friends as well! Excuse my French." She exclaims repulsion oozing out of her tone.

"Here_", I said. Pulling out a folded piece of paper from my pocket, she opens it up shaking her head like I am wasting her time. She looks at a blank piece of paper.

"So what is this supposed to mean its blank?"

"There you go again, looking at the glass half empty. Allow me to take you outside the box on this one. Imagine that this blank piece of paper represents all the space and love between us and I could never express how I truly feel about you. I have never said anything to you because I didn't want to risk losing the working friendship that we have" I point to the line going across the paper "This is company protocol" I point to all the ridges in the paper from it being crinkled in my pocket "All of the smaller creases are our coworkers, my girl, and all the other people standing between us, but when you stop focusing on the indentions in the paper you can see that Keisha I love you!" She looks at me, like I am her knight in shining armor. I reach over and turn on the radio and lean in and kiss her passionately. We kiss like our lives depend on it. She drops the paper on the floor. *Morning* by Shirley Murdock plays, softly on the radio.

She whispers in my ear, and I nibble around the nape of her neck "That is my jam." I slowly pulled off her shirt, caress and massage her body with my tongue. As I make my way to her voluptuous twins, either I was really hot, or she was very cold, because her nipples are standing like Minnie daggers cutting through her bra. With a flick of my left hand, her bra comes sliding off. She licks my ear and pulls my sweater over my head. She starts to suck on my left nipple, while caressing my six pack with my right hand. I lightly moan from the sensation of her hot tongue stroking my nipple. She opens my belt and unzips my pants, allowing gravity to pull them to the floor. I am so turned on by her, I don't have the strength to stop. I reach up her skirt and pull her panties off, I tossed them onto her desk, as I bury my face in her sweet cave. She gasps and clinches the edge of her desk. She gives me a funny smirk to finish the job that acknowledges I have done well. I stand up, she slowly pulls down my boxers and takes a personal tour, kissing me down my body. She sucks on my master cylinder, to make sure it is hard enough to withstand the pressure of her wet cavern. She leans back on her desk, pulling me towards her, repositioning her legs to receive me. It's a wrap for me, there is no turning back at this point.

"I guess you're going to win the bet." I whisper as I enter her.

"Yeah if I decide to tell, but I think I'm going to keep you all to myself." She moans. I notice one of the janitors standing near the corner watching us get our groove on smoking a cigarette. I don't think he spoke a lick of English, I pointed to my watch and then flashed him five fingers twice, wanting him to come back in about ten minutes. He nods his head and gives me the nod of his approval. Knocking on midnight's door, I finally leave work, *Damn I hope Steph had a good time hanging out and stayed out later than expected.* On the way home, Marcus calls me, "Where have you been, I've been trying to reach you all evening!"

"Ok you got me now, what's good?"

"James went to the hospital by ambulance today. We were in the gym balling and he unexpectedly passed out."

"Say what?"

"He was rushed to the hospital, they stated he had a diabetic seizure. Jamal that shit really shook me up! I just dropped James off at his house from the hospital, he said that he knew diabetes ran in his family but he didn't know he had it."

"Thanks for letting me know, I'll be sure to let Derrick know too. Sorry I missed your call, I was at work taking care of some last minute business."

"No need to apologize to me, times are hard make that money while you can." He replies.

"Oh by the way James didn't mention anything about me did he?" I try to ask casually.

"No why?"

"Well he called me a few nights ago and said we had to talk, but he didn't say about what. I called him the last few days but he never answered."

When I finally pulled into my drive way, I couldn't wait to get in the house so I could eat some of that left over Spaghetti in the refrigerator, but I knew it was a bad sign when I saw all the lights were out. Stephanie locked me out again.

I called derrick from my cell, "Yo dawg! It's me, can I stay over tonight?" I asked feeling bad that I had to wake him up.

"Damn nigga, you sure you ain't homeless? I'm going to start charging your monkey ass rent!!! I wonder if I can deduct your ass on my taxes next year!" He states sounding aggravated.

"Yeah, yeah, yeah... I'll be there in about 20 minutes." I say hopping in my card heading east.

"And you better wash before you lay your ass down, I don't want my couch smelling like ass no more!"

Chapter 10

Veronica sat in the living room at my place watching a movie, on the Lifetime channel drinking appletini's.

"Derrick, do you think, it must have been fate that brought us together the evening you wrecked into my car?" She asks, noticeably feeling emotional from the situation that transpired between the lady and her husband on TV.

"I feel like it was fate, even though things have a funny way of working out. It's like we were destined to be in that accident. Now that we're together I honestly couldn't imagine my life without you." He states compassionately.

"Derrick I just want to let you know that I've had a long hard life and I am so glad that you're here now to complete me and make things better. I guess I had to have some bad things happen in my life to know when I have something good." She chuckled to herself.

"Well like it was explained to me, how do you know when you have something good in your life if you don't have something bad to compare it to?"

"Derrick, you mean the world to me and I seriously can't go another day without you. I hope nothing ever comes between us, I've seen so many things go wrong in other peoples relationship."

"Hey baby look at me... until you came along, my life wasn't as easy as it appeared to be either. My feelings were long gone and my heart was stone cold. I never thought I would ever feel or trust another woman like this again. But you've changed all that, you have made me believe in women again. I see now that I can't take out on every woman, what the last one has done to me. Thank you for showing me the light."

I slide over on the couch closer to veronica and look her in the eyes, "You have made this easy for me to say, I am ready to take our relationship to the next level." holding her hand in my hands, and hoping she feels the same way.

She takes a deep breath and exhales, "Stop, before you go any farther... there's some things you need to know about me_," She said fretfully.

"Shhh, I know what you're going to say. Look, everyone has a past and excess baggage. It's okay, really I understand." I try to clarify.

"No, my situation is different. Yes I do have a past, but there are circumstances behind it_" I interject before she can finish, "What, are you going to tell me that you have a long lost child somewhere? You were abused as a child or adopted at a young age and you have issues. Just tell me, I can handle it."

"Well to be honest with you, I…" She is once again interrupted by the phone.

"Saved by the bell, excuse me while I get the phone. Hello?"

"Yo Derrick, do you have a minute? I really need to talk to you right now." Jamal exclaimed through the phone.

"Well actually I was trying to have a serious conversation with my girl."

"Please it will only take a minute, I'm sitting in your drive way." Jamal pleaded.

"What! Dawg ya killing me!" I exclaim. I hang up the phone, "Veronica I'll be right back, I need to holler at my brother out front. I hop into Jamal's car and slam the door with plenty of attitude, for interrupting me.

"Thanks for coming out." He says, staring straight ahead.

"This better be good, I was bonding with my baby. Trying to take it to that next level with her, ya feel me."

"Nigga I know you ain't trying to commit to anybody! Whatever happened to I'm the man, the myth, the legend? I can't be held down; no one can contain my shit!" He states sarcastically beating on his chest.

"It looks like those days are over; that was the old me. I think I've found the one this time, this is real talk." I reply, convincing not only him but myself as well.

"With her, Veronica? How well do you know her anyway? Yo, just like you're always telling me, do some research. Now take your own advice and do more research."

"Nah, nah, nah. I can feel it, she is the one." I said convincingly.

"What makes her the one, it's not like she was the first piece of ass you got! So you ain't sprung for pussy."

"See that's the thing, we haven't even had intercourse yet." Derrick shot back and looked at Jamal like he was crazy. "Is this the reason you called me out here?" I asked starting to get angered.

"No, actually I think something is going on with Stephanie. She's been on this emotional roller coaster lately. One minute everything is cool and the next she can't stand being around me."

"Imagine that?" I exclaim sarcastically.

"She's different; she looks different, talks different and acts different. I feel like I'm losing her. At one point I didn't care if we split up, but it's different now that she's pulling away from me. "

"Well what difference does it make? You were always out hoeing on her anyway!"

"Yeah, I know. But now she seems like a different person and I don't know how to relate to her anymore. Granted a part of it is my fault, I'll share the blame, but I'm ready to commit to her now, I'm giving up the game. I hope it's not too late."

"So what are you going to do? Maybe you need to sit down with her, have a heart to heart and put everything on the table."

"I don't know, I've thought about that. I'm going to have to find a way to reach her somehow. I hope she will be as accepting as she's been in the past."

"Well think about it and get back to me, I still have some other business to handle."

"Alright, you go take care of that. Thanks for listening and good luck. I hope she's everything you imagined and more." I rush back into the house, excited to finish my conversation with Veronica.

"Veronica! Veronica!" I looked everywhere for her but she is gone. I find a note on the table:

Derrick,

Sorry to leave on such short notice. I let myself out the back door; I didn't want to interrupt your intense conversation with your brother. We really need to talk; I just wanted to clear my head first. I'll talk to you later, when the time is right.

Xoxo

Veronic

I can't help but wonder what is it that she has to say, can it be that bad? I decide I have to find her she can't leave me hanging like this. I call her all night long and most of the next day. She doesn't answer any of my calls.

"Veronica, if your home please pick up, we need to talk." I sit the phone down and look out the window wondering what's going on with her and then the phone rings.

"Hey baby I've been trying to reach you all day!" automatically assuming it was Veronica.

"Man you better back da hell up, it's me Jamal!"

"Sorry_, I thought you were Veronica."

"What's up with that, did you work it out with her or what?"

"No, she slipped out the back door and we never got a chance to finish our conversation. How's everything with you and Steph?" I ask, trying to take my focus off veronica for at least a few moments.

"I don't know she never came home. Have you talked to James? I talked to him earlier today and he was supposed to call me back, but I never heard from him. He's been acting a little strange lately himself. Maybe I'm just tripping, I'm losing my mind." Jamal explains through frustration.

"I saw him the other day and he seemed a little jittery to me too, you think he's on drugs?"

"Naw, I can't see him doing that. Besides, he had an uncle that was heavy into drugs and he saw how it did him before he died. Actually I think it scared him away from doing drugs."

"Jamal I'll talk to you later, its Veronica on the other line." I say with my hand on the button ready to click over.

"Hey baby, what's going on I have been trying to reach you all day! You scared me running out on me like that."

"I know, look we have a lot to talk about. I knew this day was going to come. And I should have been more prepared for it." She explains.

"What day? What are you talking about?" I ask anxiously.

"Derrick you know how people say, you really don't know a person until you've walked a mile in their shoes."

"Yeah, but_"

"Well sometimes you need to walk an extra mile or in my case maybe even two."

"Huh?"

"Look Derrick, I don't know if I'm the right person for you." Veronica explains. "Well I'm hoping I am, but_"

"What! Look I told you how I feel, so why are you saying this?"

"When I was a child, we were very poor and my mother_"

"Look, what does that have to do with anything?"

"Derrick, please! You have to hear me out. You really need to feel me on this to understand me. My mother worked long hours to take care of my two younger brothers and me. She could not afford a legit babysitter, so she always left us with this ole drunk neighbor across the hall. Often we spent the night, because we would be sleep already by the time my mother got home from work. Well as it turned out our neighbor wasn't just a drunk, he was also a child molester. He fondled with me all the time and told me that if I ever said anything, he would kill me. So, I kept my mouth shut for years, until I just couldn't keep silent about it any longer. One evening, he was watching my brothers and me while my mom was at work. He was in the kitchen drinking vodka and cooking. Then he called me in the kitchen to help out, while my brothers watched The Super friends on TV. He wanted me to help him cut up some potatoes for dinner, but what he really wanted was for me to give him some kind of satisfaction and play hide the baton, if you know what I mean. When I refused, he got mad and threatened to kill me, I grabbed the kitchen knife and stabbed him in the chest. I told the cops that he was drinking and playing with the knife trying to do tricks and stabbed himself in the chest. I was scared and pulled the knife out hoping that would save him. I don't think the officer bought the story, but he knew what was really going on. He died at the hospital, the cops ruled it an accident."

"Wow! You had such a horrific childhood. We can get you counseling to help cope, it sounds like you were traumatized about the whole ordeal. I can't even imagine what it was like to go through something like that."

"No you don't understand! The damage has been done. It's too late for me." She expresses.

"I don't understand, what are you trying to say?" I ask, feeling more confused.

"Derrick, I guess there's only one way to say what I have to say. You know how we_, only have had oral sex." She said warily.

"Yes, will you just say it?" I ask again, my patients growing thinner.

"The reason I didn't tell you before, is because I didn't think we were ready to go all the way in our relationship."

"Please stop with the charades! Say what's on your mind!" I finally snap.

"Okay, I had my name changed from Victor to Veronica..." There was a silence over the phone, the fact that veronica used to be Victor, resonated through my head.

"You what!!!" I explode.

"I used to be a man, but I had a complete sex change and now I take hormone pills. I wanted to tell you, but I didn't know how. And if you feel about me the way you do, I'm sure we can get pass this." She pleads.

"You fucking bitch, how could you deceive me like that! I better not ever see you again! I will fucking kill your ass! If I wanted to be gay, let me be gay by choice, not manipulated into it. It doesn't matter that you had a sex change, you're still a fucking dude!"

"Derrick, calm down! This is hard for me too. We can work through this, you said you loved me." She tries to coax me.

"Fuck you! I said I loved you when I thought you were a woman! I'm going beat your bitch ass when I catch up to you!" I yell in the phone.

"Please, don't do this to us. Don't destroy what we've built together." She continues to beg, but I don't want any parts of this Jerry Springer show.

"If you would have been honest in the beginning, we wouldn't be in the situation right now today! We only would have been friends."

"Derrick I am so sorry to put you through all this." She pleads

"You played me, now you're marked for life; don't ever let me catch you anywhere!" I slam the phone so hard, hoping it burst her ear drum, instead it shatters into pieces. I sit completely still dazed, lightheaded and weak. *How did I go from being so happy, to being filled with rage in such a short amount of time? That bitch misunderstood my kindness for weakness. Jamal was right, I didn't know that girl, boy, IT, after all. The first time I truthfully open my heart up to someone in years and this is what I get a whole bunch of lies and deception. That's it, it's going to be a lot harder to ever open up to another woman again. I know not every woman is up to no good, but in this case, she really wasn't a woman.* I sat on the couch, my whole body shaking with rage. Suddenly my pants leg felt sticky and wet. I lift my right hand and a solid flow of blood is running out the side of my hand.

"Damn! That stupid bitch made me cut my hand on the phone."

£   £   £

Monday morning, I call Stephanie at work to see if we can meet up and talk I want to see if she is ok.

"Can we meet for lunch, we have to talk?" I ask, hoping she will accept.

"I already made plans for lunch and besides I don't feel like talking to you right now!" She answers in a nasty tone.

"But we need to talk, can you at least tell me what you're mad about?" I exclaim. She ignores my question. Just before she hangs up, she says, "And call your boy James he's been trying to get in touch with you." At this point, I feel it is imminent that our relationship is coming to a head. In all of my past relationships almost instantly meant nothing basically became nonexistent, but with her I just can' let go. *I'm done with everyone, it's just me and Steph, from here on out. All I need is one more chance.* After work, I rush straight home hoping to see her there. She isn't home yet, I shower and begin making a romantic dinner and put some wine on ice. A few hours pass, I have not heard from nor seen anything that resembled Stephanie. I begin to worry, I call her cell, there's no answer. The food has gotten cold and the ice is melted, I feel lost and can't bring my thoughts together. I finally call James because I had to talk to someone.

"Hello?"

"Hey James... it's me, Jamal."

"Yeah." He said, as he cleared his throat. "Oh, uh hey what's up?"

"I need someone to talk to; I'm losing my baby..." I exclaim as I started to pout.

"Stephanie?" He asks uneasily.

"Yeah, she locked me out the other night, because I came home late and I haven't seen her since."

"Damn." James said lightly, like he was not grasping the concept or was distracted by something else."

"I've been waiting for her to come home, but she hasn't come or called yet and it's already 10:30 pm. I called her sister's house but she hasn't heard from her either. Is it cool if I come over for a few? I'm losing my mind, I gotta get out of this house, do something, before I go crazy in here."

"Uh_ uh well I don't think that's a good idea. What if she comes home and you're not there again, or she tries to call you. She'll really think that you don't care." I ponder what he said and it makes sense.

"I guess you're right," I mumble.

"I would come over there, but I'm kind of in the middle of something right now. I'll make a few calls and see what I can find out." He states, rushing me off the phone.

"Thanks dog..." I said. "Hey James?"

"Yeah?"

"You're a good friend, what would I ever do without you?" I told him, he pauses for a moment before replying.

"Don't talk like that; I got your back to the end."

"Good looking out."

"Take care." I sat there thinking about Stephanie, wondering if we could reconcile our relationship. A part of me wanted to start over with her but the other part is telling me to throw in the towel. I try to wait up all night for her to come home but she never shows, not even so much as a phone call that she was not coming. I know what my heart is feeling, but the reality of this whole ordeal is overpowering.

£   £   £

I lay in bed restless, getting up every other minute or so looking out the window for Stephanie's car in the drive way. I pick up my phone, stroke my thumb across the keys not sure whom I should be calling. It is a long shot but I call Stephanie's number, it goes straight to her voice mail.

"Hey Steph, it's me. I am starting to get the picture that it's over between us. I hate for things to end on such a bad note like this, but it's apparent that you don't want anything else to do with me. I hope you would at least have the common decency and respect to give us proper closure. If I don't hear from you in the next few days, I'll assume you have moved on with your life and I'll donate your clothes to Goodwill. Bye I guess." I thought about what I had just said on her voice mail, *It's out of my hands now. I can't take it back.* As distraught as I am I can't help but to laugh hysterically to myself.

"Now don't you sound like a hypocrite?" I blurt aloud.

"You have the nerve to tell Stephanie if she has some common decency, to do the right thing. And look at all the shit you've done since you were with her! You were never up front with her, what kind of decency is that?" I speak as if I am actually talking to a real person.

"Mom you are right once again, I guess like all kids I didn't want to listen to what my parents have to say, until after it's too late." I hit the speed dial button to call my mother, but my watery vision made me hit the wrong button.

"Hello?" A sleeping male's voice answered. I looked at the phone like what is a man doing answering my mother's phone.

"Who is this? I called my mother's house." I stated waiting for an answer.

"Jamal? This is Marcus, you ass clown you called the wrong number Boy you are lucky I couldn't sleep or I would be cussing you out right now." Octavia rolled over into another position, trying to block the sound of the loud voice.

"My bad sorry to bother you, but since I got you on the phone I think it's over between Stephanie and I."

"Sorry to hear that." Marcus said, as he rolled his eyes up in his head, not trying to be insensitive he just didn't want to be bothered right now.

"She up and left a few days ago and I haven't seen her since."

"Well Jamal, maybe you should have treated her differently and you wouldn't have the drama you have now."

"I know I wish I could just start over with her and do everything different, I would be that guy that she thought I was."

"Yeah if life was only that simple, just hit the rewind button! I wish I could hit the rewind button for my mother! Maybe she would still be here. Don't take this personal, but at least you and Stephanie still have your parents to turn too. I have no one. I guess it's easy to take things for granted when you've always had it. You guys need to put all this bull shit behind you and make the most of the time your time you have left together, because tomorrow isn't promised to you. Now I'm not trying to down play your situation, but I have bigger things to worry about so if you don't mind I'll talk to you later."

"Your right, sorry to_" Before I could apologize to Marcus he had already hung up on me. Still feeling upset, I thought about calling my mother again. I looked at the time, the clock illuminated the numbers 2:15 which meant it was 5:15 am in Baltimore. I sat the phone down and laid across my bed, *there's no need to wake up the whole country because of my problems. After all, it's my fault I'm in this mess in the first place.*

£   £   £

Tuesday morning, I'm sitting at my desk with my head slump down, with about my production for the day in the red. All I can do is think about Stephanie. About 12:15 pm the phone rings at my desk.

"Hello?" I speak slowly.

"Jamal…" I perk up instantly at the sound of Stephanie's voice.

"Steph? Is that you? Thank God." I state feeling relieved that she finally called me.

"Yes."

"Where are you, I've been worried sick about you!" I exclaim.

"Can you come home, we have to talk, now!" She states, sounding very straightforward.

"Sure I'll be right there. Bye." I hang up the phone and jump out of my seat, then I realize I don't have any vacation time left, I need to think of something that will get me out of work. *I got it!* I run to the snack room and bought a microwave can of beef ravioli, I stuff as much as I can in my mouth, and start chewing it forcibly. I walk pass the boss's office making sure he sees me. I grab my stomach as if I am in pain.

"May I_" Was all that I could get out.

"Jamal are you okay?" I turned towards him and through up all over his 300 dollar shoes.

"My God!" He yells, jumping back.

I looked up at him feeling pitiful, "I'm_ Sorry…" I say with a very weak voice. "I think I have one of those stomach viruses. I'll clean up the mess sir."

"The hell you will, that's what janitors get paid for. You're taking your ass home to get some rest!" He told me, kicking off his freshly polished shoes.

"But I have…"

He cut me off, "Jamal I wasn't asking you. That was an order!"

"That paper_" I pretend to explain.

"I'll take care of that, now go!" He says pointing towards the exit doors.

"Yes sir."

"Call me in a few days when you feel better." He yells at me down the hall.

"Okay, thank you sir." Within 20 minutes, I am whipping into my driveway. *I haven't used that throwing up trick, since middle school and it still works.* The more reality sets in that I am about to be face to face with Stephanie, the more aware I am that my nerves are tugging at me, my hands are sweaty and my heart is beating fast. I walk in the door, "Steph?" There is no answer. I search the house looking for her, until I find her in the bedroom packing. I want to rush in and hug her tightly, but this isn't exactly the best time for trying to be cuddly.

"Hey!" She jumps, as I enter the room. "I didn't hear you come in."

"Sorry I didn't mean to startle you. Why are you packing, please don't leave?" I beg.

"Sorry Jamal, I have to, things will be better this way. I love you but I'm not in love with you anymore."

"Steph I want to marry you?" I gasp in desperation, she drops some of her clothes on the floor. "It's time we settle down get married and start our own little family, just like you've always wanted." I pull out a ring. "Will you marry me?" Stephanie wearing a shocked look turns away from me. I know that's not a good sign. She slowly turns back to face me with her eyes filling up with enough water to create another great lake.

"Jamal…" She softly begins.

"Yes," I take a step toward her, making sure I hear her every word. She lowers her head and continues, "I'm pregnant." I smile at her, but it doesn't explain the long face she is expressing. I brace myself and asked, "Is that all you want to tell me?"

"No_, It's…" She looks up searching for the right words to say like they are going to drop down from the ceiling, enter her mouth and make everything okay.

"It's what?" I ask tensely.

"Jamal, it's not yours." She exclaims fearfully, bringing one hand up covering her mouth.

"Huh!" I gasp for air; all of a sudden, I feel my body overheat and I become light headed, I am about to pass out.

"What! How could this be?"

"Well you were always out with your friends partying! And I was left home alone, night after night. Waiting on you to come home, we hardly did anything together. But you seemed to always have time for this person and that person." I watch as her fear turns to anger. "So I started making myself available for someone else!" She spat at me with her hands on her hips.

"What!" I struggle for another breath searching for more air. "Then whose baby is it?" She pauses for a minute, her eyes piercing through me.

"James." She said in a cold-hearted clear voice.

"James?" I yell. "James, who?" she looks down, my heart sinks I feel my knees begin to buckle and the room darkle. My mind races over the events the calls the avoidance it all makes sense. I was so busy playing games all the while the ultimate move was made on check mate, Game over and I lose.

"Damn, he was supposed to be my boy!" My anger ignites.

"Yeah, that's why I fucked him! We didn't start having sex right away. It kinda just happened over time."

"I don't understand what kind of shit is that! What kind of woman are you, screwing around on your man with his friends!" I yell.

"Well you keep your friends close and your enemies closer. And he seemed to be the weakest link in your crew. I knew it was too good to be true, with all that time you proclaimed to be hanging with your boys. Something just didn't seem right."

"What the fuck is that supposed to mean?" My blood shot eyes stab through her. She takes a few steps back, looking at me like I am some deranged stranger she's encountering on a dark lonely street. After regaining her composure, she clears her throat and tries another approach.

"I suspected you were cheating on me... so I needed a mole to keep me abreast of what you were doing." She replies lowly.

"Oh! I presume, a few blow jobs later, he was singing like a drunken canary!" I mumble sarcastically, throwing my hands up in the air.

"At first he told me that you weren't doing anything, but if he was my man he would be spending more time with me than spending time in the streets. After a while, we developed a connection, and because of all the times we talked and spent together things just happened. It wasn't meant for us to sleep together, he was only supposed to be delivering me the information. One night he stopped pass the house to tell me about some bitch you were with, I couldn't believe what I was hearing. I was so distraught I felt like killing myself_, I gave you my all! And you degraded me by sleeping with other women. You couldn't even be the man I thought you were and tell me about it." She stopped for a moment, thinking back on that night. "I remember, he held me so tight. He told me the only way he could make me feel like a lady again was to make love to me. I swear it just happened. At first I didn't want to, but as the anger set in I wanted to hurt you the way you hurt me." I sat down on the bed and started to zone out. I could see Stephanie's lips moving, but I couldn't hear anything she was saying. I went deeper into my own thoughts. *It was clear as muddy water my own partner in crime sold me out for a piece of ass, a man's quickest down fall. I guess it makes more sense, he knew everything about me and he and Steph were close as well. I guess it wasn't too hard for them to be together. Even though I am in the wrong too, I feel so hurt and betrayed. It reminds me of my previous relationship and now history is repeating itself. She played me harder than virgin plastic whirling down a bowling lane for a perfect strike, I've never fully recovered from* *all the dirt she did on me, maybe that is why I never fully committed to Stephanie. My grandfather once told me **I don't care how long a road is, there's always an end to it.** Stephanie* and I are definitely at the end of this road.

"Hey, Jamal, can you hear me, are you okay?" She said snapping her fingers at me.

"Uh_, yeah, I'll be alright." I reply holding my head with both hands.

"Jamal, I'm sorry I never meant for this to happen this way. But…" I look up at her as if more bad news was to follow, as if things couldn't get any worse. "James asked me to marry him last night and I accepted. I'm moving in with him." My mouth flew open, I had to catch my bottom jaw before it hit the floor.

"Ain't this a bitch!" I said through clenched teeth. This heifer is fucking me hard and don't even have the common courtesy of giving me a reach around!"

"Look there's no easy way to say it…"

"Well you don't seem to have too much of a problem with saying anything else!" I interject.

"Jamal I just came to get my clothes and tell you it's over. I can get the rest of my stuff later." She solemnly states.

"Well allow me to grab the fucking door! It's the least I can do." I say popping up off the bed. Stephanie walks out the door and turns to say something to me, I slam it in her face not wanting her to say another word to me. I lean against the door with my back. *I know I mistreated her first, I'm not even sure if I have a right to be mad, right now. This is unbelievable. As soon as I decide to change my life around and do what's right, this is what happens.* Ha, ha, I chuckled to myself. *I don't know if my mom warned me or jinxed me, she told me this would happen if I didn't change my ways I would get it back tenfold. I guess the thing that hurts the most is that, James was my friend. Maybe if I didn't know the guy, it wouldn't bother me as much. This is one lesson that I'll never forget, you're only going to get back what you put out!*

£   £   £

Two weeks have passed, since Stephanie and I last saw each other. Another slow day at the office and all I can do is think about what she did to me. I am mad as hell at her, but at the same time, I am more upset that she's no longer in my life. I can't talk to Derrick about it, because he has his own problems within his situation. It sucks that Veronica, Victor or whatever the name is, had him thrown in jail for terroristic threatening and trespassing. But it did feel good that he needed me for a change to bail him out. Maybe he will leave her alone, now that she has had a protection from abuse served to him. I can't call James, it's simple were not talking anymore. I have already talked Marcus's right ear off, even though he zones off and still thinks about his mother, when we're talking. The sad part is I know I don't want her back, I just really miss having her around. I head home to lie on the couch and sip Southern comfort & cranberry juice. Which has become my daily ritual since trying to put my mind at ease amongst all this chaos and confusion feels almost impossible. I start watching the Lakers pummel Miami on ESPN. The doorbell rings, *great like I really felt like having company today*! I opened the door and to my surprise, it's Stephanie looking depressed and her eyes all puffy.

"What do you want?" I snap, feeling my anger return like an old friend back from a long stay. "Large item pick up was yesterday for trash day!" Stephanie drops her head, absorbing my verbal abuse.

"I guess I deserve that, I had it coming. But you've done your dirt too! Remember." She explains in her defense.

"Steph what do want? I don't have time to stand here and argue with you." I had nothing else in the world to do, but she didn't need to know that.

She humbly mumbles, "James and I split up, he said I was taking up too much of his time but it was just an excuse for him to mess with someone else. He never loved me he just wanted me because I was a new piece of ass. Besides no one is ever going to treat me as good as you did, I am really missing you." I wanted to sympathize with her, after all we did have a history together. But I didn't want her to take my kindness for weakness.

"So now that you're back to being an old piece of ass, what do you want me to do about it?" I ask condescendingly.

"Well I just wanted to know if I could come back home?" She states apologetically.

"In order for you to come back and for this to work, I would have to allow myself to be vulnerable to you and share my inner most feelings with you like I never have before. I know I can no longer do that. You betrayed me far beyond just sleeping with another person he was my friend. How would you feel if I was sleeping around with your sister?" I rhetorically asked.

"I really miss you and want to be with you! You weren't perfect but you did well. I think we can start over and rebuild our relationship." She pleads.

"Hold on a sec.," I ran to the mirror, took a good look at my face and then returned, "I knew I erased fucking stupid off my forehead already. Bitch, you must really think that I'm that dumb! And if you do then you're about to learn a lot from a dummy! I thought we had a fairly good relationship up to a certain point and that point stopped with you and James. Of all people, you had sex with my best friend and I can't accept that."

Stephanie's sadness turned to rage. "Well you were screwing around on me too! I guess you have to win all the time!" She snaps.

"No not this time. There are no winners to this game. We're both losers." I reply sadly.

"No, fuck you Jamal! I don't know why I tried to come back to your sorry ass anyway!" Then she turns and walked away.

"Hey Steph_"

"What!" She snapped.

"The number is (858) 279-0425." She looks back putting her hands on her hips.

"Now what's that for, a fucking homeless shelter?"

"No, it's the Balboa veterinarian hospital."

"And what do I need that for?" She asked curiously.

"All wild dogs should be spaded and since you run in packs I figured you could get a group rate!"

Chapter 11

Octavia pulls into the driveway. "Marcus, who the fuck was that girl and what was she doing here?" She yells jumping out of her car.

"Woman chill out. She's just a friend of mine." I explain nonchalantly.

"Well who the hell am I? And why was she hugging all on you like that?" She asks.

"Look girl I'm a grown man, I don't have to explain every single thing I do to you!" I spat out.

"Oh so now I guess I'm just some bitch you're fucking off the street!"

"If you see it like that, fuck it you're a jump off." I state, as I head back in the house.

"Marcus what's going on with you? Ever since your mother died, you've been treating everybody like shit. You're going down in flames and you're dragging me with you! I want to help, but you won't let me help you! You're making this difficult, I don't know if I should run while I can or crash and burn alongside you."

"Jump off then, jump off! I don't need you and I don't need this shit!" I yell back.

"If you're angry about your mother passing, it's ok. Everyone can sympathize with you. But you don't have to be angry at the world." I thought about what Octavia said and she is right, I feel myself breaking down and crying. I hold my head up and suck back my tears, if I stop caring for other people then I'll never feel this pain again. I look at Octavia, "I don't need your help. I can do everything on my own, besides there's something I've been meaning to tell you."

Octavia looks at me with water in her eyes, "Don't do this Marcus, you're in mourning. You need to calm down and think this through." She pleads with me.

"I've already done all the thinking I'm going to do. I think we need to take a break for a while, I need some space, some time to think." I continue, not giving her words a second thought.

"Space, is that want you want all of a sudden?" The tears continue to stream down her face. "Is it because of that bitch! Your so called friend that you're making all this_ space for?" Holding up her hands making the quotation signs.

"That bitch name is Shayla. And she's none of your business." Octavia took off her ring and threw it at me.

"You can give this to Shayla, since she is so important to you. You've changed so much, it's like I don't know you anymore." Octavia turns to walk away, then stops. "If you need me I will be your friend, I'll always be there for you. But I refuse to be treated like this, I will never be your lover again." She says expressively.

"I'm not looking for a lover, life is too short to be settled down with just one person. I'm going to start living life to the fullest. So have a nice life, cause mine is about to get a lot better." I reply in a macho manly voice. Octavia's heart was definitely shattered and her facial expression expressed every new crack in her now broken heart. I feel her pain but I hide it as much as I can.

"I understand you're hurting and going through a big transition in your life, but this is not the way you treat people that you say you love. If you ever need to talk call me, you know how to contact me. Good bye Marcus." Octavia walks away with her head down. I know I hurt her bad and I don't know if I'll ever make it right. I wish that she hated me for what I did, so that it didn't hurt so bad watching her walk out of my life. I stood all alone watching her car drive away, I take a deep breath and sigh, *You fool, you let her get away, I hope it's for the best. I* know I was straight violating with Octavia, but it's better that she leaves now and saves herself, then to suffer more damage in the long run.

£   £   £

Octavia walks in the door of Dawn's house.

"Lucy I'm home!" She tries to joke covering the pain she is feeling.

"Thanks for letting me crash at your crib on short notice." She says giving Dawn a big hug.

"Girl don't even trip, I know you would do the same for me." downplaying the fact that she had just went out of her way for her friend.

"I am so surprised that he acted the way he did. I know all this is stemming from his mother's death, maybe this is just the only way he feels he can deal with it."

"Girl give him some time to blow off that steam, he'll be calling you in a few days." She states casually.

"He can call and I'll talk to him. But I am through with his shit, I am not going to be a door mat for him to walk all over me whenever he wants to."

"I feel you on that sistah girl!" Octavia pulls out her cell phone contemplating calling Jamal to give him a heads up on Marcus.

"Dawn can you excuse me for a minute, I need to make a call. Thank you." I dialed Jamal's number.

"Hello." He answers picking up on the first ring.

"Jamal, how are you doing? This is Octavia." He knows something is wrong he can hear the tension in her voice.

"What's going on is something wrong?" He asked apprehensively.

"Marcus and I spilt up." I exhaled.

"Sorry to hear that, but I'm not surprised with the way he has been acting. I know he's been having a hard time coping with things lately. How are you holding up?"

"I'm upset, but I'm making it." I replied softly.

"That's good. If you need anything just let me know."

"Well actually there is one thing you can do for me."

"What's that?" He asked.

"Make sure you keep checking on Marcus, so he doesn't do anything stupid."

"Yup, I sure will. Thanks for the heads up. Give him some time to blow over y'all be back together."

"I don't think so. I'm done, there is only so much a person can take."

"Sorry you feel that way. I want you to know that just because y'all aren't together anymore, doesn't mean that I am not going to be your friend. Feel free to call me anytime, you're still my lil sis." Jamal joke with her, to make her feel a little better.

"I didn't think you were that kind of person anyway. Thanks for your support though. I'll talk to you later, I need to get settled in at Dawn's."

"So that's where you're staying?"

"Just for a few days, until I can find my own place."

"Okay, well I'll check on you, in a few days to see how you're doing. I'll check on Marcus tomorrow. You take care."

"Okay, bye."

"Bye." Dawn came back in the room, "Is everything okay?" She asks.

"Yeah, everything is fine now." I stated, pulling out a small compact mirror to check my makeup.

"Hey Octavia, I have a great idea, let's go out to dinner? My treat, we can catch up on things."

"I don't know, I'm really not in the mood."

"That's exactly why you need to come out with me. If you don't, then I'll be forced to eat by myself and constantly have my dinner interrupted by other men trying to hit on me."

"Okay you talked me into it. But I don't want to be out all night."

"There's this nice restaurant called Jack's about three blocks from here and they have a wonderful atmosphere inside that will take your mind off all your worries. Plus the food is really cheap." When we first walked in, I just stared all around the entire room, looking at all the beautiful abstracts.

"It's beautiful in here." I said in amazement.

"Yeah I know. I call this place the lime light. This is where I like to come when I have a problem. Because once I get here, it doesn't even matter anymore. Come on let's sit over there." I took my seat near the entrance by all the multi-cultural artwork on the walls.

"Dawn, how is your mother doing? Looking at all these pictures reminded me of her. Does she still have all those African pictures?"

"She's doing fine and those pictures will go with her to her grave." She laughs.

"I used to love to go to her house and look at those pictures. It made me feel like I was on vacation in a safari or somewhere."

"I'm glad someone liked it there. She kept the house looking nice but we were dirt poor."

"Girl you think you were the only poor people in the neighborhood?"

"I remember we were so poor that we had to wash our clothes and take a bath in the same water because we couldn't afford to go to the Laundromat." Dawn exclaimed, laughing about it.

"And what about wearing the same pair of jeans three days in a row, but with different shirts and shoes to make it look like you had more than one pair."

We look at each other and say in unison, "Dirty jeans can be worn again, but funky ones you can't." Then we burst out laughing.

"Dawn, I haven't had a good deep laugh like that in a long time. I am so glad you talked me into coming out. Can you believe we've been here almost two hours already?"

"Time flies when you're having fun." She replies, sucking up the last drop of her electric lemonade.

"I'm ready to go when you are."

"I'll be ready in a few minutes." Dawn said looking over my shoulder. I heard people singing, clapping and getting louder like they were walking towards us. When I turned around the entire staff was standing behind me with a small cake in hand singing happy birthday. I tried to tell them that it wasn't my birthday but they ignore me and keep on singing. I turn and look at Dawn, she has tears running down her face from laughing so hard. I knew she was up to her old tricks again.

When they finished singing Dawn yells, "Happy birthday Octavia!"

"You're going to pay big time for this!" I say to her through a forced smile.

Dawn starts laughing again, "Have a little fun. No harm done."

"I can't believe you did that to me that was so embarrassing."

"You're welcome. There's no sense in buying a cake, when you can get one free. Now can you share your cake with me birthday girl?" She states swiping some icing with her finger.

£   £   £

Being at Dawn's place for a few days was chill and had its moments, now it's time to move on, I don't want to impose any longer, than I have to. Around 7:30 pm I return to Dawn's house from apartment hunting. As I walk towards the door, I hear screams coming from inside the house.

"Oh no, not again!" I ran in the house to see Dawn's man standing over her fetal positioned body about to deliver another blow.

"Hey!" I exclaim lurching my body in front of his blow. "What in the hell is going on in here, all the neighbors can here you screaming!"

"Octavia is back." Dawn's boyfriend exclaims. "You're just in time, Dawn and I were just having a disagreement about a woman's place in the home. Maybe you can enlighten your friend." He says mockingly.

"Darryl, you're drunk again, is this how you show affection towards the woman you want to be with? Dawn, how can you stay with a man that continues to beat on you like that?" Dawn struggles to get to her feet, she wipes some of the blood off of her nose with the backside of her hand.

"He doesn't mean it." Dawn mumbles with a fat busted lip. "He's just angry, he'll calm down shortly. Right baby? We'll be ok in a few minutes." She implied fixing her clothes.

"No you'll be alright in a few pieces." I mumble.

"Yeah, I had a long bad day that's all." Darryl states, picking up his beer off the floor. "Baby can you clean this mess up for me?" Dawn went to get a towel to clean up the beer, while Darryl sat down on the couch. I'm looking at the two of them act as if nothing ever happened a moment ago, *this ain't normal.*

"Dawn, you need to stop making excuses for your man to whip your ass. You're giving a whole new meaning to the phrase no pain no gain, there can't be that much love in the world. And as for you Darryl, my man has never put his hands on me!" I yell at him.

"What fucking man? He dumped you remember?" He retorts laughing on the couch.

"It doesn't matter, he's never touched me. You guys are pathetic! You for beating on a woman and Dawn you for justifying his ass whoopings. Dawn, you need to get out of this before he hurts you bad or even worse kill you. I am begging you to please leave him."

"And go where?" She states causally, sitting next to him on the couch.

"Anywhere is better than here. Go to a shelter for battered woman or come with me." I beg.

"And where you going, you're homeless?" Darryl says sarcastically.

"Well for your information I found an apartment and I'll be moving in tomorrow. I know you were there for me when I needed you most and now I'm giving you a shoulder to lean on. Please come with me Dawn?"

"Thanks, but things will be all right, he's getting better at controlling his anger." She replies, rubbing on his leg draped across her.

"But you don't understand, he has a problem and he won't get better until he gets some professional help. I don't want to read about you in the paper one day." I plead with her.

"Lady, what are you talking about? I do get counseling from a guy named Jack_ Jack Daniels." He said holding up a nearly empty bottle with pride.

"Dawn, please come with me just for tonight, I'm getting a hotel room, I can't stay here any longer."

"No thanks, I'm staying here. He needs me right now, plus I don't want him to be mad at." She explains, giving him a kiss and smiling at me.

"What he needs is a punching bag at the gym. Don't do this to yourself, you deserve better. I'm leaving now, I would like to see you in my car beside me, by the time I pull off." *This is too much. I'm surrounded by drama. I need to get away from here!* I thought walking out the door.

Two days later, I move into my one bedroom apartment. Saturday afternoon I have a weird feeling in the pit of my stomach, about Dawn and decided to go check on her after I eat lunch and read the paper. I scan through the paper sipping on my hot tea. My heart fills with sadness as I read an article that hits close to home and reminds me of how I left Dawn. The title literally jumped of the page at me,

STOP THE ABUSE OF OUR WOMAN AND CHILDREN.
We as a nation must work together to take back control and stop abusing our woman and children. There are too many people being abused around us and we as society time after time, turn a blind eye to the violence this has become an epidemic, eroding away at today's American fabric. Thursday afternoon an argument between battered woman and her live in boyfriend, took a turn for the worst and she is not expected to make it. 27 year old Dawn Freeman was admitted into the hospital late Thursday evening.

"Oh my god!" I exclaim in terror, panting for more air.

When her live in boyfriend Darryl Thomas brought her into the emergency room stating that he found her at the bottom of the stairs when he got home from work. However, medical reports state that the bruises were inconsistent with bruises that she would have attained by falling down the stairs. The boyfriend is now being detained at the San Diego Police Station and is being questioned by police. Police spokes-person Cpl. Tremble, states that formal charges will more than likely be filed by later today. Darryl Thomas is facing assault and attempted murder and he will be re indicted on to first degree murder charges if the victim dies. I am hysterical and can barely keep my breath. I am overcome with guilt this is my fault why didn't I do more to help her. *I should have called the cops on that bastard, when I had the chance! Then my friend would still be alive.* Now I may never have another chance talk to her again. I grab my phone immediately to call the hospital and see if I will be able to come visit her, but they state that she will not have any visitors today and instructed me to call back tomorrow. Later that day, I am watching the evening news to see if there was any more information about Dawn.

Reported by the newsroom anchor, "Dawn Freeman's chances of surviving became dismal as she slipped into a comma a few hours ago. Doctors are preparing an emergency operation to take her baby, there's a fifty / fifty chance that the baby will not survive due to the stress and trauma the mother has endured." I put my hands over my face, in complete shock.

"I can't believe that she was pregnant and never said a word. This is not supposed to happen." I feel lost and am clueless as to what I should do, I stand up and move in front of the TV, to finish watching the news.

"Sources say that Dawn's boyfriend Darryl Howard age 29, has a history of abusing women. The District Attorney's office will still have a tough time proving its case, because the cops were never called for the alleged abuse and a paper trail of his violent acts have never been recorded. In 2006 alone it was estimated that five women a day were murdered in the U.S. by a husband or boyfriend, only 31% of U.S. woman reported being physically or sexually abused and 30% of Americans know of a woman that's abused by her husband or boyfriend in the last year. It's time we take action now. You can report abuse by calling the national domestic violence hotline at 1-800-799-7233. Your name is optional." I call the hospital again, but they won't give me any information over the phone and told me to talk to the charge nurse tomorrow morning during visiting hours. I head to the hospital bright and early the next morning, waiting almost an hour before someone comes to talk to me. The doctor pulls me into an office so we can talk privately.

"Ma'am what is your name and your relationship to the patient?" She asked curiously.

"My name is Octavia Sterling and I am Dawn's best friend." I answer nervously.

"Well does she have a next of kin, or any family members I can talk to?"

"No she doesn't have any family, I guess you could say I was her only family." I explain.

"Octavia, I'm not trying to be rude but we have procedures we have to follow. I could get into a lot of trouble for talking to you." She explains sternly.

"Look, I have known Dawn for many years and she has never been in contact with her family or even spoke of them, for that matter. So you can either talk to me or spend the next however many weeks or months trying to find her real family that probably don't care about her anyway. Look at her she doesn't have that kind of time to work with. I'm all you've got." The doctor looks at me for a brief period and then decides to list me as her cousin.

"First I must tell you, Dawn died almost an hour ago. Her body couldn't hang on any longer she suffered from heart failure. I'm sorry." I start crying barley getting my words out.

"Did the baby survive?" She mumbles.

"Yes the baby is in critical condition, in the neonatal unit. The baby will spend a few months here until she can sustain life on her own. Then she will be turned over to children services for adoption."

"No, I want her. I want to adopt her." I fought to say, through my sobbing. The doctor wrote down a name and a number and gave it to me.

"Call Carol Mitchell she works at children services, she will help you out with all the proper paper work that you will need. Tell her I sent you, she owes me a favor." She said as she smiles at me.

"Thank you, thank you so much. Can I go see the baby now?" I ask desperately.

"Yes I'll take you. And after you complete your paper work you can legally give her a name as well." I force a small smile on my face, "I think I'll name her Zaida, meaning survivor."

Chapter 12

8:30 pm on Friday night, Stephanie now gone for good and it's time for me to start moving on with my life. The phone rang. "Hello?"

"Don't sound so happy to hear from me!" A sexy voice emitted through the phone.

"Patrice?"

"Yeah, I know it's been awhile but I didn't think I was that easy to forget." She jokes.

"Hey baby how are you doing?" I exclaim, with sheer joy.

"I'm doing fine. I get a little home sick every so often, but I'm making it." She said thoughtfully. "Oh yeah, I am almost finished with my masters in computer science. Thank you for giving me the strength to go to school and follow my dreams."

"I always had faith in you Patrice. You were always calm, cool and level headed, just what it takes to make it in this undomesticated world."

"Jamal, I want to thank you for all that you've done for me." She speaks excitedly into the phone.

"That's not necessary, your friendship is all the thanks I need."

"No I have too. I have round trip tickets for 2 to Hawaii."

"Sorry, I can't accept that from you."

"Yes you can, it's the least I can do." She stated forcing the tickets on me.

"Besides I don't have anyone to go with."

"What happened to Stephanie?" She asked inquisitively.

"I canceled her ass a little more than a month ago. I found out that she was messing around with James and get this, now she's pregnant by him."

"Wow, I didn't see that coming! James seemed like the type of person that would do something that shady. There was always something about him, I didn't like. Call it woman's intuition."

"Yeah I noticed the way he made you feel uneasy. I wish you could have warned me about him back then."

"Better late than never, have you talked to Stephanie since she left?" She asks curiously.

"She came by a few weeks ago, to reconcile after he kicked her out."

"Shut your mouth! She's got bigger balls than you. Look at it this way, there's a reason why certain people are in your past, hint, hint, because that's where they need to be. Jamal, I can only imagine what you're going through and that's why this trip could help you relax and get your life back on track. You can cash in the other ticket and use it to upgrade your room or use it as extra spending money. But I won't take no for an answer." She demands.

"You know what, you're right maybe this is just what I need." I state with confidence.

"So you'll take the tickets?" She asks hopefully.

"Yes I'll take the tickets."

"Good, there is one thing I forgot to mention. You have to use the tickets by Monday."

"Monday, are you kidding! But I have to work!" I exclaim.

"I know, can you just make up something?"

"Well I_."

"Thanks I knew you could. I love you have a nice trip. Bye." Over the weekend, I tried to tie up all my loose ends, so there wouldn't be any problems while I was gone next week. Sunday evening I was relaxing, with everything taken care of and then my phone rang.

"Hello?"

"Hey Jamal, how are you doing its Octavia."

"I'm hanging in there, I'm flying out to Hawaii tomorrow."

"Well I have some good news." She said warmly.

"What's that?"

"All my paper work went through successfully. I am now the proud mother of baby Zaida."

"Wow congratulations!" I exclaim.

"Yes I'm so happy. It's just a shame that her real mother isn't here to enjoy this precious miracle of life." She states sadly.

"How is the baby doing?"

"She's doing fine, getting stronger every day and she gained another two pounds. She should be coming home in the next two or three months. That will give me enough time to save up some money and get her nursery room together."

"Just love her, feed her and clothe her. The bigger things will take care of itself."

"Those were such kind words. You have a lot of compassion for kids and that's why I want you to be Zaida's godfather."

"Excuse me!" I choke caught completely off guard.

"That's right. I want you to be her godfather. I want to be assured that if something happens to me, Zaida will be well taken care of. And you have something special inside of you that will help her grow into an exceptional young woman."

"I don't think I'm the right guy for the job, I can't even control my own relationships. You sure there ain't no one else you can ask?"

"Jamal, look nothing is easy. You will grow and learn as the child will grow and learn. As in a relationship, you will grow together and learn together. I've never taken care of a child before in my life and now I'm about to raise one all by myself. I am terrified to death, I guess this is my way of giving back. You're so silly, you only have to take care of her if something happens to me." She said

"You're right, it's about time we start giving back. So yes I will take on the responsibility of being her godfather." I announce proudly.

"Thank you so much."

"Just let me know when and where and I'll be there for the Christening." I knew if I was going to be in that child's life and take part in raising her, then I better get my life together and give her the stable environment she's going to need. I called my boss first thing Monday morning while I was packing some last minute items.

"Mr. Shellenberger. Yes, this is Jamal, I am sorry to call you on such short notice, but I have a death in the family, yes sir. It's first my cousin, he was in the navy stationed in Hawaii. He was in a car accident. My family is in chaos right now and I'm pretty torn up myself, he was like a brother to me. So I am going to have to go to Hawaii for about a week or so, but if everything goes well, I should be back by next Monday. If I have to stay any longer, I'll call you."

"Sorry to hear about your cousin, do what you have to do to take care of your family. I must remind you however, you know company policy I will need proof of death."

"Yes sir. I'll take care of that." I quickly jotted down cut out an obituary, on my things to do list for the week in Hawaii.

"You have a safe trip and be careful." My flight left at 11: 27 am and it was already 8: 15 am, I knew I had to do some fancy driving to the airport, to make up for all the security checks that were created from 9/11. I brought my entire luggage to the front door for my trip, I opened the door and saw a young clean cut gentleman heading in my direction with a black out dated suit on.

"Ooh no! Please let this guy be anybody but a Jehovah's Witness."

"Hello sir, my name is Thomas. How are you doing today?"

"I'm fine, but I am pretty busy right now." As I hobbled out to the car with most of my luggage.

"Well sir I will make this brief. Do you accept Jesus Christ as your Lord and Savior?"

"Yes, I go to church and believe in the union of the three persons of the holy trinity the father, the son and the Holy Spirit." I exclaim, because of his persistent annoyance. Thomas tailed behind me on my final trip to the car from the house.

"Well we as Jehovah witness, don't believe in the doctrine of the Holy Trinity_"

"Look! I really don't think it matters how you get to heaven. Your way is not the only right way to get there! Now if you will excuse me I have to go."

"But_" He tried to interject.

"I'm sorry, I'm in a big hurry to get to the airport." I reached into my car and grabbed a pencil and paper. "Obviously there is a lot more about religion that you would like to discuss. So if you would just give me your address, I'll be sure to stop pass your house later when I return."

"What?"

"Give me your address?" I insisted.

"I can't give you my address, it's against our rules." He replied, as if he was shocked that I asked for it.

"Well why not? You came to my house you know where I live. Why can't I get your address?"

"Because I'm not supposed to give out my address." He states firmly.

"Ok, I get it. It's okay for you to come to my house and harass me, but you don't want me coming to your house and harassing you. So what does your good book say about practicing what you preach?"

"Huh?" He fumbled over his words.

"That's what I thought too. I tell you what, look it up, think it through and get back to me in a few weeks. I'd love to hear what you have to say." I hop into my car and speed down the street towards the freeway. I look at Thomas through the rear view mirror, he is standing by the curb trying to figure out what just happened. I said a quick prayer asking God for forgiveness, I didn't mean to be so rude. Everybody has the right to their own religious preference and I even understand the concept of saving souls from going to hell. However, to just show up on someone's doorstep and expect him or her to rearrange their entire schedule, so you can talk to them is not acceptable. I made it to the airport with a few minutes to spare. I am determined to make this a good trip. So I whip into long term parking, grab my bags and hop on the shuttle to take me to the AA's departure area. I ran to get in line and waited almost 40 minutes for my turn at the ticket counter, I gave the lady my ticket as I slapped most of my bags on the scale.

Taking a look at the ticket, "You're late! Your plane is already boarding."

"Well ma'am, I did the best I could. I was stuck in traffic." I explained, hoping that would be the end of our discussion.

"It's people like you that make me sick, you show up at the last minute and expect me to work miracles!" She clicks on her computer as she complains. *Damn it lady! If you don't like your job than quit, because no one wants to hear a loud mouth belligerent bitch first thing in the morning. Just because your morning isn't going the way you want it to, doesn't mean that you have to be a bitch to everyone else.* But since she held my vacation in her hands and I was out of time. I just smiled as best I could, "I understand what you're going through, I work in the customer service field also and we're very much unappreciated." I said sympathetically, because I didn't have time to argue. She looks up at me and then calmly said, "Your flight number is 27495 you're leaving out of gate D- 17. Have a nice flight, I'll call and let them know you're on your way."

"Thank you for your assistance." I grab my ticket and walk away. I guess it is true, you can catch more bees with honey. I finally make it to my boarding gate, with sweat pouring down my face, I can't wait to get to my seat so I can relax. But it isn't that simple, as I walk toward the back of the plane to my seat, I am abruptly stopped by two slightly oversized women arguing in the middle aisle about who is going to use the middle seat between them. I feel like I am watching an episode of Jerry Springer. The problem is quickly resolved when the flight attendant told the two passengers that whoever used the middle seat would have to pay full price for that extra seat. Finally, I made it to my seat and there was no one sitting next to me. I sat in my chair and reclined it back and twisted the little overhead air nozzle to full blast, I close my eyes and exhale. The seat belt and no smoking sign came on, the captain spoke on the intercom to instruct us to put on our seatbelts and there was no smoking aboard this flight by federal law. Just as I was relaxing and starting to dose off, I felt a tap.

"Excuse me can I get to my seat please?" The soft spoken woman asks, I slowly open my eyes to see who is standing there. At first she looks blurry, then slowly comes into focus.

"Natasha?"

"Long time no see Jamal." She replies with a smile.

"Apparently not long enough." I fretfully state. Damn! Of all the billions of people in this world, how in the hell do I end up on a plane next to my ex-wife.

"Well it's nice to see you too," As she shoves past me to get to her seat. I thought to myself, *the next nine hours just won't go by fast enough.* "Jamal! I can tell by the disdained look on your face that you'll never be happy to see me. I know that I've hurt you bad and for what it's worth, I am truly sorry." She apologizes to me, half-heartedly. *I hope she doesn't think that a simple apology will do, after she ruined my credit and left me with maxed out credit cards that she opened up in my name to start a new life with her future ex-husband. And I'm supposed to be ok with that!* I thought, looking at my watch already hoping this flight was about to end. But we had only begun to taxi down the runway.

"Jamal don't be like this, you're going to shorten years off your life with so much hatred in your heart. I was young, stupid and didn't know how good I had it. I didn't miss the well until it ran dry. For what it's worth, a few months later I found out that he was already married. And he used me just like I had used you." She starts to sob, holding a tissue up to her face. I almost feel sorry for her, but then I remembered how she used to cry to me when she wanted something to go her way. I turn my head and pretend as if I don't see her expression and can't feel her grief. The plane leveled off at twenty-eight thousand feet and the seatbelt sign goes off, "I wish I could do one more thing in this world that would make you happy one last time. Then I'd feel like I righted a wrong." I am angry but feel mercy for her, at the same time. Maybe I have been too hard on her, it is possible that people can change. I feel her staring at me, I turn to face her way. She looks into my eyes,

"Jamal this might sound crazy to you, but I feel as though we never had exit sex prior to ending our marriage. Will you give me one last chance to pleasure you?" I stare at her like she has left her mind back at the airport, I really want nothing more to do with her. But I allow my little head to take over thinking for me and begin to consider it, *I'm not physically or emotionally involved with anyone and I've always wanted to join the mile high club.* I look at the people across from us and they are already sound asleep. I turn towards Natasha and she starts kissing me. It's good to feel something so familiar again, but I know it isn't something I want to get used to. This is going to be purely physical, as far as I am concerned. She opens up a couple of buttons on my shirt and starts making her way south of the border, I try to touch her but she keeps pushing my hands away. She begins to take her temperature with my thermometer. After several minutes of becoming intimately familiar with my Lever part 216. I hike her skirt up around her waist and look around one last time to make sure no one is watching us. She has a half-bitten strawberry tattooed on the inside of her upper thigh. The drips of the strawberry juice really make me want to get a piece of her. It doesn't help that berryliscious is written underneath. That makes it more intriguing than anything. Natasha is wearing a pair of lace Brazilian blue hip huggers. With a light scent of sweet honey dew, body splash from Victoria Secret. I pull her panties down and raise her legs in my direction. As I open her legs slowly to catch a glimpse of that savory swelled labia, only to realize that she has a lot of red bumps and blisters all around her genital area.

"What is that shit, you crazy bitch..." I jumped up throwing her legs down. Natasha looked at me with a conniving look.

"A few more minutes and we would have shared something other than a bank account. We would have shared the herpes virus collectively. I hate you so much, I wish you would feel the pain that I felt after we split up. If you wouldn't have let me go, maybe I wouldn't have this disease to carry around for the rest of my life." Natasha explains how she contracted the virus from a guy she met a couple of months after I kicked her out, like it was my fault. *Can you believe this bitch is really blaming me for her infidelity, like I told her to run the streets and be a hoe!* I thought to myself, *she went too far this time and has to be put down.* Before I realized what I am doing, I have Natasha's neck secured tightly in my hands. I feel her body going limp, but I can't break my hold. The last thing I remember is a thump on the back of my head. An Air Marshal had knocked me unconscious, when I woke up, I was in hand cuffs in a special holding area of the plane. The Marshal told me that I was going to be formally charged once we landed in Hawaii for assault. At least the rest of the flight was peaceful and Natasha free. I spent the first two days locked in jail. I sat there and had to laugh to myself, *how could she blame me for what happened to her*. Wednesday morning, they released me and some overweight police Sergeant that was more concerned with the different variety of the donuts than my case, told me that my charges had been dropped. I spent the rest of my week low key and Natasha was nowhere to be found. When I returned to San Diego, I called Patrice and told her how my trip went. Patrice couldn't stop laughing. Then she told me that I needed to assess the people that I am willing to have sex with and stop putting the cart before the horse, my life may depend on it. My boss was upset that I didn't bring back a copy of the obituary, but he was willing to overlook that small infraction since production picked up after I returned. My work performance was better than ever, in view of the fact that I didn't have women on my mind anymore. Not having anyone to think about, made me really put my mind into my work. Tony had stopped pass my desk to tell me that it was a matter of time before he took over the company. He almost felt sorry for Mr. Shellenberger. He didn't plan to fail he just failed to plan.

£   £   £

Checking out my physique in the mirror flexing, from all the extra hours I have put into working out. "Damn my shit is tight! If I knew this would have been the result that I was going to get, putting in a little extra work I would have done it a long time ago. The phone rings as I was flexing my traps and biceps admiring the cuts and grooves.

"Talk to me!" I state answering the phone.

"Yo lil bro, I got your message. So other than running into your psycho ex, the trip was cool?" Derrick asks laughing into the phone.

"All these people running around on the earth and I had to run into her on the plane, imagine that!" I reply taking a sip of some warm water in my water bottle.

"I bet you forgot my postcard and shot glass, didn't you?" He asks.

"As expensive as everything was out there, I barely could afford to eat. Thank goodness they had buffets and I could pay one price to eat all day long. What's up with you playboy?"

"Oh no I hung up my playing shoes, that Veronica situation scared the hell out of me. But that was partially my fault, if I would have taken the time to get to know her, him I wouldn't have been caught up in a compromising position. I've been taking some time to reassess my playing field with woman." He announces with a hint of sensitivity in his voice.

"Wow it takes a really big person to admit their faults, I'm really proud of you. like momma used to say, if you keep playing with fire eventually you'll get burned." I congratulate and scold him at the same time.

"And that's what happened to me, I got burned this time. That was a real slap in the face, telling me to wake da fuck up. By the way I saw Stephanie the other day walking down the street, she looked like she lost her best friend."

"Oh yeah, I'm sorry to hear that. I know we'll never be together again, but I don't wish her no harm. I hope she gets herself together, at least for the child's sake."

"I see you're not holding any hard feelings towards her."

"I did at first, but that's no way to live. I'll never forget what she did, but I won't let it consume me." I explain.

"Well I guess I have to give you your props as well, being able to put all that drama behind and moving on with your life. So are you cool with James now?"

"Naw, I haven't talked to him since. And I'm still not sure if I'll ever talk to him. Women come and go, but true friends should be there forever! And he broke a major cardinal rule."

"I hope y'all straighten everything out, look I'll talk to you later. I have some business to take care of."

We both say in unison, "Peace out!"

Chapter 13

Valentine's Day is less than two weeks away. Since it falls on a Saturday, I decided to surprise Patrice and go visit her in Lake City. I call Derrick to see what he has been up to, since I haven't heard from him in almost two weeks.

"Yo Derrick, what's good, what's been going on?"

"Hey J, hang on for a second." He put me on hold for about two minutes, I was about to hang up when he clicked back over. "Jamal?"

"Yeah." I say the irritation lingering in my voice.

"Sorry about that. I'm trying to get everything together down here at the club for my third annual Valentine's Day party. I'm calling it, Valentine's Day Pleasure in Paradise this year."

"You sure have a way of connecting with your patrons. You're a true business man."

"This year I'm going to do it differently. I have gift baskets with two wine glasses, a bottle of champagne, two towels, candles, flavored condoms with a bottle of heresy's chocolate syrup for raffle. I even installed a few VIP private booths for people who want to get real cuddly and romantic, if you catch my drift."

"Sounds like you got it all together let me know how it turns out."

"What! What do you mean? You're not coming?" He asks with a surprise reaction.

"No, not this year. I am going to Lake City to visit Patrice."

"Hell, I should have known she had something to do with it. I don't know why you're torturing yourself like that. I don't see why you let her move in the first place. I never told you this, but I think you two look very good together. And she brought out the best in you, when y'all were dating.

It's a shame yous let it end."

"What do you mean?" I ask curiously.

"Everybody knows it was meant for you and her to be together. Maybe you guys should concentrate more on redefining your relationship, instead of always defying it." I was taken aback, by what Derrick was saying. He is right and I need to stop denying it.

"You have a valid point, I never should have let her go to begin with. I think she's seeing someone right now and I'm not trying to get involved in some kind of love triangle."

"You can't continue to not know about the reality of you and her. She's like the lotto, you can't win if you don't play."

"Enough about me already what about you? Do you have a lil shorty lined up for the special night?"

"As a matter of fact I do, she's mature and a well-established young lady I met a few weeks ago at the gym. In fact she has her own business as well."

"Sounds nice so far, does she_"

"Don't worry, I've done a thorough background investigation on her. I could tell you how many times she sneezed in the last year and how many strands of hair she has on her head." He interjects laughing.

"That's good. I don't want anything to go wrong on Valentine's Day, of all days."

"I know what you mean, now I hate to cut this little tea party short but I have to get back to work and order some supplies, I'll call you later."

£   £   £

While sitting at home watching an episode of Girlfriends. I had to get my Persia White fix for the night. Not expecting anyone to call me, I was startled when my phone starts ringing.

"Hello?"

"Hey Jamal, it's me Octavia."

"How are you doing today, lovely lady?" I ask focusing more on the TV than her.

"I got some more good news, the baby is coming home in three weeks. I'm so excited I won't be able to sleep."

"That's good, so now you won't have to run back and forth to the hospital every day."

"I was really calling you to tell you that I've set a date for Zaida's Christening. It will be on March 6th. I wish you and Stephanie were still together, then it would have been easier to pick a God mom." She pauses for a second waiting for my reply, but there was nothing but silence between us. "Sorry, I see that's still a sore subject for you."

"Huh?" I ask, for her to repeat what she said. I slightly shifted the phone so I can hear the argument between Joan and William.

"Is that Girlfriends, you're watching there?" She states with attitude.

"I said the Christening will be on March 6th!" She yells through the phone.

161

"Okay, I'm writing it down right now Persia_ I mean Octavia."

"Oh yea, that's right I forgot how much you love that show. I'm surprised that I held your attention for as long as I did, with Persia on the TV screen. I'll talk to you later"

"Okay see you later Persia_ sorry! I mean Octavia. I Apologize for that."

"Bye!" Octavia replies, sounding a little perturbed by my rudeness, And hangs up the phone before I had a chance to say bye. I continue to hold the phone to my ear as Lynn came in complaining about being bored. The phone started buzzing in my ear, from holding it off the hook too long.

£   £   £

I worked extra hours during the week, so that I could take a vacation day on Friday the 13th, I want to catch an early flight to see Patrice. Everybody was in frenzy, because today was supposed to be a bad luck day. I am not intimidated though, I've had way too many bad days that weren't on a Friday nor on the 13th to specifically label Friday the 13th as a dooms day. My flight left at 9:04 am, I made sure I would arrive at the airport in plenty of time to not have to rush to my gate. To my surprise, the airport was a little empty. Maybe I should travel more on this day, because it's turning out to be a better day then I expected. There were only six people on the entire plane so everyone was allowed to sit in first class and have all the free food, gum and drinks for the whole trip. I finally made it into Lake City by 4:30 pm. I started to go straight to Patrice's apartment, and then I thought that might not be such a good idea. I know Patrice and I were cool like that, but I didn't know her boyfriend. I want to at least give him the same respect that I'd want if some guy came to my home to see my significant other. What if she has company and my showing up unannounced causes a problem? I decide to stop off and have a drink to articulate my approach properly. There ends up being a bar and grill restaurant a few blocks from her apartment, I stop and order a Michelob ultra-light on tap and a chicken tender platter. I sit in a booth in the back of the bar so I don't have any distractions while I think this through. I am sitting here contemplating on my next move, I see a beautiful woman and a man walk in together and sit down at a table on the other side of the room. I am thinking about Patrice so hard, I thought I was hallucination that the girl who just came in was Patrice. I took another good look and realized that it was her. I guess the gentleman escorting her, was the boyfriend. Of course, I had to size him up and compare him to myself. Watching those two together, makes me slightly jealous. It reminds me of how good our relationship was and how I should have never let her go. He was dark skinned six feet plus, short hair, well groomed and he dressed very nice. I figured Patrice had done well this time and I sat there wishing it was me talking to her on the other side of the table. I planned on finishing my beer and slipping out before she recognized me, so I popped the last two fries into my mouth and downed the last of my beer. I paid my bill and left a few dollars on the table, I was about to leave when I noticed Patrice's friend saying something to her and by the expression on his face, it wasn't pleasant. Feeling more concerned for Patrice, I sat at the bar to see how this love scene was going to play out. Patrice was getting upset and started to shed tears, the thought of someone intentionally making her cry had me smoking inside. I couldn't take it any more I felt it was time to intervene. By the time I got to the table, Patrice's friend was yelling at her and his hand was waved in the air extended ready to slap her. I caught it midstream from coming into contact with her face as she cringed, bracing herself for impact. He was surprised that someone had grabbed his hand, but not as surprised as Patrice was to see me standing there, holding his arm in my hand.

Looking Patrice's friend square in his eyes, "Wrong attitude, unequivocally the wrong woman!" I exclaim, growling through my clinched teeth.

Standing up and getting in my face, yanking his arm away. "Don't stick your business where it doesn't belong! And this is none of your business!" He mouths off to me, with spit flying in every direction.

"Nigga she's all my business! She never stopped being my business from the first time I laid eyes on her." Patrice's friend looked somewhat stunned by my statement as his eyes widened.

Patrice interrupted us, "Jamal this is Aaron, Aaron, Jamal." Aaron's facial expression changes from surprise to anger.

"Oh, so this is the infamous Jamal that I've heard so much about. I've heard so much about you, sometimes I wondered if I was dating Patrice or you."

"Aaron stop. You don't have to be like that, Jamal is just a really good friend of mine. And He will always be my friend no matter who I'm with." She tries to explain.

"Not anymore, its either going to be him or me. Make your choice now!" Aaron spits out his ultimatum.

"Aaron no!" Patrice begs, dropping her head down.

"Come on now I'm waiting!" Patrice looks at me with a river fall of tears running down her face, she speaks sympathetically.

"I'm sorry Jamal." I thought this was it, I will be out of her life forever. I guess I should have taken heed for Friday the 13th after all. I was about to tell Patrice good-bye and I'll always be there if she needs me, when she cuts me off.

"I'm sorry Jamal, but Aaron you have to go. I will never choose another man over him." She said gripping onto my arm. The feeling that I have at this moment, is greater than all the gold stored in Fort Knox. I looked at Aaron one last time,

"You've got your answer and you heard the lady. I guess we don't need to finish this conversation." Aaron was in awe about the whole situation. He stormed out of the bar, knocking over a few chairs on the way. Patrice looks at me and gives me a big hug, "Where in the hell did you come from? I told you that you were my guardian angel! You've always had perfect timing." She exclaims, squeezing all the air out of my body.

"I came up here to surprise you. I told you I was going to visit you when you least expect it."

"It worked, I am surprised." Patrice says with a huge grin on her face.

"Are you okay?" She asks holding the side of my face with her hand.

"Yeah, I'm fine." I say trying to sound all macho.

"What was that all about?" I ask, referring to her now ex.

"I'll tell you all about it later, but let's get out of here. Now I can finally show you my cozy little apartment. Walking into her apartment, "Please excuse the mess, if I knew you were coming I would have cleaned up." Her apartment was immaculate, I don't think her apartment could have been any cleaner. But I guess that is something she felt she had to say.

"Jamal, do you want something to drink?" She asks heading towards the kitchen.

"Yes please, a glass of ice water will be fine." While Patrice was getting my glass of water, I was admiring the view from her apartment window. I saw some little girls a few buildings down playing double dutch in the street, an old man sweeping in front of his mom and pop store and a guy swinging on his porch swing with his daughter reading her a book. I think to myself, *this is the kind of place I would love to settle down and raise a family.* Then I see a street cleaning truck speeding down the middle of the street, stirring up dust into the air but not necessarily cleaning anything. I shake my head in disgust.

"That's our tax dollars hard at work", I mutter sarcastically. I sit down on the couch after she hands me my ice water, and Patrice sits right underneath me.

"You have made my day once again, I am so glad you came to visit." She exhales.

"I'm glad too, but I don't think that Aaron guy was too happy to see me." I chuckle and opened the window for her to explain what was going on.

"Yeah_ about him, I met him a few months ago at a wedding. He was a real gentleman, never raised his hand or voice at me. We never had sex and he never pushed the issue."

"So what was that all about at the bar?" I said with a concerned look on my face.

"He's a very nice guy, but I felt he wasn't living up to his potential. He had so much more to offer life, but he didn't want to hear it. I tried to explain to him, even if he is on the right track he could still get ran over, if he's just standing there. That's when he snapped, I never saw it coming. There were no signs or anything." Patrice broke down, "I have such horrible luck with men, tell me, is it me? Am I doing something wrong? I don't know what to do, am I being punished or what? I don't think it's meant for me to date men for a_" I grab Patrice and kiss her passionately. Even though I catch her off guard, she immediately responds to me. She starts tearing my clothes off while she kissed me down my body. I return the favor and start pulling her clothes off. I am nervous at the fact that I am actually going to have sex with Patrice again, because I want it to be perfect. I lay on top of her, butterball naked absorbing the heat that escaping from her body. I am about to enter her, when she stops me.

"Jamal do you have a condom?" She asks, I looked at her because I can't believe that she waited till now to ask.

"Uh_ no. I hadn't planned on coming up here and having sex with you." I answer impatiently.

"Look in the drawer right here. It should be a couple in there." I tore open the Trojan wrapper and unroll the condom onto my erect penis. I am about to penetrate Patrice and pause.

"What's wrong baby?"

"Nothing, are you sure you want to do this?" I ask, sincerely.

"Yes, I'm absolutely sure. You don't know how many times I've fantasized about us making love again. Now stop playing and give it to me." I gently slide my rock inside of her, I move slowly and she immediately moistens up and her juices start flowing. Patrice looked at me and whispers, "Jamal, we can make love as often as you like, but right now I just want you to fuck me! Give it to me hard and fast." For the rest of the evening we had wild sex all over the apartment trying to christen every room. We lay on the floor next to the sofa, wrapped in sheets from the bedroom.

Patrice looks to me, "You were breathtaking and I was in need of some serious maintenance. Thanks."

"I'm glad I still meet your seal of approval." I joke.

"I wish you lived closer so we could have sex more often." Patrice says as she exhales. I watch her sweat stream together flowing down the curves of her body.

"Patrice_ there's something that's been on my mind for a little while. And I really need to talk to you about it." Patrice turns over to face me.

"You have my attention, what's on your mind."

"You know how we've always had this special bond."

"Yes."

"I think it's more than a bond, I think it's our destiny to be together. Many things have changed in our lives, but our feelings have remained constant. To be honest with you, you're the only person that has made my life feel complete."

"Jamal are you saying what I think your saying?"

"Yes, I want to risk it all. I don't want just a friendship with you anymore. I want an exclusive relationship with you, but I don't want to stop there. I want to make it official, Patrice will you marry me?" She couldn't believe what she just heard, as her mouth flew open.

"I don't know what to say."

"You could start by saying yes."

"Yes, I'll marry you! This is the best Valentine's Day I ever had."

"This is going to work out. We weren't together before because it wasn't meant to be then. I guess there were life lessons we had to learn first. Now it's time for us to be together."

"We had to go through some rough times, to truly appreciate the good times we're going to have together."

"Well I guess one of us is going to have to move." I blurt out.

"I guess you're right." Patrice says sounding apprehensive.

"So when you are moving back to San Diego?" I joke with her.

"What!" She exclaims in horror.

"Just playing, I tell you what. I am going to flip that quarter on the table. If you win, I'll move. If I win, then you'll move. So what do you want, heads or tails?" I ask her, flipping the quarter between my knuckles. She stares at the quarter for a few moments, wondering if she should let a quarter decide her fate.

"Heads." She answers nervously. I flip the coin in the air and catch it, then slap it on the back of my hand. Patrice is so worked up she is holding her breath the entire time. I look at the coin and then at Patrice, it was tales. But I couldn't stand to break her heart and make her move back to San Diego.

"Patrice I'm sorry to inform you, but, its heads. You win! I guess I'll be moving to Lake City, Pennsylvania with you. I just have to go back to San Diego to tie up some lose ends. And then I'm yours forever." Patrice grabs me and hugs me as if her life depends on it.

"Thank you, you mean the world to me Jamal."

£   £   £

Sunday night I flew back into San Diego and started packing all of my belongings right away. I call Derrick and tell him what has happened and that I am moving away. He doesn't particularly like the fact that I am moving back to the east coast after I convinced him to move out to San Diego to be closer to me, we have a brotherly bond, that no one understands, but he understood that I have to go. Then I called Marcus and tell him what is up. He also had a surprise for me, him and Octavia have reconciled their differences and got back together on Valentine's Day, so they can raise the baby together. I was hoping that they would get back together, they both were miserable without each other. Now baby Zaida has a complete family to care for her. I went in to work early Monday morning. First, I got my boss to approve my two weeks' vacation and then I gave him my written two weeks' notice. Mr. Shellenberger almost blew an artery, yelling about how much money it's costing him to pay me for vacation and then I quit on top of that. But there was nothing he could do, he has already approved my vacation. I told a few other people that I had just quit. Keisha cried a little, gave me a hug and told me she would miss me the most. Then she told me to call occasionally to give her all the juicy gossip. Valerie came out of her cubical to talk to me, "So you're no longer employed here huh?" She states, as she sized me up.

"I guess you can say that." I reply cautiously, knowing what was about to come next.

"Does that mean a sistah can finally get some one on one time, with that hard sexy body of yours?" She seductively asks, biting on the tip of her glasses.

"Sorry, I've been taken off the market, permanently." I reply in relief.

Dropping her head and mumbling, "Tell the lucky lady she has something good and she better not ever let you go."

"Thanks, but she already knows that." Then I hear a female's voice yelling across the room before I walk out the door.

"Wait a minute who's going to get all that money in the pot, that we've been saving up? And how will we ever know if you were worth it?" I thought about telling them to split the money up, but I saw that Keisha could use a boost up.

"I'm confident that Keisha has enough experience to give you intimate details of whether I was worth it or not." I say with a smile as I gave Keisha a wink, her whole face lit up like a Christmas tree. I walked out the door, just as her mouth flew open in amazement that I had let the cat out the bag. She didn't want anyone to know, so that she could cherish that moment by herself. All the girls were starting to form around her desk asking for all the succulent details. I stood next to my car looking at the building one last time. I smiled thinking to myself, *This building holds a lot of memories, some I hope I'll never forget.* Just before I get in my car, I see Tony walking in the front door. I call out to him, but he doesn't hear me. He is walking like he is on a mission for God. I reminisce about all the fun we had while working there on and off the clock, but it was time to move on to bigger and better things. I get into my car and about to pull out the parking lot when I see an ambulance flying down the street with its lights and sirens on. I decide to wait until it passes to pull out. But I was shocked to see them stop right in front of the building.

I mutter to myself, "I know it didn't happen already, that Tony doesn't waste any time when his mind is made up." I couldn't resist, I had to wait to see who they were bringing out on the stretcher. After ten minutes, they rushed Mr. Shellenberger out, with his face beet red and his oxygen mask sliding from side to side on his face as he tried to talk. They took him away in the ambulance.

I cracked up laughing, "I can't believe that son of a bitch pulled it off! He actually took the company from Mr. Shellenberger. Tony is certainly a man of his words." No sooner, after I said that, a maintenance man came out the front door and started removing the name of the company off the door. Then put a new business title on the door, with Tony's full name over top.

£   £   £

I wanted to get the whole crew together one last time before I moved away. First, I called Derrick, "Hey it's me, I want to have one last get together before I roll out. Can you bring over some fried chicken and two bottles of Verdi when you come?" I ask excitedly.

"Sure I'll pick it up on the way over." He answers. I call Marcus next, "Hey Marc, its Jamal. I'm trying to get the original crew together one last time. Who knows when we'll all be together again. You think you can make it over?"

"Sounds like a plan, but you know I have to check with the boss first. I'm sure it will be ok, considering." He states.

"Tell her I only want a few hours of your time. In fact, tell her she can bring the baby along too if she wants. They can hang out in the den and watch TV." Marcus yells to Octavia to tell her what I said.

"She said thanks but no thanks. She just gave the baby a bath and plus it sounds like a lot of male bonding will be going on. And she doesn't want to get hit when all that testosterone starts flying around."

We both started laughing. "I will be on my way in a few minutes. By the way how would you feel if I picked up James on the way over?" The phone was silent for a few seconds. I hadn't thought about making amends with James since the incident with him and Stephanie. I didn't hate James, but I knew we would never be as close as we'd used to be. He could never be in my inner circle of friends, but I could be cordial. I am turning over a new leaf as I start a new life with Patrice.

"I_ guess you can bring him along. I'll see you when you get here." Derrick was the first one to arrive, right after the pizza delivery guy left.

"I sure hope one of those pizzas have ham and pineapples on it?" He exclaims, walking in the door.

"I hope you grabbed some beer to wash it down?" I shoot back at him.

"I sure did. I take it no one else has arrived yet?" Derrick says digging into one of the pizza boxes.

"Marcus will be here in a few more minutes. He said he was going to stop by and pick up James." Derrick stops what he is doing and looks at me to see if I am serious or not.

"James is supposed to be coming where, here?" He asks with a concerned look. "Do I need to pull out my referee shirt?"

"Yeah he's really coming, but it won't be no problems. I have bigger things in my life to look forward to. Actually he might be a blessing in disguise, if it wasn't for him Patrice and I probably wouldn't be together right now." I answer calmly.

"Now that's balls, he must have balls the size of grapefruits, wanting to come back up in here." He exclaims, biting off a pineapple from his pizza.

"Well despite what he did, I can't totally blame him."

"Why not?" He asks.

"Because I wasn't in a relationship with him, I was in a relationship with Stephanie. She screwed up when she invited someone else to cross the line into our relationship. But to some degree I can blame him, because he knew."

"That's true, I never thought about it in that sense." Derrick says not giving much thought to the boundaries of a relationship.

"But don't get it twisted, James broke the cardinal rule. And once you lose that trust, it's impossible to get it back." Just then, the door swung open. Marcus and James were coming in the door.

Marcus yells out, "I thought there was supposed to be a party going on up in here! Where are the strippers? Jamal this is the last time we're ever having a party at your house. You are no longer in command!"

"Yeah, good choice of words, now get your lanky ass in here and close the door." You could feel the tension in the air as James came in and meekly said hello with his head down. I shot him a head nod to acknowledge him. He sat down on the couch, after he said his hello to Derrick. We all sat around eating pizza and drinking beer and reminiscing about the crazy things we did in the past. Marcus was not as withdrawn as he normally is, which was a good sign, that he was moving on from his mother's death. Before everyone left, I broke out the Verdi to make one last toast.

I poured everybody a full glass, then raised mine in the air, "To a new beginning and a new journey. As I close one chapter in my life and open another. I hope that you guys find that special person in your life, to make you feel like

Patrice has made me feel. And I am also thankful to have had friends like you guys to occupy my life in the meantime." I raise my glass and everyone does the same.

Derrick stood up, "Wait, now it's my turn. I wish you all the love and happiness with Patrice. May the two of you last forever,\and your kids grow up to be as bad as you were when you were growing up. Furthermore, just for the record, I am now exclusively dating Dominique. We made it official on Valentine's Day. Even though I am in no rush for anything, I do believe she is potentially the one for me. So this will also be a new start for me as well."

Then Marcus stood up, "Don't leave me out, I got something to say too. I want to thank you for the beer and pizza and for getting me out the house because I don't know when the next time my black ass will be aloud outside other than to go to work. Oh and about you and Patrice, I always thought that you guys were going to end up together. You were so far up her ass, I couldn't tell when she ended and you began. And I can tell you just got out of her ass recently, because you smell like sweet shit." Everyone looked at me and started laughing.

Then Marcus got serious, "Now on to a more personal note, I want to thank God for taking my mother's pain away and moving her to a better place to live. Even though you took her away from me, you've blessed me with Octavia and a new born baby girl. I thank you for helping me to realize that, before it was too late." We were all about to tap our glasses and drink to our toasts, when James spoke up.

"Believe it or not I have something to say too." We all looked around the room at each other with a surprise look on our faces and then we sat back down to let him continue. "First, I want to start off by saying I'm sorry to you Jamal, I have betrayed your trust and I don't blame you for not accepting my apology. I think if I were in your shoes I wouldn't either_" He spoke with a heavy heart.

"I_"

"Wait, let me finish. This is hard enough to say man to man. It took me a long time to comprehend the fact that I respected you to your face and envied you behind your back. I wanted the girls like you had, I wanted the success that you had, I wanted the luck to fall in my favor like it did for you, I wanted to be you. By the time I realized just how good life was, it was too late. While I was out there running around like a chicken with my head cut off, sticking my dick in everything that had some resemblance of a hole. Until I stuck my dick in something I can never pull it out of_" James started to cry and everyone was looking at each other trying to figure out what he is talking about. "I tested positive for HIV. In a few years I will have full blown AIDS, I have just signed my own death certificate." At that moment, all the bad things he had ever done to me meant nothing. I couldn't begin to sympathize with him. There was no way I could feel the way he must have felt. Trying to be strong, James wiped away his tears and held his head up high, as he raised his glass up in the air.

"God I am thankful for the wisdom that you've given me, to share this dreadful experience with my friends. I hope that my tragedy becomes their treasure and they appreciate their relationships, so they will never have to suffer the way I'm suffering right now."

We all said, "Here, here." Somberly. We drunk our champagne, but we were all devastated by James testimony. I gave him a hug and my condolences. And told him if there's anything I can do for him to let me know.

£   £   £

Two weeks later Patrice and I flew back into San Diego, for baby Zaida's christening. Patrice and I were named the Godparents and Derrick was unofficially named the God uncle, I finally got a chance to meet Dominique for the first time. I was impressed, I couldn't find one single thing wrong with her. I gave her a hug and welcomed her to our family. After the ceremony, Octavia announced that she was pregnant and that she and Marcus were getting married in May of next year. I was particularly happy for Marcus and Octavia, they complimented each other very well. I had a gut feeling they were going to make it this time. We all decided to go out to dinner to celebrate the accomplishments that we all achieved over the past couple of months. I was particularly overjoyed to be hanging out with the gang again. I did feel a little sad that James never came to the Christening, what he did to me was wrong but he shouldn't have to suffer alone. Patrice and I had to get back to Lake City so we could finish unpacking all the boxes that we have all over our new home. Derrick and Dominique decided to move in together and combine their finances, so they could open up a Hotel resort for people vacationing in the San Diego area.

£   £   £

A few days had pasted, since Patrice and I had returned to Lake City from Zaida's Christening. I was still ecstatic at how Marcus and Octavia's life had changed. I sat up on the bed watching Patrice lying so peacefully next to me. My sight began to blur from the water building up in my eyes. My heart banged against my chest as the concept seeped flawlessly through my mind, of me spending the rest of my life with a woman like her. *This is too good to be true. After all the damage I have caused in other women's lives, treating them like a cheap drank that you would buy in a nightclub on a Friday night. I've drained every bit of their God given talents out of them, then discharging them like a bad case of diarrhea. Without giving a second though about their feelings or the emptiness they were left to deal with inside. Now that I have a second chance at life, I am not going to mess it up this time. I will respect my relationship with the honor, dignity and respect it deserves.* Being with Patrice, my days of playing games with women were over the moment that I achieved absolute fulfillment with her. She rolls over and looks at me staring at her with moistened eyes.

"Honey are you okay? You're sweating and crying." Patrice sat up next to me, unintentionally exposing her luscious, firm, exquisite breast.

"There's nothing wrong. I'm just so happy that my life turned out the way it did. I'm not even sure if I deserve a woman like you." I muttered out.

"But you're sitting here crying. That's so unlike you."

"Honey, these are tears of joy. I can finally stop searching for that place, were I no longer feel like half a person. It was you all along, you were the missing link to my puzzle of life. Now my half equals a whole with you. I should have never let you go before. I was too busy looking for that special someone that doesn't exist, when all along it was you right before my very eyes."

"Jamal, maybe it was meant for us not to be together then. If we had stayed together then, we probably wouldn't be together now. There's no need to think about what you could have had then, you have me now so let's enjoy it." Patrice wipes the tears from my eyes as she begins to shed tears as well.

Grabbing her hands, "Patrice look, now that you have giving me something I can't get anywhere else. I don't ever want to lose this."

"Jamal you'll never lose me, I'm yours for as long as we both shall live." She says gently. She was trying to orchestrate the correct words to say, she didn't want to leave no doubt in his mind.

I pull away, "Patrice, there's one more thing." I watch as a look of worry consumes her face. "Don't worry it's not anything bad, unless you say no."

"Jamal, just say it!" She exclaims.

"I think we should get married today." Patrice looks at me in total shock." Her mouth flies open, like she forgot how to breathe.

"Jamal why so sudden? I always had this vision of getting married in Jamaica, on New Year's Day."

"Patrice, it's not like we don't already know each other. And to be honest no one has ever touched my soul the way you have, let's make this legitimate. Please be my soul mate." Patrice looks into my eyes for traces of sincerity, looking for justification something to latch onto. I feel the surge of her soul embracing mine, making love to me emotionally. We share the same fixation, as if we are twins sharing the same thought. Patrice finds what she is looking for, as she reaches a psychological orgasm.

"Okay." She says, capturing her breath. Shortly after twelve in the afternoon, I call my mother and ask for her blessings as well as Patrice's parents, they both approve instantly. Then we are off to the justice of the peace to be married. The ceremony is short sweet and memorable, I did promise her that we would have another ceremony for all of our friends and family to attend. Patrice and I walk out of the building hand in hand, I am officially married to the woman that changed my world forever.

We are about to cross the street, I grab her and pull her close to me, "If I die right now, I'd die a happy man!"

Patrice looks at me, with the most beautiful brown eyes.

"You should be careful what you ask for, you just might get it." She laughs, then leans in to kiss me. Patrice goes limp in my arms and falls to the ground, her face covered in blood and brain matter. Her white dress turned to a stained crimson. I fall on top of her, not able to pull her up. I feel drained, tired and cold. I gasp for air but could not catch my breath. *How could this have happened? How could the best day of my life, be stripped away from me like that?* Aaron stood over us. I could no longer see Patrice, because there was too much blood in the way. I started to feel strange, like a vacuum had sucked Patrice away from me. There's something in my eyes, like spaghetti. Then I realize it isn't Patrice that was shot, it was me. Aaron shot me point blank in the back of the head. My whole life flashes before my eyes, I saw thirty years of my life go by in a matter of seconds. Everything that I had done right, everything I done wrong, then all the things I was never going to be able to do. I wish that I had more time to ask for forgiveness, to everyone that I had wronged in my lifetime. Especially Patrice, I wanted to apologize to her for letting her down, I won't be able to love her and take care of her the way that I had promised her just minutes ago. It seemed like a lot but it was all over in a matter of a second. Patrice was yelling, Aaron grabbed her by the hair yanking her up to her feet.

"Bitch once you get involved with the devil's advocate, you can never leave unless you die! I want you to feel some of the pain that you caused me when you walked out of my life for him. Now it's time to meet your maker." Aaron put his chrome plated .45 caliber pistol against my head, the last thing I heard was two loud bangs before I hit the ground. The police ran out the court house investigating the sound of a gunshot and shot Aaron before he had a chance to execute me too. I lay on the ground, lost, dazed and confused. I found myself lost for words, as I yelled as loud as I could. People were moving all around me, but no one stopped to help, or to even see if I was all right. For the first time in my life I was all alone, a mute to the world. Now I must face my greatest test ever, to stand up and continue with life, and see what tomorrow's challenge will now bring.

Book club and group discussions

1. How do you feel about the way Jamal treated the women in his life? Have you ever dated a Jamal or know of someone like him?

2. Did Stephanie have the right to start cheating on Jamal, once she found out he was cheating? Why?

3. Do you think James was justifiable to engage into a relationship, with his best friend's woman? Why?

4. By contracting the deadly disease HIV, did James get what he deserved or has he become another victim of circumstances? Why?

5. If you walked in Derrick's shoes, would you have given Veronica a chance after she stated she had a sex change? Why?

6. When would have been the right time for Veronica to disclose to Derrick that she used to be a man? Why?

7. Do you feel Veronica has the right to never disclose the fact that she had a sex change to anyone? Why?

8. Do you know of anyone who has suffered at the hands of domestic violence like Dawn? How has it affected you and what have you done about it?

9. Have you ever felt that at any time, a woman deserved to be beaten by a man? Why?

10. Should Octavia have done more to save her friend Dawn? If so what?

11. Do you know of someone like Sabrina, who has willingly made someone take care of a child that wasn't theirs?

12. Even though Pastor Robinson was molested as a child, does this excuse his actions to also molest other children? Explain your reason?

13. Do you believe Jamal and Patrice were soul mates from the very start and destined to be together?

14. Which character affected you personally the most? Why?

15. Do you feel infidelity play a major role in relationships today?

16. Do you feel that someone can love someone else and still cheat on them?

Last words of advice- You only have one life to live, don't waste it on dreaming or thinking about how you want it to be. Take control of your destiny and never settle for less! God Bless...

EUPHORIC REVELATIONS
@
www.king4lifepublications.com

177

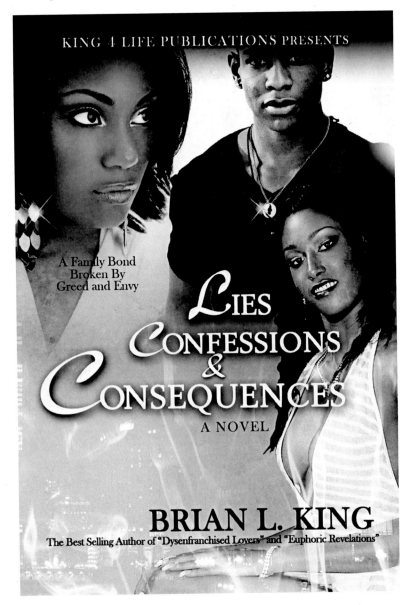

LIES, CONFESSIONS & CONSEQUENCES
@
www.king4lifepublications.com